A Kiss for the Taking

Gazing down at the beautiful, dripping-wet lass, Ryland couldn't believe he'd thought she was a lad. Standing next to her, there was no mistake she was every inch a woman. He smiled back at her, deciding he must taste that sweet mouth.

Releasing her wrist, he caught her head between his hands, tipping her chin up and closing his mouth on hers. She tasted as sweet as mead. Her lips were cool from the stream, but when she parted them, letting him delve inside, a lovely heat met his tongue. Desire coursed through his veins in spite of the cold water.

He'd thought to steal a kiss from the outlaw and be on his merry way. But instead, he found himself drawn to the lass and held there like iron to a magnet.

Her hands rose until her fingers rested upon his chest, and she deepened the kiss, tentatively at first. But then, with a soft moan of discovery, she pressed eagerly forward.

For a woman who'd been ready to beat him senseless a moment ago, she was surprisingly amenable to the kiss.

DESIRE'S RANSOM

Cover design by Richard Campbell
Formatting by Author E.M.S.

Glynnis Campbell – Publisher
P.O. Box 341144
Arleta, California 91331

ISBN-13: 978-1-634800-82-2
Contact: glynnis@glynnis.net

Published in the United States of America

DESIRE'S RANSOM

Medieval Outlaws, Book 3

DEDICATION

For all those who resist
in the name of humanity
for liberty, equality, fraternity,
and the pursuit of happiness

OTHER BOOKS BY GLYNNIS CAMPBELL

THE WARRIOR MAIDS OF RIVENLOCH
The Shipwreck (novella)
Lady Danger
Captive Heart
Knight's Prize

THE KNIGHTS OF DE WARE
The Handfasting (novella)
My Champion
My Warrior
My Hero

MEDIEVAL OUTLAWS
Danger's Kiss
Passion's Exile
Desire's Ransom

THE SCOTTISH LASSES
The Outcast (novella)
MacFarland's Lass
MacAdam's Lass
MacKenzie's Lass

THE CALIFORNIA LEGENDS
Native Gold
Native Wolf
Native Hawk

ACKNOWLEDGMENTS

My dearest appreciation for
Amy Atwell, Kirby Anderson, and Melissa Deckman,
who give me time to write;
the Jewels of Historical Romance,
who keep me centered;
my friend Kimberly Cates,
who convinced me I could write an Irish book;
my beloved pal Pam Finney,
who shared her personal story;
my delightful Readers Clan,
for their insight and enthusiasm;
my husband Richard Campbell,
for driving where the streets have no names;
and Jamie Alexander and Luke Evans
for their inspiration.

CHAPTER 1

TUATH O'KEEFFE
BARONY OF DUHALLOW, IRELAND
FALL 1193

Temair O'Keeffe closed her eyes and breathed in the sweet smell of dry hay. It was peaceful here in the shadows. Lying in the straw between her two best friends in the world—Bran and Flann—she could forget everything.

Her da wouldn't think to look for her here. He seldom staggered out of the tower house after supper. Temair would hide in the stable until he drank himself out of his temper and into a stupor. Then she'd steal back into her chamber after nightfall.

She could easily find her way by the light of the full moon. Not that she was afraid of the dark—not anymore. At twelve years old, she knew there were far worse things to fear...

Like the sickness that had taken away her ma two years ago.

The brutal fists her da swung when he was in his cups.

The soft weeping of her older sister late at night.

She stroked Bran's fur, grateful for the wolfhound's company. His brother Flann, jealous, licked at her bruised face, making her laugh.

"I love ye too, Flann," she said, giving him a good scrub behind the ear.

She doted on the two hounds, which she'd raised from pups. They'd wandered onto O'Keeffe land on the day after her ma died. If her da hadn't been drinking away his melancholy, he probably would have drowned them, saying he didn't need more mouths to feed.

But Temair had hidden them here in the stable, fed them scraps from supper, and sobbed out her own secret grief over their warm, wiggly bodies.

She'd managed to keep them secret for weeks. By the time her da discovered the hounds, it was too late. They were too big to drown. Indeed, unlike her da, who had never liked the water, the dogs actually enjoyed a good frolic in the river.

Now the enormous hounds deemed themselves her protectors, snapping at strangers who drew too close to her. Which was why they were forbidden in the tower house.

Bran yawned with a squeak. Then he shook his head. One of his flapping ears struck Temair's cheek. She sipped in a quick breath as it stung her scrape. But when he sniffed at her in concern, she smiled and scratched him under his fuzzy gray chin.

"'Tis all right, Bran."

That was a lie.

Nothing was all right.

And the older she grew, the more certain she was of that.

She'd seen the pitying looks from the servants after her da blacked her eye or cut her lip. None of the other *clann* daughters had faces so bruised and broken.

Her da said it was because she was bad. He claimed Temair had the devil inside her.

Maybe she did.

She didn't always do as she was told. She was headstrong. She had a sharp tongue.

And sometimes instead of enduring the punishment he meted out, she fought back.

Of course, that enraged him even more and earned her a much harsher beating.

But there didn't seem to be any cure for her wild spirit. She couldn't curb her willful ways.

Her older sister Aillenn fared a bit better. She was sweet and mild-mannered, agreeable and obedient. She never challenged their da's authority. She suffered the chieftain's chastisement in silence.

Maybe it was because Aillenn knew she'd be married off soon. If she could bide her time, she'd be wed to a new master, one who hopefully wouldn't clout her if she looked sideways at him.

But for Temair, marriage was a long time off. Her only reprieve from her da's anger was coming here and snuggling with her hounds.

"Ye're good lads," she said on a sigh, stroking their streaked gray fur.

They were trustworthy and loyal, better than any of her human friends.

Not that she *had* any real friends.

Since her da was chieftain, the *clann* folk ingratiated themselves to him and put up with his cruelty.

But she knew they secretly despised him.

There was not much to like. He was brutal and bad-tempered, impatient and miserly. Since the death of his wife, he'd only become worse.

Because the *clann* hated her da, by extension, many of them resented her as well. Of course, they wouldn't dare openly risk her displeasure. But she could see through their forced smiles. She witnessed the sly slant of their glances. Occasionally, she overheard their ruthless and bitter words.

Once, long ago, she'd made the mistake of passing along those words to her da.

She tensed her fingers in the hounds' fur, remembering the tragic incident.

She'd heard a crofter muttering that her da, Cormac O'Keeffe, was nothing like his brother Senach, the previous *clann* chieftain. Cormac was a greedy fool, the man had said, trying to squeeze blood out of a stone.

When she'd gone to her da with the crofter's words, wondering what they meant, he'd purpled with rage under his bright red beard. Snapping up his fighting cudgel, he'd sought out the man and punished him with a vengeance.

When he was finished, the crofter's ribs and arm were broken. His eyes were swollen shut. And he lay unconscious on the sod.

Temair had been stunned and shaken at what she'd caused to happen. In that moment, she'd vowed never again to confide in her da, no matter what aspersions were cast his way.

She shook off the painful memory and stared up at the

wooden slats of the stable ceiling. It was growing dark now. The sun was down. Soon the air would chill and the wind would whistle through the spaces between the boards.

Even her long woolen *léine*, belted with a leather *crios*, and the heavy *brat* covering it all were no match for the biting cold of Eire. But Bran and Flann would keep her warm enough.

She pressed her fingertips gingerly to the cut on her cheek. It wasn't deep, so it should heal quickly, though her eye would likely be black for a day or two. She tested her lip with her tongue. It was split. But it was almost always split. She'd grown accustomed to the coppery taste of blood. At least she still had all her teeth.

All at once, the hounds lifted their heads, suddenly alert. Temair rose up on her elbows. Bran chuffed softly in warning. Flann scrambled to his feet.

Someone was coming.

Temair's heart thrust up against her ribs.

Was it her da? Was he was coming to finish her off?

She shot to her feet and drew the dagger she'd tucked into her *crios*.

Bran rose as well, and the three of them faced the door. The hounds growled quietly. Temair braced her legs and raised her dagger.

"Temair?" came a soft cry from outside.

"Aillenn?"

Temair lowered her weapon. What was Aillenn doing here? How did her sister know where to find her?

"Back, lads," Temair commanded as she reached for the stable door. The hounds settled obediently onto their haunches.

She peered out. Aillenn was alone. She was wearing nothing but her thin white *léine*, which was torn at the shoulder, making it droop indecently low on her bosom. She had no *brat* against the cold and no *brogs* on her feet. Her face was as pale as frost, which made her lips look like a smear of drying blood. Her rust-colored hair hung in slashes over eyes that seemed empty and lifeless.

Temair's breath caught. She dropped the dagger in the straw.

"What's happened? What's he done?" There was no need to name their tormenter. When Aillenn didn't answer, Temair widened the door. Her sister could hide in here with her. "Come in. Hurry."

Aillenn glanced at the interior of the stable. For an instant, her pale blue eyes flickered with hope.

Then the spark extinguished. She shook her head.

"Come on, Aillenn," Temair urged. "Your *léine* is torn. Ye'll freeze out there. Bran and Flann can keep us warm until…until he goes to bed."

Aillenn winced as if Temair had struck her. She fingered the edge of her torn *léine*. Then, very slowly, an ironic and unsettling smile tugged at her lips. "He's already in bed."

Temair frowned. Aillenn was scaring her. Temair had never seen her sister look so strange, so disconnected, so lost in some other world.

"Please come in, Aillenn," she begged.

"Nay," she said woodenly. "'Tis too late."

"What do ye mean?"

Aillenn's eyes focused on her and then drifted away. "'Tis too late for me."

After a moment, her sister's brows pinched and she locked eyes with Temair. She abruptly seized Temair's wrist in her icy hand, hard enough to make her gasp. "But 'tisn't too late for ye," she said, her gaze burning with intensity. "Go, Temair. Get away. Now. Tonight. Save yourself."

Temair blinked. "What? Why?"

"Just go," Aillenn insisted, squeezing Temair's wrist with bone-crushing strength.

"Aillenn, what are ye sayin'? I can't just leave," Temair said, wrenching her hand out of her sister's grip. "Where would I go? Besides, my home is—"

"Temair! Promise me!" Aillenn snarled.

The hounds rose off their haunches in alarm. Temair flinched from her soft-spoken sister's unexpected harsh tone.

"Promise me ye'll go, Temair," she repeated. "Leave the *tuath*. Tonight."

Temair's first impulse was to dig in her heels. She wasn't about to let her older sister tell her what to do. Especially when it involved kicking her out of her own home.

But she feared the longer she stood here arguing, the more upset Aillenn would become. And the more agitated her sister grew, the more attention she'd draw to Temair's hiding place. The last thing she wanted was for her da to find out about the stable. If he found out about her safe haven, she'd have nowhere else to go.

"Promise me, Temair!" Aillenn demanded. "Promise me on our dear ma's grave." Her voice cracked over the words, and tears formed in her eyes.

Temair frowned. Whatever troubled Aillenn, it must be serious for her to invoke the memory of their ma.

There was no way to refuse her now. Temair reasoned

that she could always spend one uncomfortable night in the forest and then return to the *tuath* in the morn when Aillenn saw the folly of her fears. At least the hounds would keep her safe and warm in the woods.

And she wouldn't be breaking her promise. Aillenn had asked her to go away. She hadn't said anything about *staying* away.

"Fine," Temair said with a sigh. "I promise."

Aillenn's eyes spilled over with grateful tears. "Good. Good. Ye'll be safe then. At least ye'll be safe." She stared at Temair as if memorizing her face. "I will miss ye, darlin' Temair."

"Come with me then." Temair furrowed her brows. She didn't want to leave Aillenn alone, not when she was acting so strange. "Bran and Flann can keep us warm. I'll throw my *brat* o'er the both of us. We can snuggle together like we did when we were—"

"Nay. I can't." Aillenn shook her head in sorrow. "'Tis simple for ye, dear sister, but for me..."

Temair thought Aillenn was being overly dramatic and a bit insensitive. After all, their da never beat Aillenn half as badly as he wailed on Temair. Aillenn's *léine* might be torn, but her face didn't have a scratch on it. Surely on the morrow, by the light of day, Aillenn would realize she'd been making much out of nothing.

Temair always found that the world looked bleaker when the sun dimmed and the shadows grew long. With the coming of dawn, even a black eye and a split lip seemed trivial.

Aillenn's eyes softened. She reached out to pluck a piece of straw from Temair's hair.

"One more thing," she said gently. Her voice had grown

eerily resigned. "Don't look back. Promise me. Tonight. Or ever. Never look back. Do ye understand?"

Temair nodded. But she didn't fully understand. Not yet.

Aillenn kissed her brow with lips as cold as the grave. "I love ye, sister," she whispered. "Never forget that."

Temair nodded.

Then Aillenn straightened with a faraway look in her eye. "Go now."

With an irritated sigh, Temair summoned her hounds, bundled her *brat* about her, and slipped out the stable door. She headed obediently toward the woods while her sister walked back to the tower house by the light of the rising moon.

Halfway to the trees, Temair suddenly remembered she'd left her dagger behind. Muttering a curse under her breath, she turned with the hounds to go back.

Her sister was nowhere in sight. Temair could have easily have slipped back into the stable and stayed there. Aillenn would never know. Indeed, as soon as they entered, Bran and Flann flopped onto the straw, expressing their preference to return to their warm bed.

But she'd given Aillenn her word. So after she retrieved her dagger, she clucked to the hounds to come with her and headed out again.

As she closed the stable door behind her, her glance caught on the moon. Against the dark purple sky, if she stood just so, the big pale orb appeared to perch on top of the tower house.

When she moved again, she saw a black figure suddenly eclipse the moon. She scowled. Someone was standing on top of the wall. The fool. It was five stories to the ground. A fall from that height would kill a man.

A breeze swept past, blowing Temair's long black hair over her eyes. By the time she brushed it back, the wind had rushed onward and up, catching the clothing of the figure atop the tower. The instant Temair saw the fluttering *léine*, she knew who it was.

Before she could scream Aillenn's name, her sister pitched forward with her arms outstretched. She looked as if she were diving into the *lough*, the way she and Temair always did on warm summer afternoons. But instead of splashing and sinking into cool waves, Aillenn dropped like a stone, hitting the sod with a dull thud.

CHAPTER 2

The air rushed out of Temair's lungs. Her legs buckled. She collapsed onto her knees.

She was unable to speak.

Or breathe.

Or blink.

Or look away.

She felt like she'd been punched in the stomach.

She stared in horror at the motionless heap that had been her sister.

After an agonizing span of time, the hounds, troubled by Temair's shocked silence, began nudging her, licking at her face, urging her to get up.

But she couldn't. She was stuck fast. Frozen in time.

Only the sorrowful wailing of the servants discovering Aillenn's broken body at the base of the tower finally roused Temair.

She had to go.

She'd promised Aillenn.

She had to go.

Now.

She drew in a ragged breath and rose on trembling limbs. Turning blind eyes toward the forest, barely able to command her legs, she nonetheless forced one unsteady foot in front of the other.

Eventually, she reached the trees.

Shock gave way all too soon to anguish. The path blurred in her vision as her eyes brimmed with tears. Her throat ached with grief. Her chest felt cold and hollow, as if her heart had been ripped from her body. Her limbs seemed to be made of lead as she dragged herself forward.

She staggered along the trail, using the patches of moonlight that sliced through the overlapping branches like stepping stones.

She had to get away. Far away.

If she hurried, maybe she could elude the despair threatening to engulf her.

If she ran fast enough, maybe she could escape the image that was seared into her brain...

Her sister falling.

Over.

And over.

She ran until the trees muffled the sound of the keening servants.

Until the wind no longer pierced the leafy wood.

Until the moon ceased lighting her way.

Where she was going she didn't know. Nor did she care. She only knew she needed to get as far away from the tower as possible. Hooking her fingers beneath the hounds' collars, she let them lead her deep into the wood.

She was dimly aware that there were dangers in the forest. Wolves. And outlaws. But there was no room for fear in her heart.

Fat tears rolled down her cheeks, stinging her cuts. But the pain wasn't enough to distract her from the chaos of her thoughts.

How could her sister have taken her own life?

Why had she done it?

Why hadn't she just run away with Temair?

And the most tormenting thought of all...

Could Temair have done something to stop her?

She sobbed with the burden of her guilt—deep, racking sobs that came from the tortured depths of her soul. And even at twelve years old, she knew that question would curse her forever.

She lurched onward for miles, out of *Tuath O'Keeffe*, farther than she'd ever gone afield alone.

Until the moon rose high over the trees.

Until the hounds led her off of the main path, as if they knew where they were going, taking a trail that twisted through trees and landscapes unknown to her.

Until her sides ached with fatigue.

Yet it still didn't feel far enough.

At last, when she was weary with sorrow and her fingers were half-frozen, the toe of her *brog* caught on a root, and she pitched forward, falling onto her hands and knees.

All at once the weight of her sister's death pressed down on her like a heavy hand. Unable to rise, she hung her head, weeping brokenly, letting the moss absorb her tears.

Flann nudged her with his wet nose, urging her on. But she had nothing left. She could go no farther. Her legs were useless. Her eyes were swollen and sore. Her mind was exhausted.

She collapsed atop the leafy ground, curling in on herself, pulling her *brat* around her.

Surrendering, Bran and Flann circled and bedded down in the ferns beside her. The last thought Temair had before she fell into the blissful oblivion of sleep was that if she died tonight, at least it would be in the company of her last two friends in the world.

Nobody woke Cormac O'Keeffe. Anyone who dared to wake him from slumber learned quickly what a grave mistake they'd made. Which was why the *clann* chieftain didn't hear the news until late the next morn.

When he finally pried open his groggy eyelids, it was to the sight of his sniveling servant, hovering over his bed. The man bunched his cap in white-knuckled hands. His eyes were red and raw. His chin was quivering. The man looked as if he might piss his *trius* at any moment.

Cormac growled low in his throat. He wondered how long the dullard had been standing there, watching him sleep. Long enough, apparently, to prod the banked fire on the hearth to life.

"What?" Cormac grunted, wincing at the throbbing in his head.

He'd indulged in the brew from the monastery again last night. The strong stuff made him forget his troubles easily enough. But it punished him like the devil the next morn.

"Sorrowful tidin's, m'lord."

Cormac scrubbed at his eyes. What was it this time? Escaped cattle? A pregnant servant? Bugs in the wheat stores? "Spill it."

The man looked ready to crumble. "I regret to inform ye...your daughter is...she's dead, m'lord."

Cormac halted. Surely he'd heard wrong. He gave his head a shake. "Say that again."

The servant wiped his wet nose with the back of his hand. "She's dead, m'lord. Your daughter's gone."

Cormac blinked.

He felt nothing.

Not regret. Not even surprise.

To be blunt, he'd never really liked the lass anyway. Temair was a useless wench and too mouthy for her own good. It was no shock to him that that mouth of hers had finally gotten her killed.

He tried to remember what had happened last night. It was all blurry in his mind. He'd knocked the lass around a bit. But he was sure he hadn't beaten her that badly. Temair was a tough imp.

If she was dead, it wasn't by his hand.

"The lass was lucky to live as long as she did," he grumbled. "Temair's wayward tongue was bound to—"

"Oh, nay, m'lord, not her." And then, as if to soften his bad news, he added hopefully, "I'm sure Temair is alive and well."

Which didn't cheer Cormac in the least. He narrowed his eyes. His breath stilled. "Not Aillenn?"

The servant nodded. "She fell from the top o' the tower last night."

Cormac's heart dropped.

Nay. It couldn't be. Aillenn couldn't be dead.

He compressed his lips and began to grind his teeth. He could feel the blood start to simmer in his veins.

The servant must have sensed the coming storm. He

excused himself with a hasty, "I'll leave ye to your grief, m'lord." Then he scurried from the chamber.

Cormac's bushy beard quivered as the rage built inside him. Nay. Aillenn could not be dead. Not his oldest child. Not the heir to his land. Not the bride he intended as barter for a rich English lord.

How dared she? How dared she die?

He snatched up the crock of ale beside his bed, intent on taking a bracing swig. It was empty. With a curse, he flung it across the room. It shattered against the plaster wall.

How had this happened? How could Aillenn be dead?

She wasn't the type of girl to clamber on top of the tower wall. That was something Temair would...

His brow clouded.

Temair.

Could she have pushed her sister from the tower? It did seem like the sort of foul deed the wicked whelp might perpetrate.

He felt the steam roiling between his ears.

If Temair was indeed to blame for Aillenn's death, he'd give her such a beating, she'd be lucky to survive it.

Beside himself with ire, he hurled off the coverlet.

It was then he spied the crimson stain on the bed linens.

The breath caught in his lungs.

Now he remembered.

CHAPTER 3

ormac stared at the stain.

Aillenn had been in his bed last night. The lass hadn't wanted to lie with him. She'd begged him to stop. But he'd been deep in his cups and as randy as a goat. And Aillenn had always reminded him so much of his wife—his dear, departed Lerben. They had the same fair skin and blue eyes, the same ripe body, the same warm...

Cormac gulped. He ran a shaky hand over his mouth. Sweat oozed from his brow.

He'd fondled the lass before. It had been all in fun. After all, what hale man could resist Aillenn's plump breasts and curvy arse?

But fornication—that was a sin. One of the most heinous. Forbidden by the Celtic gods and the Christian one as well.

Shite. That was the last time he'd drink the monastery ale.

But he couldn't afford to dwell on his unfortunate mistake. He had to think of more important things.

Like who else knew about it.

Aillenn. Aillenn knew. But she was dead. So maybe that was for the best, after all.

Had she told anyone before she died? Had she confided to her maidservant? Had she confessed to her sister?

He glanced again at the damning stain. No one had seen it yet.

He scrambled up and tossed the coverlet onto the floor. Then he tore the linens from the bed, balling them into a gruesome bundle.

Quickly, before the evidence of his crime could betray him, he shoved the sheets into the fire. The flames licked hungrily at the cloth, consuming the linen—and his guilt—in one fiery gulp.

He dropped to a naked crouch by the blaze to watch it burn, letting the heat scorch his knees.

It wasn't fair, he decided, gazing into the fire. It seemed he'd been born under unfavorable stars, that he was ever fortune's foe.

Long ago, when his older brother Senach had died, leaving Cormac to take his place as *clann* chieftain, Cormac had thought it an unexpected gift. After a lifetime of languishing in the shadow of his illustrious sibling, he finally had the chance to prove his worth.

He should have known he'd never fill his brother's *brogs*.

Cormac spit his bitterness into the fire, making it sizzle.

Senach's death hadn't been a blessing. It had been a curse.

The *clann* had adored his brother. Strong and handsome, bold and just, Senach had been the pride of the O'Keeffes, a hero to the people.

No matter how hard Cormac tried, he could never quite measure up to Senach, whose heroic legend had only grown after his death. Cormac had never been able to earn the respect or affection that had been freely given to his brother.

Until he'd taken Lerben to wife.

It had been a clever decision. At least he'd thought so at the time. The *clann* loved Lerben's gentle gaze and winsome smile, her kind heart and sweet nature. With Lerben at his side, Cormac was reborn as a chieftain the *clann* could follow and obey.

But that hadn't lasted. Lerben had failed to provide him with the sons he needed to continue his precious chieftain line. She'd given him two daughters. And then she'd died.

After that, he drowned his misery in ale and hardened his heart against the *clann*—some who secretly blamed him for Lerben's death.

He couldn't afford to diminish his honor price—the status he was afforded through his bloodline. He might not possess the reputation of his brother, the charm of his wife, or the legacy of sons. But what he couldn't woo to his hand, he could command.

He forced the *clann* to bow to his will. He seized power by amassing riches. By hook and crook, he bought himself higher and higher rank, clawing his way into the good graces of Lord John—Eire's overlord and the son of the English King Henry.

His plan was to curry favor with Lord John by offering his daughter Aillenn to an English bridegroom, thus securing *Tuath O'Keeffe* for King Henry.

There were those in the *clann* who would have

condemned his actions as treason against their Gaelic birthright. They were determined to fight tooth and nail against the creeping invasion of foreign forces.

But Cormac wasn't stupid. He knew the English would eventually have their way. King Henry's hunger for land was insatiable. He might devour it one bite at a time. But he *would* devour it.

Henry's son John already reigned over most of the eastern coast, which made the young man's nickname, Lackland, laughable. It was only a matter of time before all of Eire would be subject to the English king.

It was Cormac's intention to come out on the right side of the inevitable battle. And to do that, he needed to prove his loyalty to the crown. What could be more convincing than bartering away his oldest daughter and the heiress to *Tuath O'Keeffe* to a vassal of King Henry?

But now, curse his fate, he had nothing to barter.

He stared hard into the bright flames—his gaze and his options narrowing.

Cormac could take another bride. A young bride. One who could give him sons.

But by the time a son of his grew to manhood, Cormac would be a doddering old fool. Nay, he needed leverage now, something to secure and solidify the bond between Lord John and the O'Keeffes, something to prove his allegiance.

Temair.

He sneered with distaste.

The lass was unfit to be any man's bride. Willful and bullheaded, conniving and sly, she was as slippery as an eel and as tenacious as a wild boar.

She was ugly as well. Unlike her delicate, milky-fleshed,

red-haired sister, Temair had raven-black hair and spooky gray eyes that smoldered like ashen coals. It was little wonder Cormac's fist found her face so often. She had the kind of cocky countenance that looked in need of a good clout. With looks like hers, the lass invited brutality.

But she was his only hope.

He sighed. He would have to pray she would grow breasts, for she was currently as flat as a plank. And he would have to find a way to tame her, to mold her into the kind of meek, mild bride her sister would have made. Which would be no easy task.

Beating the lass didn't work. Besides, if he was to make a bride of her, he'd have to preserve what little beauty she had. He couldn't send her to her betrothed with a black eye and missing teeth.

He scratched at his flea-bitten arse.

How else could he make her behave?

As the last bit of linen curled and burned and smoked itself to gray ash, destroying the proof of his sin, the answer occurred to him.

Her hounds.

The lass might not care what happened to her. But she protected those dogs of hers with an unnatural ferocity. Master the hounds, and he could master the lass.

He rose to piss on the fire, feeling better already.

Temair awoke to the sound of the hounds growling low in their throats. It took her a moment to remember where she was. She blinked into the blinding dawn, trying to see what had upset the dogs.

She rose on her elbows. The hounds were standing

watch at her feet, snarling a warning to something beyond.

She shielded her eyes with her arm, trying to make out what it was.

Someone yelled, "Call them off!"

She sat up all the way and gasped. A ragged band of archers had their arrows trained on Bran and Flann.

"Nay!" she cried. "Don't shoot! Please!"

No one lowered their bow.

"Please!" Temair begged again.

"Then ye'd better call them off!" one of the men barked.

"Aye, I will," she assured them. "But ye'll have to lower your bows." Temair knew that as long as the hounds perceived a threat to her, they wouldn't let down their guard.

Another man grumbled, "Not likely."

"I won't let them hurt ye," Temair said.

"So ye say," came a woman's dubious voice.

Bran chose that unfortunate moment to lunge forward with a snap of his jaws, casting doubt on her promise.

"Nay, Bran!"

Someone fired an arrow. Temair gasped as it landed an inch in front of Bran's paws. Of course, that was all it took for both hounds to erupt in panicked barks.

She knew it was hopeless, but she had to try to control the hounds before they got injured...or worse. She shot to her feet.

"Bran! Flann! Come!"

They ignored her.

She whistled, the loud whistle she used to retrieve them when they roved too far from the tower.

That didn't work. Their instincts to protect her were too strong. They continued to snap and snarl at the archers.

"Please," Temair pleaded. "If ye'll put down your bows, they'll stop."

A man replied with a smirk. "No doubt they're gnawin' on the bones o' the last man who believed that."

Temair felt her normally tough shell begin to crack. She'd already lost her sister. Now this band of archers wanted to kill her hounds. A knot of despair clogged her throat, and she felt her eyes fill with tears. What was she to do?

Suddenly, an older woman with silvery hair emerged from the trees. She wore a *léine* of soft green and carried a bow over her shoulder.

"What's all the clamor?" the woman asked.

"Wolfhounds," a man replied.

Another remarked, "The kind rich nobles own."

Temair furrowed her brow as she realized this must be one of the bands of woodkerns that were said to plague the forest. She'd never seen woodkerns before, but everyone knew of their thievery. Mostly misfits, byblows, disinherited nobles, and battle-scarred soldiers, they dwelled in the woods, preying on passersby.

If they indeed meant to rob her, they were out of luck. She hadn't a single coin on her person.

Temair lifted her chin and tried to keep up a brave face as the woman cocked her head and studied her from head to toe.

"Put away your bows," the woman finally said in a soft and trembling voice. Then her lips curved into a curious smile. "This lass is *the one*."

"The one?" one of the men asked.

"Nay," declared another. "Impossible."

"This tiny mouse?" a woman asked.

"It can't be," said a man.

The silver-haired woman was looking strangely at her. "'Tis."

"Ye're sure?" someone said.

"The sight has never failed me," the woman replied. Then she narrowed twinkling eyes at Temair. "Ye've been visitin' my dreams, lass."

Temair didn't know what the woman was talking about. But to her relief, one by one, the archers complied. The hounds calmed, and as Temair had promised, she grabbed their collars to rein them in.

"Sit," she said. "Stay."

"What's your name?" a woman asked.

"Temair."

"Temair?" said one of the men. "Not the chieftain's daughter?"

She gulped. What was the best answer? Maybe if they knew she was the daughter of the O'Keeffe, they'd leave her be and send her on her way.

"Aye," she said cautiously.

The man's lip curled up in a way that made her wish she hadn't told the truth. "She can't be the one then, Orlaith. But 'tis our lucky day. No doubt the O'Keeffe will offer a handsome reward to get his daughter back."

Temair doubted it. Cormac O'Keeffe clung to coin like moss to an oak. Besides, why would he pay to get back the daughter he claimed had the devil inside her?

The older woman, Orlaith, was watching her carefully. "Ye don't believe that. Do ye, lass?"

Temair shook her head.

"'Tis only fair," a man sneered. "The filchin' cur has bled us dry."

"Aye," another chimed in. "'Tis time the scales were balanced."

A third man added, "If he doesn't pay the ransom, we'll take it out o' her flesh."

Temair wasn't exactly sure what the man meant, but it didn't sound good.

The silver-haired woman whirled to them in fury. "Are ye so blind? Can't ye see he's already done that?"

The woodkerns fell silent.

When Orlaith turned back to Temair, her eyes had softened. "Ye don't want to go back, do ye?"

Temair swallowed and shook her head again.

"Ye're runnin' away?"

Temair supposed she was, although it hadn't occurred to her before this moment that she probably would never return.

The woman spoke quietly. "He beats ye, doesn't he—your da?"

Temair blinked. Nobody had ever said it aloud before. As the silence between them lengthened, the stark words seemed to hang in the air like snowflakes. As if the merest breath might melt them away like they'd never existed.

She was afraid to respond. Afraid and embarrassed. This woman had dragged the truth out of the shadows, exposing it for all to see.

No one had ever done that.

The servants always tended to her cuts in silence. The *clannsmen* frowned but didn't breathe a word. Her sister never mentioned the abuse they both suffered. Even Temair didn't like to talk about it, because she half believed she deserved it.

"'Tis all right," Orlaith cooed. "Ye're safe with us."

Something deep inside Temair shuddered dangerously like a wall threatening to crumble.

She dared not let it fall. God only knew what vulnerable thing it protected. And it took all her strength to keep that barrier intact as the woman murmured words of comfort. Words that Temair's hungry soul had been starving to hear.

"Ye can stay as long as ye like," Orlaith gently told her, coming forward. "Ye'll be safe here." She took Temair's trembling hand in her own. "And your da?" The woman locked eyes with the woodkerns, one by one, as if securing each one's loyalty. "As long as we've breath in our bodies, I swear he'll never lay a hand on ye again."

CHAPTER 4

SUMMER 1199 – SIX YEARS LATER

"**I**f ye want to keep your bloody hand," Temair warned, taking careful aim with her bow, "ye'd best drop your purse."

The red-faced nobleman grimaced in frustration. He probably assumed she'd miss at this distance. But he was wise enough not to wager the precious appendage at the end of his arm on that. He dropped the bag of coins onto the forest floor.

She could have easily made the shot.

Lefthanded.

With her eyes closed.

For six years she'd been practicing with the longbow, trained by Cambeal, the finest archer among the woodkerns. Now the weapon felt like an extension of her arm. And she rarely missed.

In fact, she probably could have pinned his hand to the tree with one arrow and—while he hopped about, screaming in pain—fired a second into his heart.

But she wouldn't.

Temair didn't like spilling blood. Fortunately, she rarely had to.

Her uncommon height, combined with her speed and the gray hood and scarf she wore to mask her feminine features, were usually enough to make all but the most foolish of men back down.

"You won't get away with this," the man bit out.

Aye, she would. She always did.

She gave him a dismissive wave of her hand. "Off with ye now."

He suddenly narrowed his eyes at her. "Wait," he growled in consternation. "Are you a wench? You're a damned wench, aren't you?"

She barked out a laugh. "Does it matter?"

He hesitated a moment. Finally, he must have realized that when an arrow was aimed at his heart, it made no difference who stood at the shooting end of the bow.

"You're the mistress of the devil," he snarled as he turned to go.

"Ye're not the first to say so," she called after him, arching an unimpressed brow.

The men she robbed were ridiculously predictable. She'd heard that insult so often, it rolled off of her like rain off her waxed leather armor.

After he'd scurried away, she opened the brown velvet bag and peered in at the coins. It was a decent cache of silver. There was enough here to see the mac Aida family through the winter. She closed the bag again in satisfaction.

Six years ago, if anyone had told her the daughter of the *clann* chieftain would grow up to be the leader of a band of outlaws, she would have called them mad.

Now she took pride in her profession.

It wasn't only because she was good with a bow and the *bata*. Fast on her feet. Clever at entangling greedy men in their own vices.

It was also because, as Orlaith had foretold from the beginning, from the first day she'd met Temair, it was she who was destined to take Orlaith's place as leader of the woodkerns and balance the accounts her father had set awry.

Temair never took a farthing for herself. None of the outlaws did. They hunted their own food and bartered for whatever else they required. The silver they stole came from those who had much more than they needed. And the woodkerns gave it to those who had much less than they deserved.

For Temair, it was revenge of sorts. Gratifying revenge.

Her father, no longer in possession of daughters to use for political gain, had resorted to bribing the English nobles with coin seized from the *clannfolk*.

In return, Temair had resorted to meeting those bribed English nobles in the woods, confiscating their ill-gotten wealth, and giving the coin back to those from whom it had been stolen.

Of course, only the woodkerns knew it was the *clann* chieftain's own flesh and blood wreaking havoc with the O'Keeffe accounts.

The ugly rumor in the *tuath* was that it had been young Temair who had pushed her sister to her death six years ago. The fact that no one in the *clann* had seen Temair after that night lent credibility to the rumor.

But her father, too proud to admit that a murderer had managed to slip through his fingers, claimed instead that that he'd put Temair in chains and kept her under lock and key in the tower.

Having to take the blame for Aillenn's death tormented Temair—especially since she felt partly responsible. And part of her longed to prove her father a liar by turning up, free as a bird, on his threshold.

But as silver-haired Orlaith used to remind her, Temair could exact sweeter vengeance upon her father, keeping her distance and taking away his precious coin, than if she lived under his nose again, subject to his control.

She tied the velvet bag onto her belt and shouldered her bow.

Petty thievery would do for now. But her father owed much more than what his coffers would yield.

Now that she was older, she'd worked out what had happened to her sister. Their father may not have beat Aillenn the way he did Temair. But the damage he'd done to the innocent young lass had been far worse. Aillenn's wounds went far deeper than Temair's bruises. Her sister had been abused and violated. She'd borne scars that would never heal.

Temair furrowed her brows as she trudged along the narrow deer trail that intersected the main road, heading back toward the hidden cave the woodkerns called home.

It made her sick to think of what her sister must have endured. Of the pain that had driven Aillenn to take her life rather than face the revolting truth of what had been done to her by her own father.

The fact that her sister lay in a grave while Cormac O'Keeffe was still breathing gnawed at Temair's soul.

She often dreamed of storming out of the forest, marching brazenly up to the tower house, bursting in upon her father, and shooting him straight through his black heart for what he'd done to her sister.

But any time her temper rose—when she'd had a little bit too much ale or when she was waxing melancholy over Aillenn—wise old Orlaith had spoken to her with the stern affection of a mother, telling her that revenge wasn't worth throwing away her life.

She said Temair's time would come. Her father's deeds would not go unpunished. For the moment, however, there was more power in anonymity.

Orlaith had been right. And even though the old woman was two years gone now, Temair tried to keep her wisdom close at hand.

Still, it didn't keep Temair from being impatient for revenge. And it didn't stop the guilt that haunted her on cold and starless nights.

She should have done more.

She *could* have done more.

If only she hadn't agreed to leave the stable that night...

If only she hadn't thought her sister was exaggerating...

If only she'd convinced Aillenn to run away with her...

Temair might have prevented her sister from taking her own life.

She steeled her jaw against the unrelenting guilt. That guilt would be with her for the rest of her life, she knew.

"If only" would follow her forever. Even taking vengeance upon her father couldn't make it disappear.

She was still deep in thought when Bran and Flann came bounding out of the trees toward her, nearly knocking her down with their enthusiastic greetings.

"Any luck, Gray?" Tall Conall grinned as Temair approached the encampment.

To protect her identity, the woodkerns had given her that nickname, referring to the color of her eyes, which was usually all her victims ever saw of her.

She tossed back her hood and pulled the scarf down from her face, squirming away from the hounds' excited licks. Then she untied the bag of coin and tossed it to him. "A safe winter for the mac Aidas."

Fair-haired Niall came up behind Conall. "They'll be glad to know."

Temair tussled with her hounds. "How are ye, lads?" she cooed at the dogs. "Did ye miss me?"

She'd learned not to take her hounds with her when she was waylaying strangers. Though the enormous dogs were excellent protectors and expert hunting animals, they tended to frighten her victims away before she had the chance to harvest their riches.

Lady Mor and Friar Brian came into the clearing.

"What's for supper?" Temair asked.

Lady Mor nodded toward the oak grove as she tied up her lush red hair. "Maelan and Domnall should return soon with somethin'."

The hunting was good this time of year. With any luck, they'd bring back a brace of rabbits or a deer.

Matronly Sorcha, who had been brewing ale, emerged from the cave, which was almost invisible because of the thick vines hanging over the entrance. An ideal spot for brewing, it also served as a good hideaway. As well as being nearly impossible to find, the interior cavern was large enough to house all twelve members of the woodkern family in comfort.

Of course, at this time of year, they usually slept under or in the trees, taking advantage of the balmy weather and sweet evening air.

Temair liked to curl up with the hounds just outside the mouth of the cave, which was the best vantage point for protecting the camp.

"Has Aife returned yet?" she asked.

Lady Mor and Friar Brian shook their heads.

Plain, quiet, unassuming Aife served as an important connection to the outside world. Armed with a basket of eggs, a bundle of herbs, or a sack of rags, she could steal in and out of the *tuath* without attracting notice.

It had been Aife all those years ago who'd gently informed Temair about the rumors at the tower house and the story her father had made up to cover her disappearance.

Today, Temair had sent Aife to follow up on a rumor about some change afoot in the *tuath*. Temair guessed it might have something to do with the fact that Lord John of Ireland had only a few months ago become King John of England. Perhaps her father's bribing of the English nobles was finally going to pay off in the form of extra land for O'Keeffe.

Temair told herself it didn't matter. She'd left the *tuath* six years ago. Even Aillenn had advised her to go and never look back.

But she knew the land and the *clann* were hers by

rights. There was still a part of her that longed for justice—revenge for her sister and redemption for herself.

Eventually Temair would return to O'Keeffe and claim what was hers. She still had a soft spot for the servants who had shown her empathy and the crofters whom her father had impoverished. But the only true friends she'd ever had in her old life were Bran, Flann, and Aillenn. She'd brought the two hounds with her, and her sister she'd left in death's arms.

Now that the sun was on its way down, the woodkerns began to return to the encampment from their various enterprises.

Young Fergus and merry Cambeal turned up first. Fergus's eyes lit up as he boasted about how they'd tricked a pair of cocky lads out of their jeweled daggers. Lady Mor snapped up one of the stolen blades to examine it, confirming that she could pry loose the jewels and sell them at the next fair for a tidy profit.

Next, sour-faced Maelan arrived, mumbling that he'd snared a half dozen fat rabbits for supper. Bald-pated Domnall followed, shouldering a young wild goat he'd speared. The band of outlaws would eat well for a few days.

Just before sunset, black-bearded Ronan marched into the clearing and tossed a small wooden trunk onto the ground. It tipped, spilling out its contents of silver coins.

Young Fergus whooped with glee. "'Tis enough for all the Sinna orphans, isn't it? What happened, Ronan? Tell us!"

Maelan let out an annoyed grumble, then stirred the fire to life. Friar Brian rolled up his cassock sleeves and started to prepare supper, chopping up wild leeks and garlic. Ronan settled his long frame on a log, rubbed his hands together, and began telling his tale with relish.

Everyone gathered around the fire to hear the story. Temair settled down on a mossy spot between her hounds.

"The particular villain I met today claimed he was a priest," Ronan said. "He said he'd been wanderin' the woods and lost his way, and would I be so good as to show him the way out?" He shrugged. "Naturally, god-fearin', helpful man that I am…"

Young Fergus snickered at that. Everyone knew that Ronan was as mischievous as a marten.

Ronan gave him a chiding scowl. "God-fearin' and helpful man that I am," he asserted, "I started describin' the windin' curves o' the woodland path." He made a grand gesture to demonstrate. "But a curious thing happened when, in the midst o' my instructions, my wayward arm happened to catch his hood and dislodge it." He raised his brows dramatically. "'Ah, good father,' said I, 'ye must have been wanderin' a very long time.' 'Why?' said he. Said I, 'Because it seems your priest's tonsure has all grown in.'"

"Ha!' young Fergus exclaimed.

Temair grinned.

The friar clucked his tongue.

"He turned as red as your hair, Lady Mor," Ronan continued, giving her a wink. "But he still insisted the trunk o' silver I found in his satchel was alms for the poor."

"What did ye do then?" young Fergus asked eagerly.

Ronan gave him a smug smile. "I told him I'd be sure the silver got where 'twas headed then."

Young Fergus burst out in giggles, which made the rest of the company join in. Even grouchy Maelan managed a chuckle.

As the others recounted their adventures for the day and the fire began to merrily crackle and burn, Temair's gaze circled the ring of woodkerns with fondness. They were her friends now, the best companions a lass could hope for. She trusted them with her life. And now that they'd taught her how to defend herself with bow, dagger, *bata*, and fists, they could trust her with theirs.

Lawless and free, the woodkerns recognized no chieftain, though, by old Orlaith's decree, they looked to Temair for leadership. And their *tuath* was the entire forest.

Their needs were few.

Their talents were many.

And they lived by an unwritten code of honor.

Lady Mor, Niall, and Cambeal had all come from noble houses. Long ago, Conall, Ronan, and Aife had been merchants. Friar Brian had been deposed by an English priest. In another life, Maelan and Domnall had been soldiers. The old alewife Sorcha had lost her entire family to sickness. And young Fergus had been a beggar.

But none of that mattered. Now they were brothers and sisters of the woodkern *clann*. What bonded them was their simple mission—to make the world as fair and just as possible by whatever means they had at their disposal.

Temair scratched the hounds beneath their collars. She thought she'd never been luckier than the day she'd stumbled onto the woodkerns' encampment, the day they'd taken her in as their own. She smiled, remembering that it was actually Bran and Flann who had led her here in the first place, likely drawn by the smell of whatever the woodkerns had been cooking over their evening fire.

In the midst of her warm recollections and the woodkerns' merriment, old Sorcha abruptly rose, sobering as she looked toward the road. Temair followed her gaze.

Aife had returned. Her face was grave and pale. For one terrible moment, Temair was reminded of her sister. Her heart spasmed at the horrifying possibility that Cormac O'Keeffe had ravaged Aife the way he had Aillenn.

But she knew she was being ridiculous. Aife might appear mild-mannered. But she would have cut Cormac's fingers off before she'd let him touch her.

"What is it, Aife?" Temair asked.

The woodkerns silenced.

Aife sent one brief, revealing glance toward Temair before she spoke to the group. "I fear 'tis unwelcome tidin's."

Temair blurted out her dark wish. "Is he dead?"

Aife creased her brow. "Who?"

"My father," Temair said.

The friar flashed Temair a glare of reprimand, wordlessly reminding her it was sinful to wish for a person's death.

Aife shook her head.

Temair was ashamed to admit she felt a pang of disappointment.

Sorcha asked, "What are the bad tidin's then?"

Aife glanced briefly again at Temair. "The O'Keeffe has agreed to ally with the English."

The woodkerns looked to Temair for a response.

"'Tis no surprise," Temair told them with a shrug. "Where do ye think he's been spendin' all the coin he collects from the *clann*? He's been courtin' Lackland's favor for years. And now that Lackland's king..."

"There's more," Aife ventured, setting down her basket of eggs. "A...a man has been sent to form the alliance."

"A man," Temair said. "What man?"

Aife's brows creased. "His name is Ryland de Ware. He's King John's man. He's on his way from England even now, and he's come for a bride. He's been sent to wed...the O'Keeffe heiress."

No one said a word.

But Temair snorted at that. "The stupid fool. Did no one tell him Aillenn's been dead for six years?"

She smirked. The Englishman was going to be very disappointed, having traveled all that way, showing up at the tower house to discover his bride was lying cold in her grave. She shook her head.

When Temair looked up, no one else was smiling.

CHAPTER 5

"I'm only repeating what I've heard, m'lord," Sir Warin claimed as the five knights rode along the sun-speckled, tree-lined road.

Sir Ryland de Ware wasn't fooled for an instant. Warin's words might sound innocent. But his eyes twinkled with mischief.

"Enough, Warin." He glowered at his right-hand man. "I know very well that Irish wenches do *not* have tails."

Sir Osgood chimed in behind them. "Are you certain, my lord? I've heard those claims as well."

"Oh, aye," Sir Godwin added solemnly. "Tails...and flippers, some of them."

Osgood couldn't contain his laughter. He burst out with it, earning him a cuff from his brother Godwin for ruining the jest.

"Are you knaves quite finished?" Ryland grumbled.

It was easy for them to taunt him about the matter. None of them had been betrothed by the king to a woman they'd never met.

Of course, he was well aware, as the firstborn son of

an old and noble family, he had no choice when it came to marriage. Men like him were instruments to be used for power and influence. Brides were carefully selected to create political alliances. In Ryland's case, that political alliance included leaving his beloved England and laying claim to a castle in a strange and savage country. Nay, not a castle—a tower house. In Eire, their strongholds were made of plastered timber, not impenetrable stone.

He supposed he should be grateful. It was an honor, after all. The king had chosen Ryland as the knight he most trusted to claim and tame the wild folk of Ireland.

But he didn't feel grateful. He felt trapped.

He sighed as his men snickered around him. His bride-to-be might not have a tail, but she probably had the sickly pale skin and fiery red hair so many Irish lasses seemed to possess. Worse, she might have the fiery temper to go with it.

But what no one dared utter, what Warin was trying desperately to distract him from, was a more unsettling claim about his Irish betrothed.

"What about the other matter?" Sir Laurence finally murmured. "That she's a murderer?"

The other men turned on him.

"God's eyes, Laurence!" Warin spat. "Why did you have to bring that up?"

Laurence scowled. He preferred to have things out in the open, to face his enemies head-on. He'd been brooding over the match ever since Ryland had announced it.

"Pah!" Godwin scoffed. "There's no proof of the claim."

"The lady was a child," his brother Osgood added. "'Twas an accident, certainly."

Ryland frowned. He wasn't so sure. Since coming

ashore and getting his first taste of Irish wenches—a foul-mouthed innkeeper, a sharp-tongued brewster, and a bitter harpy selling fish—he was convinced the whole lot of them were capable of murder.

But Warin, for all his jesting, had a sensible head on his shoulders.

"Look, m'lords, if it were true," he reasoned, "wouldn't they have hanged her for the crime? Instead, they've promised her to the most glorious, noble, and upstanding knight in all of England."

The others groaned.

"Come, come, gentlemen!" Warin exclaimed with an impish glint in his eye. "Do you not agree?"

Godwin gave Warin a cuff on the shoulder. "Slathering it on a bit thick, aren't you?"

"Sir Ryland *is* the most glorious, noble, and upstanding knight in all of England," Warin protested with a wink. "And he'll fight any man who says he isn't."

The men laughed at that.

"And Warin will no doubt be wagering his purse on the outcome," Osgood added.

Ryland shook his head, but he had to give Warin a grudging smile. Warin might be full of folly, but no man could ask for a more loyal companion.

Indeed, Ryland was grateful for all of his knights. When they'd learned he was being banished to Ireland, all three dozen of them had fought for the dubious privilege of accompanying him on his initial visit. Ultimately, he'd chosen these four.

They were stouthearted men and fierce warriors. It was good to know he wasn't heading into the unknown alone. Whether he'd be greeted by the O'Keeffe *clann* as friend or foe, Ryland was well equipped for either an alliance or a battle.

At least the Irish countryside was welcoming. The day was sunny, and the oaks and elms made a leafy canopy overhead. Moss and ferns softened the forest floor, though the loam was already so yielding that their horses' hooves on the sod were nearly silent.

Now and then a stream wandered toward the road and then diverged into the wood, like a silvery snake slithering into the shadows. Sparrow and wrens, robins and dunnocks chirped from the trees, and an occasional lizard wriggled through the stems of bluebells.

As they continued to ride lazily along in idle conversation, Ryland began to feel a tingling along the back of his neck. A vague sense that they were not alone. But when he glanced into the wood, he saw only flitting finches and blackbirds.

Still, his hand was never far from the hilt of his sword.

Laurence must have sensed it too. He cast a wary gaze along the edges of the path, as if he expected a wolf to spring out at them.

According to the foul-mouthed lass at the inn, the forest was "full o' feckin' faerie folk—the sort to lure a man deep into the wood to steal his bloody soul."

Ryland had naturally dismissed her claims. He was a man of reason. He didn't believe in faerie folk.

But as they rode past round rocks completely covered in plush moss, strange rings of tiny red mushrooms, glistening threads of water that seemed to weep from the earth, and branches overhead so dense they formed tunnels, it was easy to imagine the forest was populated by otherworldly creatures.

It was far more likely, however, that there were more *worldly* creatures in the wood. He'd been warned that the forests of Ireland were rife with outlaws.

That he believed. Outlaws were the bane of *every* forest.

He wasn't much worried about thieves. They were five strong, fully armed knights on horseback. They were more than a match for any miscreants roaming the woods.

But the queer sensation wasn't going away. He couldn't shake the feeling that he and his knights were being watched. And if anything made him restless, it was a threat he couldn't see.

Without turning his head, he let his gaze slide to the side. For an instant, he thought he saw an odd flicker of movement through the trees. But on second glance, he saw it was only a red squirrel hopping from branch to branch.

The path began to narrow so that the knights had to ride in a single line behind Ryland. If there *were* outlaws in the woods, this was the kind of spot they'd most likely use to intercept their victims. His men must have thought so as well, for they grew quiet and watchful.

But though he still felt eyes following him, no thief with a dagger slipped from behind the tree trunks. No archer leaped out into the road ahead to take aim at his heart.

Once the path widened again, they all breathed easier. They reached a place where, to one side of the road, the ground sloped gradually down, opening into a sunlit glade where a deep stream rushed past. Here they could rest a while and water their horses.

He motioned his men to follow and eased his horse off the road and down the shallow embankment.

The clearing was drenched with light and dotted with daisies, hardly the kind of spot where an outlaw could hide. So they dismounted, stretching their legs.

While the others began unpacking food from their satchels—scones, sheep's milk cheese, salted pork, and ale they'd brought from the inn, Warin led the horses to the water.

Ryland needed to stretch his legs and relieve himself, so he set off downstream. As he trudged farther and farther along the wet bank, the burbling stream took a turn. He followed it around the bend, where the water deepened and the current smoothed into a swift, rippling sheet.

Trout probably swam in the green depths, far below the reach of the sunlight dancing atop the waves. Ryland half wished he had a fishing pole. He'd much prefer to spend the afternoon dabbling a line in the stream than face his new and possibly murderous bride.

Sighing, he continued on.

Farther along, on the opposite side of the stream, he spotted a patch of brambles. Blackberries. And they appeared to be juicy and ripe. His mouth watered at the sight.

The stream was too wide to leap across and too deep to ford.

But just beyond the berry patch was a giant fallen pine log that created a makeshift bridge between the two banks.

Clambering over the mossy rocks, he climbed atop the log. It felt sturdy enough to support him, and it looked well-used. The branches had long since broken off, and the bark had worn away on the top in places, exposing the blond wood beneath. It was manageably wide along its entire twenty-foot length, where it found anchor on the opposite bank. If he took his time, he could make a safe crossing.

Foot over foot, he made his way above the lazy current, faltering only once when his heel slipped on a slick spot on the log. Finally, he traversed the last few inches and landed on the far bank. Deciding to take care of necessities first, he relieved himself on a willow sapling, then washed his hands and face in the cold stream.

Gathering the blackberries was quick work. The plump purple fruit grew thick on the vines. When he was done, his fingers and the bottom of his dark green surcoat, which he'd used to collect the berries, were stained with juice, and he'd pricked his knuckles a few times on the thorns. But the couple of berries he popped into his mouth burst with sweetness, proving his efforts were not in vain. He'd take the rest of the blackberries back to his men.

He was a quarter of the way back across the log when he heard a movement from the other side. He froze. It was probably just a deer. But by the sound, it was advancing rather quickly. He hoped the beast would look up before it charged onto the log.

Temair hadn't made a successful score in three days. Ever since that night the woodkerns had explained that it was *she* and not her sister whom her father had sold to the English, she'd been unable to concentrate on anything else.

Why would her father do such a thing? Bloody hell, he

couldn't even be sure she was alive. To be honest, she liked it that way. At least for the moment.

Now, barreling home through the forest after yet another fruitless day of thieving, she couldn't help but be exasperated about the whole situation.

Cormac O'Keeffe claimed to have locked Temair away in a cell at the tower. But they both knew that wasn't true. So how he planned to make his daughter magically appear on her wedding day, she couldn't imagine. After all, he had no idea where she really was or what had become of her.

She batted aside a blackthorn branch and frowned down at the leaf-littered path.

What did the *clann* chieftain intend? How would he keep his promise?

Would he send *clannsmen* to hunt her down?

Or did he mean to pass someone else off as his daughter and heir?

It was the last possibility that had kept her awake at night, staring at the stars and grinding her teeth in frustration.

As much as she thought she'd divorced herself from the *clann*, the blood of the O'Keeffe ran thick in her veins. A part of her was tied to the *tuath*, to the tower house, to the good people who might not have been her friends, but who were definitely her family.

In her heart of hearts, she longed to see justice prevail, to see her sister avenged, and to reclaim what she'd lost. But she refused to be forced to marry the man of her father's choice to do it.

And she definitely didn't want an imposter to usurp her legacy.

She scurried along the trail, edging past holly and hawthorn bushes, eager to learn what news Aife had brought back from the castle today.

So distracted was she by her thoughts that she was halfway across the log bridge when she realized it was already occupied.

CHAPTER 6

emair came to a skidding halt.

It was a man.

He was scowling.

A quick glance at his attire told her he was English, a noble knight by the looks of him. Ordinarily, she would have nocked an arrow into her bow before he could say "good day" and insist that he share some of his wealth with the local Irish folk.

But for a split second, his dark good looks alarmed her.

Silently cursing her own foolishness, she scowled back.

"Out o' my way!" she barked through the scarf covering her face.

The man, clearly startled, wobbled a bit on the log. She glanced down. His outer tunic was filled with blackberries. The *woodkerns'* blackberries.

She clenched her jaw. How dared he pilfer their blackberries?

"Back up," she snarled.

Maybe she *would* train an arrow on him after all, once they were off the log. She'd had no luck with coin for the past three days. The least she could do was steal back the berries and bring home a tasty treat for the rest of the woodkerns.

But to her annoyance, the man didn't budge an inch.

"*You* back up," he said.

Her jaw dropped.

Was he jesting? She was halfway across the log already, and he'd only taken a few steps. Besides, this was *her* forest. And she could tell by his accent that he was definitely English. If anyone should retreat, it was him.

"Move." She narrowed angry eyes at him.

Ryland drew his brows together. He wasn't about to let a scrawny Irish whelp of an outlaw give him orders. He was a commander of knights.

"Don't be a fool. Out of my way," he growled, skewering the youth with a fierce glare that usually sent his men cowering away in fear.

But the masked and hooded lad only stared back, standing his ground.

Ryland felt the muscle ticking along his jaw. He didn't have time for this.

Keeping his surcoat carefully aloft to contain the berries, he took a step forward. The youth was tall, but Ryland outweighed him by half at least. If the lad refused to move, Ryland would just shoulder him out of the way...provided he didn't lose his own balance in the attempt.

But though Ryland strode forward, the lad never budged or backed away.

When there was but a yard between them, Ryland shook his head. "You know you're going in the water, lad."

The lad clucked his tongue. "Don't be so bloody sure."

The youth's voice brought to mind the Irish whiskey Ryland had sipped at the inn—rough and smoky.

Before Ryland could take another step, the lad whipped a knobbed wooden stick from over his shoulder, holding it in both hands before him.

"Last chance, English," the brash youth warned.

Half-incensed and half-amused by the lad's self-assured boast, Ryland decided it was up to him to teach the Irish outlaw a lesson. After all, if he was to reign over these lands one day, he might as well start laying down the law now.

Determining that this lesson was more important than the blackberries he'd picked, he let go of his surcoat and let the fruit spill into the stream.

This seemed to vex the outlaw even more. Above the gray scarf, the lad's steely eyes flashed with pure rage. He flipped the stick forward, and Ryland just had time to dodge back out of the way. He felt the breeze as the weapon missed his head by inches.

On instinct, he drew his sword.

The lad gasped once, but recovered quickly, holding the flimsy stick before him as if it were somehow a match for Ryland's three feet of sharp Spanish steel.

Of course, Ryland hadn't earned his illustrious reputation by being cruel. He would never slay a lad at such a disadvantage. But he didn't mind teaching him a lesson.

"Never trifle with a noble swordsman," he said. Perhaps the next time, the young churl would think twice before he attacked a seasoned warrior.

Just as Ryland was about to give the lad's thigh a punishing whack with the flat of his sword, the lad's infernal stick flipped forward through the air. This time the knob landed with a painful crack against Ryland's ear.

The unexpected clout from someone so clearly his inferior goaded the normally even-tempered Ryland to fury. He raised his sword, biting back the urge to lop the cocky lad's head from his shoulders.

The youth clucked his tongue again. "Noble, are ye? Usin' a bloody blade against a *bata* hardly seems noble."

Ryland colored in shame, but managed a biting retort. "So says the *outlaw*." He'd never heard of a *bata*, but his ear still stung where the damned wooden stick had unexpectedly hit him.

"Now out o' my way, churl," the lad said, "ere I rob ye o' your coin *and* your dignity."

The lad's brashness stunned him. At least that was Ryland's excuse when, before he could lift his blade, the narrow end of the lad's stick shot through his defenses to poke him hard in the chest.

Ryland staggered back a foot. He ground his teeth and tightened his fist around the hilt of his sword, determined not to let a paltry lad get the best of him.

But when he tried to cleave the offending weapon in two with his sword, the stick seemed to suddenly retract into the outlaw's hand. Ryland's blade whistled through empty air. A flick of the lad's wrist, and the knobbed end of his stick flew round again, knocking Ryland in the ribs.

Bloody hell!

Ryland almost lost his balance. Only pride kept him upright. His side throbbed where the club had struck him. He could tell his ribs were badly bruised.

He had to admit to a grudging respect for the lad's fighting skills, as unorthodox as they were. For a scrawny lad, the outlaw held his own fairly well.

Ryland had retreated. He was so close to his own bank, he could have easily stepped aside to let the youth pass. But now winning was a matter of pride. He'd cut that bloody stick in half if it was the last thing he did.

He wasn't about to let an outlaw win the day.

Temair thought she'd never met a more stubborn fighter. She'd forced him to retreat until he was nearly all the way back across the log bridge now. It made no sense for the man to keep insisting on the right of way. It was obvious he was going to lose.

Of course, he didn't believe that. Not for an instant. She could see that in the resolute set of his jaw and the burning determination in his eyes. He still thought he could best her.

Most men did. They saw her lack of size as a lack of power. And they always underestimated the advantage of speed. In particular, English swordsmen never anticipated the element of trickery that was second nature to Irish fighters.

She should probably just club the poor fool senseless with a good clout to his head, steal his purse, and leave him at the water's edge. She didn't have time for such nonsense. The day was growing late, and she needed to learn what Aife had discovered at the tower house today.

But something prevented her from making quick work of him.

There was something about him—the smoldering intensity of his gaze, the wild sweep of his dark, unruly hair, the broad command of his shoulders, the quiet strength in his hands—that intrigued her.

She'd prefer to play with him awhile.

So she let him advance.

When he lunged forward, she leaped back. When he pressed his advantage, she retreated. Gradually, she drew him back along the log to the middle of the stream.

The man cut a fine figure. His tooled leather armor fit snugly over his wide chest and narrowed at his waist, emphasizing the breadth and muscle of his arms. Under his long tabard, his powerful legs strained at the confines of his thick woolen *chausses*. Lush waves of hickory brown hair fell carelessly over his high, broad forehead and caressed his angular, resolute jaw, which was softened by the dusky shadow of a beard. His eyes were as deep and dark as chestnuts, and at the moment, there was a furrow between them.

To be honest, despite that furrow, he was one of the most handsome men she'd ever seen. Indeed, he was so alluring that as he came closer and the sun bathed him in golden light, her heart staggered in breathless wonder.

Only the swift pass of his blade startled her from her wayward daydreaming. At the last instant, she diverted the blow with her *bata* and took a giant step backward.

He abruptly lowered his sword. "Had enough?"

"Are ye jestin'?" she scoffed.

"I've driven you halfway back already," he reasoned. "You may as well surrender."

Was that what he thought? She arched a brow. "Never. Besides, I *let* ye drive me back."

He narrowed quizzical eyes at her. Then his face blossomed into the most unexpected and brilliant smile she'd ever seen. His teeth gleamed white, and his eyes sparkled with amusement. "Is that so?"

"Aye," she told him, though her thoughts were so scattered by his charming grin that she could hardly think straight. "I haven't even begun to fight."

Suddenly, his chuckle filled the air, as rich and warm as sunshine after a spring shower. He shook his head. "I hope you know how to swim, lad."

Of course she knew how to swim. Like a fish. But she wouldn't need to. She had no intention of letting him push her off the log.

She braced her feet and raised her *bata* as the thrill of impending victory filled her veins.

He flipped the haft of his sword once within his palm. Where he gripped the hilt, she could see his knuckles bore the scars of battle. He was clearly no stranger to warfare.

But he'd also clearly never fought an Irish outlaw with a *bata* before. If he had, he would have realized he'd be better off discarding his heavy sword and using his quicker fists...or his dazzling smile.

Ryland hadn't been this entertained in a long time.

He'd assumed conquering the lad would be easy, like swatting a pesky fly out of the way.

But this fly was more crafty and clever than he'd anticipated.

Though he hated to admit it, back in England, Ryland had grown weary of battling the same knights, day after day. He'd tired of the tournaments, where every opponent's strengths and flaws were known to him. He might not be—as Warin claimed—"the most glorious, noble, and upstanding knight in all of England." But he had yet to meet the man he couldn't defeat.

This, however—fighting against a foreigner wielding a strange weapon—added a whole new challenge. Despite his intention to reach the O'Keeffe lands and get on with his business, Ryland suddenly looked forward to waging war with this unpredictable opponent.

He'd be cautious, of course. This land would soon belong to him. While it was wise to make his leadership felt, there was no need to be heavy-handed about it. Like the land, the lad had a lively, if somewhat swaggering, spirit. There was no point in crushing it.

"Come on then," Ryland urged with a smirk, bracing his feet on the log and holding his blade aloft. "See if you can cut my sword in two with your stick."

The lad wasted no time. But he didn't aim for Ryland's sword. Instead, he feinted forward with the narrower end of the stick, retracted it, and then flipped it suddenly backward, rapping Ryland's sore ribs again with the knobbed end.

Ryland grimaced and took a step back, forcing the lad to keep his distance by lashing the space between them with his blade.

The second sweep of his sword came within inches of the stick. But before he could return with a third slash that would cleave the weapon in half, it slipped around to his unguarded side and smacked him in the neck.

Peeved at his own error in judgment, Ryland shook off the clout with a curse and braced himself to attempt another charge.

This time he stabbed straight forward. If the lad hadn't quickly leaped back, the point might have scratched his belly. But with an inch to spare, the youth dodged the stroke. Before Ryland could return from his lunge, the lad used one arm to knock Ryland's blade straight up and jabbed the stick forward with the other.

The knobbed end punched Ryland's stomach with breath-stealing force. If not for his leather armor, he would have been folded in half from the blow.

"Had enough, English?" the lad mocked, lowering his weapon as if he had no fear whatsoever of Ryland's much bigger, heavier sword.

But Ryland wasn't about to surrender to a puny Irish outlaw, just because he carried a big stick.

"Just warming up," he retorted.

He realized now the lad was capable of lightning-fast strikes. Ryland would have been better off with a cudgel, which would have afforded him a quicker, more responsive defense.

But while he was busy realizing this, the lad, using his stick in one hand like a lance, thrust low with it, catching Ryland's ankle and nearly tripping him.

Ryland staggered a step, flapping his arms, and barely managed to keep from falling off the log.

When he recovered, he gave the lad a grim grin of threat. "Oh, ho."

It was obvious now that the lad's most powerful weapon wasn't his stick. It was his trickery. He feinted in one direction and attacked from another. He alternated which end of the stick he used and which hand he used to wield it. He chose unconventional targets for his blows—ribs, ears, ankles. And he struck when Ryland least expected it.

For Ryland, who was accustomed to the rules of chivalry, that kind of reckless fighting went against all his instincts.

But he could learn.

And if he was going to live in Ireland with packs of unschooled savages like this one, he supposed he'd have to learn fast.

"Ye know," the lad taunted, casually resting the stick across both shoulders, "'twould be a bloody shame to lose such a fine blade in the stream. I'll give ye one last chance to throw it back on the bank ere I toss ye in."

Ryland grinned and shook his head. He'd never heard such ludicrous boasting, especially from one so unseasoned.

It was apparent he wasn't going to win this battle using regular tactics of sword fighting. He'd have to improvise. And he'd have to catch his opponent off-guard.

The lad had quite a reach with that stick of his. The knobbed end packed a wallop when given sufficient momentum. But if Ryland could get in close, he could minimize the lad's ability to strike. Of course, he'd also be unable to use his sword effectively at that proximity. But he had another idea.

The lad swung the stick off his shoulders and whipped it through the air so swiftly it whistled. Ryland let him approach, using his blade defensively, encouraging the lad to draw nearer.

When the lad cocked his arm back with the stick,

Ryland lowered his blade and rushed in suddenly to stand toe-to-toe with the outlaw.

The move startled the lad. Ryland heard his sharp intake of breath. At this proximity, though the lad's forearm struck Ryland's shoulder, his stick swished ineffectually at the empty air behind him.

Ryland could have ended the battle then and there by giving the outlaw a good shove. The lad was nearly as tall as he, but he seemed to be mostly skin and bones. A light push would have sent the foolish wretch sprawling in the water.

But Ryland wanted to see the look on the cocky outlaw's face when he realized he'd been bested.

So before the lad could recover, Ryland reached up and snagged the hem of the gray scarf covering his face, wrenching it down in triumph.

But the outlaw had one last weapon in reserve. A weapon that stunned Ryland just long enough to make him hesitate. And that hesitation cost him the battle.

As Ryland gaped in shock, one swift kick dislodged his foot. He wheeled his arms wildly and careened sideways into the stream with a great splash.

His final thought before the water closed over his astonished head was that it wasn't possible. How could Sir Ryland de Ware have been bested by a wench?

CHAPTER 7

Temair was unhappy that she'd let the knight unmask her. She'd been careless, allowing him to steal under her defenses and take her by surprise.

Abarta's ballocks! It was the kind of mistake a beginner would make. If her feminine face hadn't made the man hesitate when he did, she might have been the one tumbling into the stream. Or, she thought with a shudder, being run through with a sword.

Fortunately, she was able to react quickly and take advantage of his astonishment.

But now she was exposed. He'd seen her face.

That was never a good thing.

Nonetheless, watching the pompous knight plunge beneath the waves amused her. And when he rose to the surface with his dark hair plastered to his head and his mouth agape in wonder, she couldn't help but crow a little.

"I warned ye to throw your sword on the bank."

She stood sideways on the log, gripping the *bata* in both hands, gloating down at him.

He tossed the hair from his eyes and stood up in the chest-deep water, lifting his dripping sword. "'Twill dry." He gave it a toss. It slid onto the grass by the water's edge.

Then he squinted up at her. A half-smile graced his mouth.

Her heart skipped. She was used to being the target of furious glares, sputters of outrage, and vile curses whenever a man discovered he'd been bested by a lass.

This man wasn't angry. There was something else in his sparkling eyes.

Amusement.

Delight.

Perhaps even admiration.

"I suppose you think you're rather clever," he said.

She shrugged, but a smug smile tugged at her lips.

He slicked the wet hair back from his forehead and then shook the water from his fingers. "Where did a lass learn to fight like that?"

It *was* admiration. She stifled a flattered smile. It had been a long time since anyone had admired her.

She tossed it off with an arch of her brow. "Ye mean with brain and not brawn?"

"Ha!" he barked. Then he clapped a humble hand to his chest and gave her a nod of respect. "'Tis a worthy warrior who knows his...or her...strengths and weaknesses."

Gazing down into his twinkling eyes, she began to feel one of those weaknesses now. It was hard not to be charmed by the man. Not only was he pretty to look at. He had a pretty way with words.

Still, she wouldn't be gulled by wiles. Instead, she

offered him a compliment in return. "'Tis a worthy warrior who's unafraid to admit defeat."

He chuckled.

The sound sent a warm shiver through her.

"Of course," he chided, "we both know you cheated."

Her brows shot up.

"Cheated?" she scoffed. "And just how did I cheat?"

One side of his mouth curved up in a knowing smile. "You know very well that if I hadn't been startled by your sudden...revelation...*I'd* be the one standing on the log, and *you'd* be soaked to the skin." He punctuated his words with an armload of water.

She gasped as the cold water splashed her legs. "My revelation? Ha!" She dipped the knobbed end of her *bata* in the stream, flicking vengeful splashes back at him. "I don't recall havin' a choice in the matter, ye bloody oaf."

"Oaf?" Deflecting her splashes with his forearm, he waded forward until he stood below the log at her feet. Then he grinned up at her, flashing teeth so bright it made her heart flutter. "So a cheat *and* a name-caller."

"'Tisn't name-callin' if 'tis true," she said breathlessly.

He clucked his tongue. But as he gazed up at her, his dark eyes danced with devilry. "I believe you've insulted my honor. And you should know, as a noble knight, I can't let such an insult go unanswered."

She smirked. His threat could not have been more empty. After all, he'd tossed away his sword. And he was practically groveling at her feet.

She leaned forward to whisper. "I believe ye've already answered an insult with an insult. After all, ye called me a cheat."

"But you *did* cheat."

"And ye *are* an oaf."

"Hmm." He gave her a thoughtful frown. "So you reckon we're even then?"

Not quite. She still intended to relieve him of his coin. But she couldn't do that while he was chest-deep in the stream.

So she gave him a conciliatory smile, tossed her *bata* onto the bank, and offered her hand to help him up out of the water. "Aye, I reckon we're even."

The instant she felt his hand close around hers and saw the glimmer of mischief in his eyes, she knew she'd made a terrible mistake.

"Well, I don't," he said. "You see, you're still dry."

"Ye wouldn't." Reading his intentions, she tried to pull her hand back, to no avail. "Ogma's arse, don't ye dare."

"You know," he confided, tugging her inexorably toward the water, "I think 'tis for the best." He frowned in false concern. "It seems to me a dirty mouth like yours could use a good washing."

She scrabbled backward, looking for purchase. "Ye bloody bastard! Let go o'—"

"See what I mean?"

"Nay!" she cried, though she was beginning to see the humor of the situation.

"Oh, aye," he assured her with a grin.

His grip was iron-hard as he pulled her farther and farther forward, until she was teetering on the edge of the log. By then, her squeals of protest were infected by nervous giggles.

"Nay!" she tried one last time, but the word was swallowed up when she sprawled face-first into the water.

He never let go of her hand. Indeed, he pulled her up out of the waves an instant after she went under. Apparently he didn't mean for her to drown.

She sputtered and, with her free hand, peeled the soggy hood back from her face. "Ye devil's spawn!" she cursed, though the effect was ruined by the laughter that kept bubbling up out of her.

"What's that?" he asked. "Still swearing? Do you need another dunking then?" He placed his hand on top of her head.

"Nay!" she shrieked. "Get the hell—"

"I think you *do* need another dip."

"Nay! Let go o' my bloody—"

"Such filth from such a sweet mouth," he said, clucking his tongue.

She would have cursed again, but his compliment startled her. Nobody had ever told her she had a sweet mouth.

Gazing down at the beautiful, dripping-wet lass, Ryland couldn't believe he'd thought she was a lad. Even with her uncommon height, her husky voice, and her expert fighting skills, standing next to her, there was no mistake she was every inch a woman.

The wet hair clinging to her face looked like ink artfully scrawled across the fair parchment of her skin. Her eyes, flashing silver like a sword blade, were fringed with thick black lashes. In his grip, her hand was strong yet delicate. And her mouth…

He wasn't jesting when he called her mouth sweet. Despite spouting coarse words, her lips were soft and pink, as innocent as an angel's and, at the moment, quivering with stifled laughter.

He smiled back at her, deciding he must taste that sweet mouth.

When her eyes lowered to his lips, he made his move. Releasing her wrist, he caught her head between his hands, tipping her chin up and closing his mouth on hers.

She stiffened at first. But she didn't struggle away. And he was right. She tasted as sweet as mead. Her lips were cool from the stream, but when she parted them, letting him delve inside, a lovely heat met his tongue. Desire coursed through his veins in spite of the cold water.

He'd thought to steal a kiss from the outlaw and be on his merry way. After all, he had a bride waiting for him not far from here. But instead, he found himself drawn to the lass and held there like iron to a magnet.

Her hands rose until her fingers rested upon his chest, and she deepened the kiss, tentatively at first. But then, with a soft moan of discovery, she pressed eagerly forward.

Beneath his callused thumbs, her cheeks felt like damp velvet. Her breath was soft where it blew against his face, making him shiver with pleasure. He shut his eyes tight as a searing lightning bolt of lust streaked through his body.

For a woman who'd been ready to beat him senseless a moment ago, she was surprisingly amenable to the kiss.

He too was in no hurry to end it. The contrast of the cold stream rushing about him with the warm sunlight upon his head was invigorating. The combination of her wet tresses draping his fingers and the liquid passion of her kiss made him feel as if he'd caught a seductive water nymph bathing in the enchanting Irish stream.

Her fingers crept higher, encircling his throat and threading through the locks at the nape of his neck. As their tongues waged a lusty battle and their kiss grew more intense, more desperate, he moved one of his hands down over her back, drawing her closer.

She gasped and clung to him, arching forward until their armor ground together with a leathery squeak. Where her hips contacted his, he roused against her, groaning at the divine flood of desire.

So distracted were they that neither of them noticed they were no longer alone. Until a man pointedly cleared his throat.

"Hello!"

At the sound of Conall's familiar voice, Temair wrenched out of the Englishman's embrace faster than dropping a hot coal.

What had gotten into her, she didn't know. Her head was in a daze. Her heart was pumping at an alarming rate. And she couldn't catch her breath.

The man in the stream was like a merrow—a dangerous water sprite drawing her to her doom.

Thank god Conall had intervened. Without his interruption, she might have drowned in the deep waters of the strange knight's power.

Yet, when she lifted her mortified gaze, she saw no trickery or triumph in the Englishman's eyes. He appeared to be just as astounded as she.

She had no time to consider what that meant, for in the next instant, she saw Conall was not alone.

Standing on the far bank were six of the woodkerns. And they had captives with them—four very angry men with their wrists bound behind them, all dressed in matching green tabards.

After a short, awkward silence, Conall called out, "Hey there, Gray! I hope ye were tryin' to steal more than just a kiss!"

For an instant she was flummoxed. Then she held up her empty arms and yelled back, "I was! But the bastard isn't carryin' any coin!"

One swift glance at the knight told her he knew she was lying. She hadn't been trying to rob him at all. Her hands had been too busy caressing his neck.

Conall continued. "Carryin' his coin on his horse, most likely. Their mounts are in the clearin'. I'm guessin' their saddlebags are probably full o' silver."

Beside her, the knight said a foul word under his breath.

Young Fergus rubbed his hands together. "We'll have a right proper feast tonight," he said gleefully. "And ye're all invited."

It couldn't be said that the woodkerns weren't hospitable. It was probably owing to the chivalrous example set by the noble outlaws in the band. If their victims were good-natured and cooperative, they were always offered a hearty meal and often a night's lodging after their purses were emptied.

The knight apparently wasn't interested in their hospitality. "Impossible."

His face was grim now. His brow was furrowed. His mouth was hard. Temair couldn't believe those were the same lips that had been pressed so sweetly against hers only moments ago.

"Ah, come now, we insist," Conall said with a cheeky smile.

"Aye," Fergus cheerfully explained, "'tis how we treat *all* our guests."

"Guests?" the knight scoffed, crossing his arms. "Prithee don't trouble yourself." His voice dripped with sarcasm.

Maelan sneered and replied in the same sardonic tone. "'Tis no trouble at all."

"Look, outlaw," the knight said firmly to Conall, "we have business elsewhere. I'll make you a bargain. Untie my men...and you have my word we won't kill you."

Temair's brows shot up in surprise. That had escalated quickly.

The woodkerns naturally laughed at his offer. The Englishmen were bound and at their mercy. They had nothing to bargain with.

Until the knight snagged her by the arm and dragged her back against him.

Temair gasped.

God only knew where he'd been hiding it, but he drew a dagger and pressed the cold edge against her neck.

"Let my men go at once," he commanded, "or I'll slit her throat."

The woodkerns reacted with vehement outbursts.

Some of them condemned the knight for his ignoble threat.

Some of them began pleading for her life.

But oddly, despite the sharp steel at her throat, Temair's first emotion wasn't fear.

It was betrayal.

She'd just let the man kiss her, for god's sake. She'd never let any man kiss her before.

And he'd enjoyed it.

At least she *thought* he'd enjoyed it.

She certainly had.

How dared he kiss her one moment and threaten to kill her the next?

She wanted to ask him what the hell he was doing.

But she could tell he was serious. She didn't doubt he meant to use the dagger. The woodkerns, at least, were taking him at his word. The knight's left arm secured her waist like a band of iron. While the blade hadn't pierced her flesh, she could feel its keen edge. One quick slash, and her lifeblood would gush out into the stream.

CHAPTER 8

Ryland furrowed his brow. He'd sooner cut off his own hand than slit a woman's throat.

But the woodkerns didn't know that.

So he planned to take advantage of their ignorance, as well as the fact that, by some miracle, he still had enough wits about him after that kiss to leverage the situation.

How he hadn't heard the outlaws arrive, he didn't know. His fighting instincts usually served him better than that.

But his head was still reeling from the touch of her lips. And regardless of the icy water, his blood felt like molten iron pouring through his veins.

That the honey-mouthed woman gasped in his embrace, fearing for her life, shamed him to the core. He'd never hurt a woman in his life.

But desperate situations required desperate measures. The woodkerns would believe his bluff. And he and his men could go their merry way, horses and purses intact.

He wasn't disappointed. At the sight of their woman held at dagger's point, the outlaws quickly released his men from their bonds.

Despite the fact the knights had been disarmed, one word from Ryland, and they could have finished off the outlaws then and there with their bare fists.

But a vow was a vow. And Ryland didn't want blood on his hands on the first day they were in Ireland. The woodkerns had done no lasting harm. They'd even invited him to supper. Besides, his heart was still racing from that exquisite kiss. The last thing he wanted was to taint that memory with violence.

"Throw down your weapons," he said to the outlaws.

Once they complied, he lowered his blade and let her go.

He was unprepared for the glare of hurt, anger, and betrayal in her liquid gray eyes. Her lips, at first parted in dismay, curved down in disappointment. She immediately raised her fingers to her throat, seeking blood, finding none.

He shouldn't have felt one drop of guilt. She was an outlaw, after all. He owed nothing to an outlaw. Given the chance, she would have gladly stolen his silver from him. Instead, he'd stolen a kiss from her.

Yet he couldn't bear the condemnation in her gaze. He wasn't the sort of man to slay a person in cold blood. Not a fellow knight. Not even an outlaw. And especially not a woman. It was a matter of honor.

But before he could tell her so, her eyes went flat, turning the color of hard steel. All emotion vanished, as if she'd closed a visor over her face. Nothing remained of the soft-lipped woman who had melted in his arms.

Without another word, she turned stiffly to wade out of the stream.

The woodkerns crossed the log to join her on the far bank.

Ryland felt a twinge of regret. But he supposed there was no point in dwelling on it. What did it matter what she thought of him? He'd never see her again anyway.

So he slogged out of the water toward his men.

They were in a foul mood. Being captured by a motley pack of outlaws had been a crushing blow to their pride. The fact that they'd needed Ryland to come to their rescue probably chafed at them as well.

So to salvage their dignity, as he emerged from the stream, he issued a stern warning to the woodkerns.

"I intend to count the silver in our saddlebags. If even one farthing is missing, we'll be coming back for it." He shoved his dagger forcefully into its sheath. "And next time we won't be so merciful."

It was best to put the fear of god into these ruffians before they began to believe that the English were easy targets.

That was his intention.

But he couldn't leave things alone.

After the woodkerns had safely crossed the log to the far bank, he caught a last glimpse of the sweet-mouthed outlaw. Her wet garments clung to her like a second skin, revealing her long, shapely limbs. Her hair, darkened to the color of midnight, draped over her shoulders in seductive invitation.

He must have been mad to have believed she was a lad.

And even though he knew he'd never see her again,

even though he shouldn't care what an outlaw thought, he couldn't bear to let her believe he was a monster.

What had her fellow called her? Gray?

"Gray!" he called out.

She glanced up.

"I wouldn't have done it, you know," he told her. "No English knight worth his spurs would hurt a helpless woman."

She made no reply. Nonetheless, he was glad he'd made the confession.

With a final nod, he picked up and sheathed his sword. Then he turned to follow his men back to their horses.

He'd gone two paces when something whizzed past his nose and landed with a thunk in the tree beside him. An arrow. The shaft was still quivering when he whipped his head around and saw the woman on the far bank. Her bow was aloft, and her guilty hand was raised beside her cheek.

"Then ye're a bigger fool than I took ye for," she called back.

His men came to his defense at once, growling like riled hounds. Warin wrenched the arrow out of the trunk, angry enough that he would have fired it back at her with his bare hand.

But Ryland pried the arrow from him and broke it in half between his fists, dropping the shaft to the ground. Then he calmed his men with a motion of his hand.

"If you're going to be so brazen," he warned the woman, "you'd better shoot to kill."

She slung her bow back over her shoulder. "If I'd wanted ye dead, ye'd be dead." Then she gave him a sly smirk. "But no Irish outlaw worth her bow would hurt a helpless man."

Ryland couldn't help but chuckle. Leave it to the clever sweet-and-sharp-tongued woman to throw his own words back at him.

His men, however, did not find her so amusing.

"Helpless!" Laurence spat in disgust. "I'll show her helpless."

Warin bit out an oath, barely able to suppress his rage.

"Are you going to let her get away with that?" Godwin asked in outrage.

"I am," Ryland said. His pride might be wounded, but it would heal. "They're only words, after all. I don't think we need to be starting a war when we've only just arrived." He continued along the stream. "Never fear. Once I'm chieftain over these lands, I'll put the outlaws in their place." Including, he thought, rather relishing the idea, that spirited wench with the wide gray eyes and the delicious mouth.

All the way back to the woodkern camp, Temair felt as out of sorts as a wind-bristled cat. Why, she didn't know.

After all, she'd gotten the last word. She'd even driven home her point...literally...just missing the English knight with her arrow.

But she was unsatisfied. She felt as if there was unfinished business between them.

For one magical moment, standing in the stream, in the arms of the charming knight with the wide smile and sparkling eyes, she'd experienced a curious sort of joy. Her heart had raced. Her head had spun. Every nerve in her body had come to life.

Then bumbling Conall had ruined everything.

If only the woodkerns hadn't arrived when they did...

If only they hadn't chosen those particular knights as targets...

If only they hadn't interrupted the two of them...

What? she asked herself. What would have happened?

She scuffed at the leafy path.

It was foolish to imagine things might have ended differently. The man was obviously on some knightly quest. She was going to return home with the woodkerns. They wouldn't be crossing paths again.

So why did that irritate her?

She tried to tell herself it was because she was once again returning empty-handed. After days of watching and waiting and stalking travelers, she'd reaped no reward for her efforts.

But she knew it was more than that.

She'd been strangely drawn to the man. Cocksure and clever, amusing and delightful, he was as playful as her hounds and deliciously wicked.

He was also dangerous. He was a foreigner, an invader. As swiftly as he'd stolen the kiss from her, men like him were swooping down upon her land and claiming it for their own.

If she'd forgotten that fact for a moment, the reality had come crashing down when he whipped out his dagger and held it at her throat.

His treachery had been all the more cruel because she'd trusted him. For one brief moment, she'd left herself vulnerable, believing he was a kindred spirit. The fact that he was not—that he was capable of tasting her passion one moment and ending her life in the next—crushed her.

And then he'd yelled across the stream at her, admitting he wouldn't have done it.

That had simultaneously relieved and infuriated her. She wished now she had called his bluff. Maybe then she wouldn't be walking away with empty hands and a hollow heart.

Maybe then he would have been forced to dine with the woodkerns...

And stay the night...

And possibly steal away with her in the moonlight to...

"Who do ye suppose they were?" young Fergus asked, interrupting her thoughts. Maelan growled. "More bloody foreigners come to steal our fair isle."

The others grumbled in agreement. They were as upset as Temair. But their annoyance had everything to do with the fact they hadn't managed to rob the knights. The small English retinue had probably been carrying a considerable amount of silver.

She wondered where they were headed.

Were they only knights-errant seeking their fortune in the land that would eventually belong to their new king? Or did they have a specific destination in mind? The knight had mentioned that he had business elsewhere. He'd also threatened to return if any of his silver was missing.

She cursed herself now for not taking a coin or two to ensure his return.

And then she cursed herself for having such treasonous thoughts.

These were enemies of Eire. The sooner she forgot about the knight's warm, sweet, inviting mouth, the better.

It wasn't until the woodkerns returned to the glade for supper and were settled around the fire, relaying what had happened, that Aife brought up something no one had considered.

"So ye're sayin' these men saw your face, Gray?" she asked.

Temair shrugged and ran her fingers through Bran's fur. "Aye." She didn't add that one of the knights had not only seen her face, but kissed her lips. Thankfully, nobody divulged that detail, not even impulsive Fergus. Remembering how she'd humiliated them, she added proudly, "But I doubt they want to see it *again.*"

"Still, if they got a good look at ye," old Sorcha said gravely, eyeing Temair through the flames, "they'll be able to describe ye."

Lady Mor gave a little gasp, drawing the attention of Cambeal and Conall. "What if they tell the chieftain they saw ye?"

Temair's brow creased. She hadn't considered that. For days now, she'd been fretting over the possibility that her father might send his men to hunt her down. She hadn't considered that outsiders might inform him that a young woman with peat-black hair and gray eyes was living in the woods.

Cambeal, hoping to allay her fears, argued, "The knights could have been headed anywhere, Gray. There's no reason to think they'll cross paths with the chieftain."

"Besides," Conall said, "I doubt they'll be talkin' much about the lass that tossed one o' them on his arse."

The woodkerns chuckled at that.

Conall was probably right. The cocky English knight

wouldn't be keen for anyone to know he'd been bested by a wisp of an Irish lass. The idea made Temair smile.

Until she glanced at Sorcha, who wasn't sharing in the laughter.

"It might be best if ye lie low for a bit."

Temair wanted to argue. She'd brought in nothing for the woodkerns in days. It troubled her not to be sharing the burden of providing for the band.

But she supposed Sorcha had a point. Until the English knights passed through the O'Keeffe lands, she couldn't be sure of her safety.

She cursed under her breath. She hated that her life had been turned upside down, and all because of her father and his wretched scheming.

CHAPTER 9

The moment Ryland laid eyes on Cormac O'Keeffe in the great hall of the tower house, a shudder went through him. As he'd feared, the *clann* chieftain had mottled white skin and a fiery red beard. No doubt his daughter had inherited that coloring and the hot temper to go with it.

Still, Ryland would try to withhold judgment. He hadn't met his bride yet. Despite the appearance of her father and the rumors of her violence, he intended to keep an open mind.

Cormac was not easy to like. Despite wearing a heavy silver circle of a crown and a vivid green *brat* embroidered at the edges in Irish knots of red and yellow over a fine linen *léine*, he had the appearance of a peasant disguised in the garments of a king. He stank of sweat and ale. He was soft-bellied and shifty-eyed. His nose was ruddy with excessive drinking. And he somehow managed to be imperious and fawning at the same time.

He blustered about like an angry drunkard, snapping at his *clannsmen*, berating his servants. Yet he ingratiated himself at every opportunity to Ryland and his knights. Like a poorly trained hound, he barked at his own pack, and then returned to lick his master's hand, seeking approval.

Ryland's men disapproved of Cormac as well. He could see it in their stern gazes and the way their knuckles tightened on the hilts of their swords. The chieftain was loud and volatile, bellowing at a maid one moment and confiding in the knights the next. And nothing was more unsettling to a warrior than an unpredictable foe.

Ryland tried not to concern himself too much with Cormac. After all, once he was married to the chieftain's daughter, Ryland would eventually replace him as lord. So he concentrated instead on the *clannsmen* who would be under his care.

On the whole, from what he'd seen, riding through the O'Keeffe lands on the way to the tower house, they seemed like good people, despite being downtrodden and naturally suspicious of Ryland and his men. But he was sure that once he showed them his fairness, his loyalty, and his even temper, they would learn to rely upon him. There was no need to flaunt one's power when trust could be earned through mutual respect.

"Ale!" Cormac yelled at a kitchen lad. "What's takin' ye so long, ye half-wit?"

The cowed servant bobbed his head and scurried from the hall.

Godwin's eyes narrowed in disapproval.

"Stupid lad probably can't count to six," Cormac chortled, elbowing Ryland in the ribs. Ryland winced. He'd hit one of the spots where that lady outlaw had bruised him with her club.

Laurence, who himself had been late to learn his numbers, took offense at the rude comment, growling under his breath.

Warin, ever the diplomat, intervened to turn the conversation. "The tower house is magnificent, m'lord. When did you say 'twas built?"

Cormac, easily distracted, started waxing poetic about the ancient keep, though Ryland was more interested in its sturdiness than its magnificence. He was relieved to see the plaster-covered timber walls were straight at least, though stone would make a more formidable defense. As for the pieces displayed in the hall—a silver aquamanile in the shape of a lion, a jewel-encrusted sword on the wall, an ornate wooden screen painted with hunting scenes accented in gold leaf—they seemed more pretentious and extravagant than tasteful.

He wondered if his betrothed shared her father's preferences for decoration.

Quickly losing interest in the discussion about the tapestries, Ryland began studying the denizens traveling through the hall.

Where was his bride anyway?

Every time a woman entered the hall, his breath caught.

A lass with curly blonde hair gave him a flirting glance. But she couldn't be his intended. The filthy hem of her ragged skirt and the basket of hen's eggs she was carrying marked her as a servant.

A dark-haired beauty shyly lowered her eyes. But her lover was quick to claim her, taking her arm and leading her outside.

An impossibly old woman hobbled by, and Ryland

gulped. It wasn't as if he had any choice in the matter, but only now was he beginning to realize that he knew nothing about his bride-to-be...other than the rumors about her murdering her own sister.

She could be half-lame...

Or half-mad...

Or fourteen years old, as far as he knew.

He hadn't been uneasy before. But now that he was here, about to meet the woman with whom he would spend the rest of his life, he felt as nervous as a squire at his first tournament.

As the chieftain blathered on and on about his priceless treasures, Ryland grew more and more anxious.

Where was his damned bride?

He was about to blurt out the question—in more polite language, of course—when the chieftain made a grand gesture with his arm at the very moment the servant arrived with the six ales, knocking the entire tray out of his hands.

The earthen cups shattered on the floor. Shards of clay and splashes of foaming ale burst outward.

The horrified kitchen lad seemed to shrink in his skin. The chieftain's face purpled with rage as he raised one meaty fist.

Ryland acted on instinct. He wouldn't stand idly by while the chieftain hurt an innocent servant. Before Cormac could bring down his fist, Ryland seized the man's thick forearm, halting him.

For one agonizing, uncomfortable moment, there was silence in the hall. Ryland could feel the shuddering fury in Cormac's arm as everyone looked on in horror.

Ryland knew he had no right to interfere in what

happened between the chieftain and his servant. This was not Ryland's keep—at least not yet. And his action undermined the authority of the chieftain in the eyes of all who witnessed it.

But he couldn't help himself. Above all, Ryland believed in justice, in fairness. And the kitchen lad didn't deserve punishment.

Fortunately, brilliant Warin came to the rescue. He stepped between Ryland and Cormac, grabbing the sleeve of the chieftain's garments with a gasp.

"Oh, nay, m'lord," he said to Cormac in concern, "you don't want to be getting servant's blood on that fine linen."

Startled by the comment, Cormac was distracted long enough for Ryland to give the servant a sharp, dismissive glare. The kitchen lad didn't need a second warning. He made a hasty escape.

Laurence motioned to a maidservant to clean up the mess while Warin continued fussing over the chieftain's sleeve.

"Servants are easily replaced," Warin said. "But quality linen such as this..." He clucked his tongue.

Whether the chieftain believed Warin's nonsense, Ryland didn't know. But the chieftain's rage subsided quickly. Ryland owed Warin for that favor.

"You there, lad," Godwin called out to a less skittish servant. "Fetch us ales, will you?"

The servant left to do Godwin's bidding.

Ryland decided to use the chaotic moment to casually toss out the question that had been nagging at him. "So, m'lord, when do I get to meet my beautiful bride?"

Cormac looked stunned for a moment, as if it had

totally slipped his mind. Then he eyed Ryland with a calculating squint. "Ye seem in a hurry." His lip curled up in what he probably thought passed for a smile. "Are ye so eager to toss me on my arse and take my *tuath?*"

"Not at all," Ryland said. "I only—"

"Because I don't plan to die for a long while yet."

Though Ryland thought the man's temperament and health indicated otherwise, he nodded. "Of course not."

Cormac grunted.

Ryland opened his hands in friendship. "I only wish to meet the woman who is to be my wife."

"Aye, o' course."

But Cormac made no move to remedy the situation. Instead, he glanced around the ring of knights, stroking his beard as if grinding some plan through the gears of his brain.

"About that," he finally said. "I'm afraid there may be a small...difficulty."

"Difficulty?" Ryland didn't like the sound of that.

Just then, the servant returned with their ale, thankfully without spilling a drop.

Cormac seemed grateful for the distraction. "Perhaps it should wait until after we've finished our ales."

The last thing Ryland wanted to do was stretch out the anticipation. What "small difficulty" could the chieftain possibly mean? Had the woman refused his hand? Had she run away with a lover? Was she dead? Maybe they'd finally executed her for the murder of her sister.

"As you wish," he said between his teeth.

Hiding his impatience as best he could, Ryland followed their host to the trestle table in the midst of the hall.

As they drank, his knights engaged in polite and harmless conversation with the chieftain.

They asked how the fishing was in the lakes.

They commented on the pleasant climate.

They listened to the chieftain's boasts about the plentiful game in the forest.

Through it all, Ryland sat silent. How could they speak of such trivialities when his entire future was hanging in the balance? What was Cormac's damned "small difficulty"? Where the devil was his bride?

Ryland's fingers tightened around his cup of ale. He swore if he heard one more word about the weather, he would crush the cup in his fist.

Finally, unable to stand the suspense, he steeled his nerves and asked, "Forgive my impatience, m'lord, but regarding my bride..."

The chieftain's bleary blue eyes slipped sideways, and he licked his lips, as if thinking up a good lie.

Cormac was uneasy. He'd been uneasy ever since these Englishmen had arrived. And he didn't like being uneasy. Not in his own keep.

He'd always been able to appease the English noblemen who visited, impressing them with his wealth and power. Even without an actual daughter to offer, he'd been confident that when the de Ware retinue arrived, he'd be able to come up with a substitute and an arrangement that would benefit them all, with the king none the wiser.

As far as his *clannsmen* knew, his daughter was imprisoned in a cell in the tower. But in all that time, no one had seen her. And so a few months ago, when King John had taken the throne, Cormac had put a daring plan into action.

He'd sought out a willing harlot of the right age and a reasonable resemblance to Temair to pass off as his heir, promising her untold riches and power.

Keeping her in the tower cell, he'd proceeded to fornicate with her at every opportunity, hoping to get her with child.

It was a mutually beneficial arrangement. Through her, he'd retain control of his *tuath*. And through him, she'd live a life of privilege.

His seed had finally taken hold in the lass. Wishing to see her wed in a timely fashion, he'd contacted the king and offered up his daughter and heiress to the man of John's choosing. It was the perfect deception. When the lass gave birth, no one but she and he would know whose offspring it truly was.

Now, however, he was having second thoughts.

These knights were not as manageable as he'd expected. Unlike the velvet-clad popinjays of the king's court, these men were hardened warriors. And except for the one called Warin, who showed the proper interest and respect for Cormac's acquisitions, they seemed undaunted by his power and unimpressed by his riches.

As for the man King John had sent as a bridegroom, Sir Ryland de Ware, Cormac liked him least of all. Though Sir Warin had covered for the man, he was convinced that Ryland's intervention on behalf of the servant had been a direct challenge to Cormac's authority. He couldn't risk having such a man in control of his lands.

He had to think of a different option.

He could say his daughter was dead. That would rid him of Sir Ryland. But it would also leave him with no political pawn for the future.

He could allow Sir Ryland to wed the imposter and look for a chance to murder the man later. But that was a messy business. Besides, the knight was not a man easily gulled. If he discovered his bride was a counterfeit, he would no doubt immediately report the unsavory news to King John.

A third idea suddenly came to Cormac.

It was a diabolically simple deception. He'd utterly destroy Sir Ryland by using his own untarnished chivalry against him. Even better, Cormac didn't have to lie. He only had to distort the truth.

Carefully furrowing his brows, he feigned regret. "I was hopin' I'd not have to tell ye this. But I can see there's no way around it." He paused to shake his head. "Ye see, to my great shame, my daughter, your bride, has..." He sighed. "The lass has run off."

The other knights gasped. But Sir Ryland said nothing. His eyes were stern and unwavering, and his frown was inscrutable.

Cormac continued. "When I told her she was to be wedded to an English knight, well...she sobbed and carried on." He tugged at his beard. He still couldn't read Sir Ryland's expression, so he looked for assurance from the other knights. "But I was firm with the lass. 'Aillenn,' I said, 'ye don't have a choice in the matter.'"

"You mean Temair?" one of the knights asked.

"What?"

"Your daughter," Sir Warin clarified. "You meant Temair."

"Oh, aye, o' course, Temair." Cormac cursed himself for the slip. It had been years since he'd seen either of his daughters. Their names were rusty in his mind. "I told Temair 'tis her duty to marry as the king sees fit." He shook his head again. "But the lass was havin' none of it."

When Sir Ryland finally spoke, his voice was cool and even. "Did you try beating her into submission?"

"Oh aye," Cormac replied automatically, instantly realizing his mistake as the knight's brows lowered in disapproval. "That is, nay, nay." He rubbed anxious fingers through his beard. "I should have," he said defensively. "After all, I couldn't have my own daughter refusin' the King of England." Ryland's face had gone grave again. "But ere I could lay a hand on the lass, she was out o' the keep and off into the woods."

"She fled?" Warin asked.

"Aye." Cormac's gaze veered from man to man as he tried to determine if they believed his story.

"How long ago?" another knight demanded.

"Three days," Cormac invented. That sounded reasonable to him.

A second knight asked, "Did you send men to hunt for her?"

Cormac hated to complicate his lies, so he shrugged and shook his head. "I was so sure she'd return."

Ryland frowned. "The woods are dangerous. She might be in peril." He sighed and set down his cup.

Cormac resisted crowing with glee. As he'd hoped, the knight was falling neatly into his trap. He could see Sir Ryland was considering taking matters into his own hands. He'd search for the lass himself.

Of course he'd never find her. Cormac expected

Temair was dead. And when the knight came back empty-handed, he would have only himself to blame. Cormac would be innocent. And Ryland would be too ashamed of his failure to remain in Eire.

Once the knight was gone and safely wed to someone else, Cormac's daughter could be miraculously "found." Then Cormac would once again have an heir with which to bargain. And with any luck, the next bridegroom the king sent would be more governable.

As for the pregnant imposter, Cormac would pay her for her trouble and send her on her way. Hers probably wasn't the first bastard he'd sired.

Cormac wrung his hands and tried to look distraught. "Do ye think ill may have befallen my daughter?"

Their silence was answer enough.

"We'll look for her," one of the knights decided.

"Aye," another agreed.

"Of course," Ryland said.

The first knight asked, "Can you describe her?"

Cormac opened his mouth and froze. How could he describe the daughter he'd last seen years ago? She hadn't even had breasts then. Even if she were somehow alive, she'd have grown into a woman by now.

At his hesitation, Warin guessed, "Does she have your coloring, m'lord?"

He shook his head, trying to remember. "Nay, she's a small, wildish lass with dark hair."

"Never fear," Warin said, as much to Ryland as to Cormac. "We'll find her."

One of them added, "We can start first thing in the morning."

Perfect, Cormac thought. That would give him time to

send the imposter away. After a few days, at most a week, he figured, they'd give up the search and return to England.

On the other hand, the forest was full of thieves and wolves. Maybe misfortune would befall the knights. Maybe Sir Ryland would never be heard from again. It was an attractive alternative.

CHAPTER 10

Dawn painted the topmost stones of the tower house, the spot where the older O'Keeffe daughter had apparently fallen to her death.

Ryland drew his brows together. He wondered if the rumors were true, that his bride-to-be had murdered her sister.

As he and his men shouldered their packs and set out on foot toward the trees, he took a bracing breath. If ever there was an inauspicious beginning to a marriage, this was it.

He couldn't blame the lass for running off. As a ruler, Cormac was abusive. As a father, he was likely even more vicious and demanding. The idea of submitting to a foreign bridegroom who might well be a harsher master than her father was probably horrifying. It was reason enough for Temair to flee and take her chances in the wilds.

The fact that Cormac practically admitted he beat his own daughter set Ryland's teeth on edge. Nothing was more abhorrent to him and contrary to his knightly vows than a man who preyed on those less powerful than himself.

When they found the lass, Ryland would have to convince her that he was nothing like her father, that he meant her no harm. To his relief, it sounded like Temair was nothing like her father either. She shared neither his pasty flesh nor orange hair. Hopefully, she didn't share his volatile temper.

"Where do we start?" Godwin asked.

"She can't have gone far," Ryland said. At least, he hoped not. The Irish forest was like a maze. It would be easy to get lost. He'd already decided it would be best if they didn't split up to search for her.

"'Tis a shame O'Keeffe keeps no hounds," Osgood said.

Ryland agreed. A keen-nosed hound would have been useful.

Warin nodded toward the trees. "A traveler would normally stay close to the main road."

"Not if the traveler didn't want to be found," Laurence said.

Ryland furrowed his brows. Who knew this forest? Who knew the places a fugitive might hide? Who might have stumbled across a lass lost in the woods in the last three days?

The woodkerns.

They probably noticed every time a new sparrow flitted through the boughs. They would know if a stranger had entered the wood. He'd find the outlaws and offer them a reward for information about a chieftain's daughter wandering among the fern.

Though he was loath to admit it, the possibility of encountering one particular outlaw—the beautiful, gray-eyed lass—stirred Ryland's blood in disturbing ways. As wrong as it was, his pulse quickened at the thought of matching wits with her again.

They searched for hours along the main road. They looked for footprints, scraps of cloth, ashes of a fire. There was no evidence whatsoever of a runaway bride.

At mid-day, they stopped for cheese, oatcakes, smoked trout, and ale, adding a few wild strawberries that grew along a roadside spring.

By late afternoon, they drew near to the narrows before the clearing where they'd been waylaid by the woodkerns. There was no assurance the outlaws would be there today, but it was likely they preferred to work in familiar surroundings.

"We'll question the woodkerns," he announced.

There was an outcry over that.

"Are you mad, m'lord?" Warin blinked in disbelief.

Ryland shook his head. "We've been searching all day, and we're no closer to finding her."

"The longer she's lost, the more likely..." Osgood didn't want to finish the sentence, but they all knew a woman alone in the woods was at terrible risk. Every hour counted.

Warin grimaced. "There has to be another way."

"This is really our best chance," Ryland said.

"Our best chance to be beggared," Warin muttered.

"Sir Ryland has a point," Godwin volunteered. "No one knows the forest better."

"That may be." Warin arched an indignant brow. "But why would a pack of common thieves help us?"

"Because I'll pay them to help us," Ryland said.

Laurence crossed his arms over his chest and clucked his tongue. "I don't trust them."

"Right," Warin agreed.

"Nor do I," Ryland said, "which is why I won't pay them until they lead me to my bride."

Warin still grumbled, "I don't see what's to keep them from simply robbing us blind and stealing off into the woods."

Laurence could answer that. "A band of motley outlaws is no match for five Knights of de Ware."

"Is that so?" Warin argued. "They seemed to have had little trouble yesterday."

"They had leverage then," Godwin pointed out. "Today, we won't be taken by surprise."

"Right," Ryland said, unbuckling his sword belt and handing his sword to Osgood. "This time we'll be ready for them."

Warin glared at him. "What the devil are you doing, m'lord?"

Ryland adjusted the pack on his shoulders. "Offering myself up as bait."

Warin choked.

"What?" Laurence demanded. "Unarmed?"

Ryland clapped Laurence on the shoulder and winked. "They're thieves, not murderers. I'll be fine."

"Oh, bloody hell, if anyone is going to be bait, 'twill be me," Warin decided, fumbling with the buckle of his sword belt.

"Nay." Ryland seized his arm to stop him. "This is my quest. She's my bride."

Warin bit back another oath. "If anything happens to you…"

Laurence frowned. "Take a dagger at least, my lord."

"I'll be perfectly safe," Ryland assured them. "And I

promise, if I get into any trouble, I'll give a whistle, and you can all come running to my rescue."

This seemed to mollify Godwin and Osgood. Laurence still looked displeased. And Warin looked inconsolable.

"Don't look at me like that," Ryland said, thumping Warin on the chest. "You'll make me think that perhaps I'm *not* the most glorious, noble, and upstanding knight in England after all."

With that, he ventured down the road alone. He followed the path around the bend until he lost sight of his men. Then he began to tromp loudly along toward the narrows, bellowing a tune sure to attract the attention of anyone in earshot. If his heartfelt rendition of *Le Lai du Chaitivel* didn't roust the woodkerns from the woods, nothing could.

Temair sighed as she picked the blackberries off the streamside vines and dropped them into her basket. She supposed, if she was forced to stay concealed in the woods for her own safety, at least she had the company of her wolfhounds, Bran and Flann. She tossed a berry to Flann, who snapped it up in his teeth, pretending to enjoy it. She laughed, throwing one to Bran as well, who gingerly peeled his lips back and let it drop to the ground.

Now and then her gaze strayed to the fallen log that made a bridge across the stream and the spot where she'd knocked the handsome knight into the water. Her heart skipped as she remembered his bright grin and dancing brown eyes.

She'd returned to this place today, telling herself she was going back for the blackberries. But she knew the truth. As childish as it was, she hoped by some ridiculous miracle to run into that dashing swordsman again.

Of course he wasn't coming back. Why would he? The woodkerns hadn't stolen so much as a single coin from the knights. There was no need for them to return to collect their losses. The man was likely halfway across Eire by now.

Not that it mattered if he *did* come back.

Temair had to stay out of sight. Her black hair and telltale gray eyes would instantly mark her as the chieftain's daughter. Now that she was in danger of being hunted, her mask wasn't enough of a disguise.

She'd never really minded wearing a mask, to be truthful. She'd always rather enjoyed the air of mystery it lent her. And disguising her gender usually gave her an advantage when it came to foiling foes.

She smiled as she remembered the English knight's astonished face when he'd unmasked her and realized he'd been defeated by a lass. She wished she could see his perplexed expression again.

But she couldn't.

Because she had to hide.

Damn it all. She hated hiding.

She let out another long sigh, consoling herself with a blackberry.

She was mid-bite when a sudden, loud howl from the road startled her, nearly making her upend the whole basket.

The hounds snapped to attention, but they made no sound. Temair had trained them well. They stood silent, at the ready, waiting for her signal.

She cocked her head to listen. The distant baying

sounded suspiciously like a song. She gulped down the blackberry. What fool would travel through an outlaw-infested forest, singing at the top of his lungs?

A gullible fool, she thought. Probably one with more coin than sense. Easy prey for an outlaw like Temair.

She caught her lip under her teeth. She was supposed to lie low. She could not be seen. She knew that. Anyone she encountered might send her description back to the chieftain.

But how could she resist the temptation of easy coin?

It wouldn't take long, she reasoned. She could slip out onto the road, relieve the bellowing bard of his riches, and then vanish into the woods again in the blink of an eye. She'd be there and back in a matter of moments, with none the wiser.

She could trust Flann and Bran to stay obediently behind. And she'd return immediately to camp with her spoils.

While she pondered the risks, the singing grew louder. She couldn't make out the words, though they sounded French. His voice was powerful and not unpleasant. Maybe he was a troubadour with a heavy purse.

If she didn't decide quickly whether to take the risk, he'd pass by. And the chance would be lost.

"To hell with it," she muttered, setting down the basket of berries.

She pulled her scarf up over her face and her hood down over her head. Then she turned to the hounds with a stern finger.

"Flann. Bran. Sit."

They did.

"Stay."

She placed the basket in front of them, as if it was their duty to guard it.

"Stay," she repeated.

The hounds slid down until their front paws touched the basket.

Then she slung her bow and quiver of arrows over her shoulder and tripped lightly across the log to the far bank. Following the source of the sound, she made her way soundlessly through the fern and willows. Near the narrows of the road, she hid behind the thick trunk of an oak. Silently nocking an arrow into her bow, she waited for the singer to draw close.

His truly was an outstanding voice. The melody was strong and confident. The tone was rich and rolling with just a touch of melancholy. In fact, Temair had to be careful not to get so distracted by the performance that she misjudged her timing.

She'd made the leap from behind this particular oak so many times she could do it with her eyes closed. The tree was perfectly situated to conceal an outlaw from anyone traveling along the road until the very last instant. All Temair had to do was listen for the footsteps—or in this case, the loud singing—for the ideal moment to pop out.

Just before the man grew even with the oak, Temair sprang out onto the road with her bow drawn.

"Hold, sir, and—!"

The air went out of her lungs. It was him. Somehow—impossibly—it was the English knight.

CHAPTER 11

"Ye," she breathed.

She'd startled him. His voice had ratcheted up to an alarmingly high pitch when she'd leaped out.

She lowered her bow in disbelief as a dozen questions rushed through her brain.

What was he doing here?

Why was he alone?

Where was he going?

Why was he singing?

For a moment, he looked as shocked as she was. But of course, he had less reason to be surprised. He might have expected to find her here. She, on the other hand, hadn't expected to ever see him again.

She was still reeling when his face blossomed into the adorable grin that had been haunting her daydreams.

"Why, Lady Gray," he said in amused tones, inclining his head. "We meet a—"

She raised her bow again, training her arrow on his heart. She couldn't afford to let his pretty face distract her.

She didn't know what he was doing here. But considering she was alone and didn't have the advantage of strength over him, she had to use whatever leverage possible to keep him at bay. At least until she discovered his business.

"I'm unarmed," he told her.

That remained to be seen. He'd managed to pull a dagger out of nowhere yesterday.

Still, a battle raged inside her. He was so magnificent, so handsome and full of charm. His eyes and that grin were even more enchanting than she'd remembered. And now that he stood before her on solid ground instead of swimming at her feet, he seemed more imposing, more muscular, more commanding.

Then she made the mistake of locking her gaze onto his mouth and those pressuring, yielding lips that had claimed hers and sent her pulse racing. Her fingers faltered on the drawn bow.

"Look," he bade her, slipping his pack slowly and carefully from his shoulders and letting it drop to the ground. He held up his hands in surrender. She noted he wasn't wearing his sword belt. Maybe he was telling the truth. Maybe he *was* unarmed.

But she never fooled herself about her own vulnerability. She didn't have her *bata* this time. If she lowered her bow, he could reach her in three long strides.

Bloody hell. She should have stayed in the woods. She'd been so sure she could make a quick score on the road and be on her way, as fast and invisible as a shadow.

"Where are your friends?" she asked him.

"You're not going to lower your bow?" He almost looked hurt.

"Not until I get some answers."

"I told you I'm unarmed."

She smirked. "Somehow I don't think that matters. We're not exactly evenly matched when it comes to hand-to-hand combat."

The corner of his lip drifted up slyly. "On the contrary, I think we're perfectly matched."

She blushed at the thrill that shot through her as she imagined tangling with him in less combative ways.

But she couldn't let lust get in the way of logic. She steeled her jaw and tightened her grip on the bow. "Are ye goin' to answer me?"

"My friends? I left them."

"And ye're travelin' through the wood on your own?" She doubted that.

He shrugged and looked around him. "So 'twould appear."

"What's your business?"

"I need your help."

"My help?" She frowned. So he *had* come here intentionally. "What kind o' help?"

"The kind that puts silver in your purse."

Temair gave a humorless chuckle. "I don't need to *help* ye to put silver in my purse, English. All I need to do is *rob* ye."

Indeed, she should do just that and be on her way.

But if what old Sorcha had said was true—that there could be an active search for someone matching Temair's description—then letting him go was too great a risk.

"You really won't help me?" He seemed genuinely puzzled.

"Why should I help ye?"

"I thought after...that is...after we...hmm."

"What?" She knew what he thought. He thought that maybe after that breath-stealing, world-shattering kiss they'd shared, they'd forged some sort of a connection... had a meeting of hearts...bonded on an earthy level that had rendered them forever intertwined...

He was right.

She felt it too.

A part of her *did* want to help him.

But her life was in danger. She had to help herself first.

She'd start with helping herself to his silver.

She nodded to his pack. "Hand over your coin."

He shook his head. "I'm afraid I can't do that."

She blinked. "What do ye mean?"

"If you're not going to help me, I'm not giving you a farthing." His eyes were no longer twinkling. They'd become as flat and menacing as a storm cloud.

"Then I'll have to shoot ye," she threatened.

Bloody hell, she hoped he wouldn't make her shoot him. Only two people had ever made her do that. One she'd shot in the arm, the other in the foot. It still made her sick to think about it.

He leveled a rock-steady gaze at her. "You won't kill me."

Her return stare was just as unflinching. "Who said I was goin' to kill ye?" Then she let her gaze and her arrow wander over possible targets, ending between his legs.

His eyes widened a little.

She cocked her head. "Now will ye hand o'er the coin?"

He sighed. "You give me no choice."

But instead of digging through his pack for his silver, he raised his thumb and finger to his mouth and let out an ear-splitting whistle.

For a moment nothing happened, and she wondered what game the knight was playing.

Then, like a distant rumble of thunder, she heard them come.

His four fellow knights came roaring around the bend in the road on foot in a roiling cloud of dust, brandishing their broadswords like avenging angels.

For an instant, Temair couldn't breathe. Like charging berserkers, they were bearing down on her with such force and fury that she'd be trampled in another minute if she didn't move.

Beneath her fear was an awful sense of betrayal. Damn that knight. She'd believed him when he'd said he'd left his men behind. But it had been a trick. And now she wasn't convinced it hadn't been a deadly deception.

Outnumbered, all she could do now was surrender and hope for their mercy. She didn't have a choice.

Or did she?

The moment she dropped her bow to the ground, the knight raised his arm, commanding the others to stop their charge. Still several yards away, they slowed to a walk and sheathed their swords.

It was then Temair pulled down her mask and let out a loud whistle of her own.

The knight frowned at her, and she gave him a smug smile.

No doubt he expected a handful of woodkerns to come flying out of the trees. He probably figured they could be easily dispatched by his four armed and armored knights.

Instead, two gigantic wolfhounds, all churning limbs and snarling teeth, came boiling out of the woods.

"There!" she directed them, hurling an arm in the

direction of the four knights coming down the road.

The hounds bounded toward the men at such speed that the knights had no time to draw their swords. They shrieked and scattered, leaping into the trees to escape the snapping jaws of the wolfhounds.

For a moment, the knight stood dumbfounded, staring at his treed and trembling men with his jaw agape.

Temair felt a surge of heady triumph. She'd bested him again.

Shaking his head, the man gave a sigh of surrender and reached into his pack where he kept his coins. He pulled out a small parcel tied with twine and set it on the ground. Then he gave a loud whistle, a perfect imitation of Temair's whistle.

The hounds, fooled by the sound, perked up their ears.

"Nay," Temair breathed in disbelief.

The man untied the twine and opened the parcel. Inside was something that looked suspiciously like salted pork.

"Nay," Temair said more loudly as the hounds abandoned their prey and began trotting forward.

"Look what I have for you, pups," the knight cooed fearlessly.

"Nay!" she shouted. "Nay, Bran! Nay, Flann!"

"Come on, lads," the man called out. "That's it. I've got something for you. Something that tastes much better than an English knight."

Temair bit back a scream of frustration. She'd never felt so betrayed. Her hounds were completely ignoring her. Distracted by the scent of meat, they only had eyes for that damned knight.

He used a dagger to cut the meat in half while the dogs waited impatiently, drooling and licking their chops.

"There you go," he said as the two disloyal hounds nosed forward, gobbling up the meat as if they hadn't eaten for days.

Then, just to salt her wounds, the knight gave her hounds a good scratch behind the ears. They returned his gesture of affection, licking his face as if he were their new best friend.

"Ye bloody traitors," Temair muttered at them in disgust. "Ye should be ashamed o' yourselves."

The knight laughed as the gangly wolfhounds slobbered all over him, nearly knocking him over in their enthusiasm.

Damn the unfaithful hounds. Their magnificent breed was used as war dogs in combat. They were fierce and powerful enough to drag a man in full armor off of his horse.

At the moment, however, Flann and Bran seemed more inclined to lick the man to death.

He caught their chins in his hands. "You're not traitors, are you, lads?" he crooned. "Poor things, you're just half-starved."

"Ballocks!" she protested. Her hounds ate better than she did.

He clucked his tongue. "Your mistress probably feeds you nothing but nuts and berries."

"Nuts and..." she echoed. "That's ridiculous."

He grinned. Obviously, he was teasing her.

Then he swiveled on his haunches toward his men. "Are you going to roost all day in the trees?" he asked them. "Or are any of you brave enough to meet these ferocious beasts?" He ruffled the hounds' heads again, and they wagged their tails in delight.

His men climbed reluctantly out of the trees. As they cautiously approached, her gaze flitted uncertainly between them. She hated being unarmed against five hulking knights.

"I have no coin," she warned them. "So if ye're hopin' to rob me, ye're out o' luck."

"I'm not interested in your coin," he told her. "As I said, I just need your help. And I'm willing to pay for it."

"What do ye want?"

"I'm looking for someone."

Her breath caught. But she didn't dare let her alarm show. As casually as possible, she asked, "Who?"

"A young woman."

She gulped. So it was true. Her father had hired foreign mercenaries to hunt for her. She cursed herself for not taking her own advice, for not staying hidden in the forest. If these knights dragged her back to the tower house...

"She ran into the woods three days ago," he added, "and has been missing ever since."

Temair blinked. She let out a shuddering breath of relief. "Three *days* ago?"

"Aye."

The rest of his men had come up now. None of them were interested in tangling with her hounds again. But to her aggravation, the dogs seemed content to sit beside the knight anyway, nosing at his hands and enjoying his companionable scratches.

"This woman," Temair asked. "What does she look like?"

The knight furrowed his brows. "Small. Dark. Wild."

"That's all?"

"I'm afraid so."

She need not have worried. That description fit about half of Eire. And small? These men were obviously searching for someone else.

On the other hand, all five men had seen Temair's face clearly now. They could easily take her description back to her father. If her correct age and her raven-black hair didn't convince Cormac his daughter was alive and well in the woods, her gray eyes would.

She had to find a way to keep these men away from the *clann* chieftain.

She perused the other knights. Despite being spooked by her hounds, they were a formidable group. Tall. Strong. Tough. With broad shoulders and heavy swords.

She was unarmed and alone. She couldn't very well overpower them and force them to stay in the forest.

Maybe there was another way.

CHAPTER 12

Ryland had to admit the description he'd been given of his runaway bride was of little help. But surely there weren't that many wenches loose in the woods.

"I've seen no one like that," Gray told him. "But perhaps ye'd like to come to my camp and question the others. It may be they've crossed paths with the lass."

Her suggestion stirred up instant conflict among his men, who scowled and grumbled at the idea of venturing into what Laurence referred to as "a den of thieves," what Godwin called "a trap," and what Warin claimed might be full of "feckin' faerie folk."

But he lifted his hand to silence them. "We'd be grateful."

There was a risk it *was* a trap. Her people probably knew the woods well. They could easily waylay the knights.

But Ryland didn't have much choice in the matter. He had to find his bride before something happened to her. Not only did her life hang in the balance. But the king was depending on this alliance.

Besides, he knew how to mitigate the risk.

"I'll just hold onto your hounds while we travel through the forest." His eyes twinkled with a knowing half-smile as he took a firm grip on their collars.

"O' course," she said, answering with a knowing half-smirk of her own. "Follow me."

The journey through the woods was breathtaking.

Gray led them along winding trails just wide enough for deer and past tiny streams that glistened between the pebbles like silver chain. Mounds of moss dressed the trees in skirts of emerald velvet. Luxuriant ferns brushed their legs with feathery caresses. More ribbons of water trickled down shelves of rock, disappearing into the soft earth. Mushrooms lay like tiny discarded caps on the forest floor. The smell of damp soil and fertile life filled the air. And there was a curious stillness over everything, a silence that absorbed all sound as they passed.

It was enchanting and unsettling all at once.

Indeed, he found it remarkable how the lady forged ahead with confidence through the virgin woodland, even without the help of the hounds. He was certain, without her guidance, he and his knights would have lost their way.

He hoped he could trust her to lead them *out* of the woods as well.

He thought he could.

Still, he'd been surprised at first when she'd shown no interest in helping him. Most women leaped at the opportunity to lend assistance to a noble knight.

This wench was not like the other women he knew. Maybe it was because she was Irish. Or maybe it was because she was an outlaw. But she was definitely unpredictable.

They'd hiked a few miles when they entered a shadowy downward dip in the trail. Gray gave a low whistle. His men clapped their hands to their hilts as they heard someone unseen whistle in response.

"M'lord?" Warin nervously whispered.

Gray replied to his unasked question. "I'm lettin' 'em know we're approachin' the camp." She cheekily added, "If I meant ye harm, ye'd be caught by now. They've been watchin' ye for the last quarter-mile."

Ryland wondered if that was true. If so, he was impressed by the outlaws' stealth. It was little wonder the Irish thought their forests were populated by faerie folk and spirits.

As they traveled onward, the path gradually widened. Then it opened out onto a flat, roughly circular expanse bordered on one side by a natural wall of vine-covered stone. Dense greenery surrounded the clearing. Towering yews made a leafy canopy overhead. In the center was a ring of blackened rocks where ashen coals slumbered, surrounded by several small boulders and tree stumps that were probably makeshift stools.

"Welcome," their guide announced with a somewhat insincere lift of her brow.

One by one, like bark peeling off the trees, woodkerns seemed to appear out of nowhere. Then, as if emerging out of the mountain itself, two women brushed aside the vines and stepped into the clearing. Ryland thought if he stayed in the forest much longer, he might start believing in faerie folk himself.

His men braced to face the oncoming threat.

But the outlaws showed no aggression. They didn't need to. The knights were in *their* domain now.

The same jolly woodkern who'd interrupted them at the stream greeted them now. "Well, well, if 'tisn't the 'noble' fellows we met yesterday."

A pretty red-haired woman stepped out from behind an elm, frowning. "Why have ye brought them here, Gray?"

"They need information. They're searchin' for someone. And they're willin' to pay."

A tall, slender man of noble bearing chuckled at that. "Willin' or no, they *will* pay."

Warin whispered furiously in Ryland's ear. "I told ye this was a mistake, m'lord."

Ryland hushed him with a hiss and faced the tall gentleman. If he was as noble as he appeared, perhaps Ryland could appeal to the man's sense of honor. "Sir, the information I seek will cost you nothing, and yet I offer payment for it. Surely you'll honor such a humble and courteous request."

The man straightened, moved by Ryland's chivalrous words. "Well said." Then he called out, "What say ye, all? Shall we give aid to these foreigners?"

After a few nods and grunts, the camp seemed to reach a consensus.

"Who do you seek?" one of the women asked.

Ryland politely inclined his head. "My lady, I'm searching for a woman lost in the woods."

Gray added, "He said she went missin' three days ago."

A man dressed as a friar spoke. "Three days? Is that so?" He studied the knights, one by one, sizing them up as if he were choosing a horse. "Ye're English."

"Aye." That was fairly obvious.

"And of high rank," another said.

He nodded.

"Have ye just arrived in Eire?" the red-haired beauty asked.

"We've been here a sennight."

Ryland felt like a wandering thief being interrogated by the local lawmen. But what else could he do? For all he knew, these might be the Shire-Reeves of the Woodkerns.

"Why do ye seek this lass?" another asked.

Ryland would have preferred to keep his reasons to himself. After all, there were some who might think preventing a foreigner from finding his Irish bride was a good idea.

But he had little choice. He was fairly sure if he didn't answer their questions, they'd just send the knights on their way...after they robbed them of their silver just for spite.

So he answered. "The lady is to be my bride."

A few of the outlaws stiffened.

Before Ryland could wonder why, the black-bearded outlaw spoke. His voice was laced with amusement. "So your bride ran away, did she? And what reason did ye give her for that?"

Ryland straightened with pride. He'd had about enough of prying questions. Besides, he'd never given a woman reason to flee in his entire life. "I wasn't even given the courtesy of meeting her."

It was Gray's turn to interrogate him. "Why would ye wish to wed a lass ye've never met?"

He gave her a rueful chuckle. She obviously didn't understand the responsibilities of nobility. Women like her probably married for love. "'Tisn't my wish. 'Tis my duty."

"Your duty?"

"I was commanded by the king to do so."

"The king?" the noble outlaw remarked with raised brows. "John Lackland?"

Behind him, Ryland's men stirred at the insult. He could almost feel the anger boiling off of them in silent waves.

"*King John,*" he said pointedly, "wishes to forge an alliance between our people—"

"Pah!" a sour-faced outlaw snarled. "He wishes to seize our land is what ye mean."

"Just like the English always have," grumbled a bald-pated brute.

"Aye," some of the other woodkerns chimed in.

Ryland heard the menacing growl of his men behind him, which triggered menacing growls from the two wolfhounds.

Before a fight could break out, Gray held up her hand for silence. "Bran! Flann! Hush."

The hounds calmed at once.

Ryland wished he could calm his men so quickly. But he understood their anger. He was beginning to regret engaging the outlaws' help. All this delay was troubling his spirit and trying his patience.

"Look," he told them. "This quarreling is pointless. Either you've seen the woman or you haven't. Either you'll help me or you won't. Every moment we waste, hurling insults and arguing politics, brings her closer to danger. She's out there somewhere in the woods—frightened, lost, hungry. Whether you agree with this marriage or not, I would think you'd at least want to keep your countrywoman safe."

Gray's eyes actually softened at his words. A hint of a smile graced her lips.

The gentleman outlaw let out a sigh of shame. "He's right. A good Irish lass's welfare is at stake."

"True." The tall, jolly fellow sheepishly hooked his thumbs into his woven belt. "I suppose we ought to help him, for her sake."

The others shrugged and nodded.

"Wait." Gray stepped in front of Ryland. Her beautiful silver eyes locked with his. It took all his willpower not to let his gaze slip down to her soft, kissable mouth. "This bride o' yours, does she have a name?"

For one inexplicable instant, captivated by her gaze, he couldn't remember. For one mad moment, he imagined being married to a brash and beautiful outlaw instead of a frightened bride who'd fled into the forest.

But his strong sense of duty turned the lock on that idea.

"Her name is Temair O'Keeffe."

CHAPTER 13

emair didn't dare flinch. Or blink. Or move a muscle.

She kept her gaze trained with forced nonchalance on the bold English knight, as if she had no idea he was here for *her*.

But she could barely breathe. Her heart was pounding. And her brain whirled with chaotic emotions.

The rest of the woodkerns had fallen silent. If someone didn't say something soon, he'd suspect they had something to hide.

Old Sorcha found her voice first. "Ye mean the *clann* chieftain's daughter?"

"Aye."

"So ye must be Sir Ryland de Ware," Sorcha said.

"I am."

Wild thoughts careened around in Temair's head.

This was her betrothed?

She'd been intrigued by the English knight since they'd met at the stream. Charmed by his laughter, his dancing eyes, his brawny figure, and his delicious mouth, she had to acknowledge he was just the sort of man a lass might wish to marry.

But he was English, the choice of her tyrant father and of the bloody English king. He'd been sent, not to court her, but to claim her. And while *he* might be the sort of man to wed out of duty, she'd be damned if she'd be a political pawn, forced into a marriage of convenience. No matter how handsome he was.

She narrowed her eyes. "Ye say she ran away three days ago?"

"Aye, according to her father."

"And ye never laid eyes on the lass?" she pressed.

"Nay."

"The chieftain only said she was small and dark-haired," Ryland volunteered.

"And wildish," one of his men added.

Temair frowned. Wildish? Maybe. But nobody would ever call her small. And certainly no one could overlook Temair's most defining characteristic, the one that had given her her nickname—her unique gray eyes.

But the fact that her father said this small, dark-haired, wildish Temair had run away just three days ago could mean only one thing. He'd hired an imposter.

No one in the *clann* would be fooled. Surely they remembered Temair's gray eyes. But the English knight would never suspect he was wedding a counterfeit bride. And her *clannsmen* would be too afraid to tell him.

Temair was glad the lass had run off. But how long would it be before they found her? Or if they didn't, how long would it be before her father found another imposter? There were plenty of small, dark-haired, wildish lasses to choose from.

Rage filled her so quickly she could hardly speak.

Fortunately, she was saved from having to say anything. With a soft rustle of the bushes, Aife suddenly appeared at the edge of the camp, returning from her day of spying in *Tuath O'Keeffe*.

The knights turned toward the sound.

"Temair?" Ryland asked hopefully.

Aife gave a start, both from being addressed by that name and the fact that there were five strange strapping knights occupying the clearing, all staring at her.

For some reason, the hope in Ryland's voice aggravated Temair. "Nay, that is not Temair," she muttered.

Then she suddenly realized that Aife may have news about the imposter.

"Aife, ye must be exhausted," Temair said. "Come inside and have a pint. Sorcha? Mor?" She beckoned the women to gather in the cave. "Gentlemen, if ye'll give us a moment..." She didn't wait for their approval, but she gave Cambeal a meaningful look to ensure his cooperation.

Though Temair was the leader of the woodkerns, decisions were usually made by the entire group. This situation, however, required a hasty plan. Cambeal would recognize that. He'd make sure the rest of the woodkerns stood by her decision, whatever it was.

Once the four women were inside the cave, the furious whispers began.

"What are ye goin' to do, Gray?" Lady Mor asked Temair, wringing her hands.

"I know what I'd *like* to do," Temair ground out. "I'd like to grab my *bata* and pay my father a visit."

"Why did they think I was Temair?" Aife asked.

Temair started pacing in fury. "That land has been in

O'Keeffe hands for hundreds of years. That *tuath* is my bloody legacy. How dare my father hand it off to strangers?"

Aife blinked in confusion. "What's goin' on?"

Lady Mor answered Aife. "That knight—the one who thought ye were Temair? Well, that's Sir Ryland de Ware, the English knight who's come to wed Temair. Only he doesn't know that Gray is Temair, because he's never laid eyes on her. And Cormac has told Ryland that Temair has run away when in fact—"

"Hush, Mor!" Sorcha said. "Ye're only confoundin' the matter. One thing at a time." She poured ales all around.

Temair stopped pacing and took a bracing gulp. "Aife, what news from the tower house?"

Aife cleared her throat importantly and gave her report. "'Tis woeful tidin's. This afternoon, a maid o'erheard the chieftain speakin' to someone on the stairs. He was arguin' with a lass, tellin' her his plans had changed, that he was sendin' her away."

"A lass?" Temair asked. "What lass?"

Aife shrugged. "The maid said she was certain the lass must be his daughter Temair, finally released from her cell after all these years."

"Go on."

"The lass began weepin' and wailin', sayin' the chieftain had promised she could stay at the keep. He told her to keep quiet or he'd give her a reason to weep. Then she said a curious thing. She said she'd tell everyone the truth—that the babe she was carryin' belonged to the chieftain—if he didn't keep his word."

Lady Mor gasped.

Temair felt sick. No matter how diabolical she believed

her father was, he always managed to exceed her expectations.

Aife went on. "After that, the maid heard the chieftain cloutin' the lass and the lass whimperin'. There was a dreadful thud on the stairs and then silence. The maid was afraid she'd be discovered, so she fled. But she said when she returned later, there was a great deal o' blood on the stairs. She feared the chieftain killed the lass."

They all stared silently into their ales as they absorbed the horrible news.

Lady Mor sighed in sympathy. "The poor wench."

Temair shuddered. She remembered what it was like to be beaten by Cormac. She'd been lucky to escape with her life. But to be burdened with child, then cast out like offal...

"Maybe she's better off dead," she breathed. Sometimes that was what she thought about her sister.

But the other revelation was even more insidious. Her father hadn't intended to leave the land in the hands of strangers after all. By impregnating the lass he meant to pass off as his daughter, he planned to deceive the English, to make Sir Ryland de Ware believe the child and heir was his.

Lady Mor creased her brow. "I'm confused. After the chieftain went to such trouble to find a counterfeit bride and get her with child," she mused aloud, "why would he get rid o' her?"

Sorcha nodded. "And why would he send the English knights on a fool's errand—searchin' for the lass in the woods—when he knew very well she hadn't run off?"

Temair could answer that. "The lass was threatenin' to expose his secrets. She was becomin' too difficult to control."

That was the reason her da had never expended much effort in looking for Temair after she'd fled. Her sister Aillenn he'd always been able to manage. But Temair fought back. And if there was one thing a tyrant like her father could not abide, it was someone who wasn't afraid to retaliate.

"So what do ye think the chieftain will do next?" Lady Mor asked.

"He'll find a replacement for her," Sorcha guessed.

"One he can bend to his will," Temair agreed.

Sorcha added, "Meanwhile, he's distractin' the English knights, sendin' them on a merry chase after a ghost."

After a long, pensive silence, Aife meekly suggested, "What if ye tell them the truth, Gray? What if ye tell them who ye are?"

"Nay!" Temair blurted out vehemently. "So long as my brutish father is breathin', I won't go back to the *tuath*. I won't live under his thumb again. Ever. I just won't."

Sorcha gently took her arm. "Nor will we ever make ye. Orlaith made ye a promise that first day, and we mean to keep it. Ye'll always have a safe home with us here."

Temair nodded and gave her a grateful half-smile. But she still wasn't happy. "I won't let my father hand o'er what rightfully belongs to the *clann*." She began pacing again, rubbing the back of her neck. "I need to stop this sham of a marriage and come up with a way to take the *tuath* away from him, once and for all."

"Take it away?" Aife's brows shot up. "How?"

Sorcha sighed. "Ye'd need an army."

Temair let out a sigh. Sorcha was right. It was a foolish idea.

"What if we...kept the bridegroom?" Lady Mor asked.

"Kept him?" Aife said. "Why?"

Lady Mor arched a brow. "He can't very well be married if he can't be found."

"Wait." Temair had another idea, one that made a shiver of excitement travel up her spine. "What if we held him for ransom?"

"Ransom?" Aife exclaimed.

"Aye," Temair gushed. "The last thing Cormac wants is for the king to find out things have become...messy, right?"

"Right," said Sorcha.

Temair continued. "So he'll pay to see the king's man returned safely."

"And quietly," Aife added.

"Right," said Temair.

Sorcha knitted her brows. "If he pays the ransom, then what?"

Temair smiled in triumph. "We'll use the money to hire an army o' mercenaries to take back the *tuath*."

"A *real* army?" Lady Mor said in surprise.

"Aye."

Temair felt suddenly giddy. They could do this. Orlaith had told her that one day Temair would reclaim her legacy. That time was now. Between Cambeal's warfare expertise and Domnall and Maelan's experience as soldiers, they could assemble and lead an army to storm the tower and reclaim what was hers.

Lady Mor and Aife squealed in contagious joy.

But when Temair looked at Sorcha, the woman had gone quiet.

"What is it?" Temair asked.

Sorcha tapped her lip. "Do ye think 'tis necessary to take it by force?"

"Force is the only language my father understands." Bitterness colored her words.

Sorcha studied her a long while then and finally nodded her head. "'Tis up to ye, Gray. Ye brought de Ware here. Ye should decide his fate. O'Keeffe is *your* birthright, after all."

Temair thought of it as *all* of their birthright. As far as she was concerned, the woodkerns were her *clann*. Though she'd never openly stated it, she'd always known in her heart that when she regained her title, she'd bring her band of outlaws with her to live in *Tuath O'Keeffe*.

"So what will we tell the English knights?" Aife asked.

"A lie," Temair said. "We need them to deliver the ransom message."

"And what will ye do with Sir Ryland?" Lady Mor asked.

Temair shrugged. That was the least of her worries. For the moment, all she had to decide was how much he was worth.

Ryland wasn't born yesterday. By their exaggerated air of nonchalance, he could tell the women were up to something the instant they emerged from the strange vine-covered cave.

What it was, he couldn't tell. But something was afoot.

At the moment, he couldn't do much about it. The knights were at the mercy of the woodkerns. They'd never be able to find their way out of this knot of a forest alone. But it was a calculated risk he'd taken to get the outlaws' assistance.

Indeed, while the women had been chatting about...whatever it was they were chatting about...the woodkerns had discussed a number of possible ideas about where his missing bride could be. They clearly knew the lay of the land. And to his relief, not once did they try to suggest she might have been stolen by faerie folk.

Gray gave him an elusive smile. "Aife has indeed brought news about your bride."

"News? What news?" Ryland eagerly demanded.

"Do ye mind?" she asked, sidling past him and breaking his concentration, indicating her hounds. "They haven't been watered yet."

He released the dogs, and they trotted off to her. She ushered them away, chaining them to a tree.

"Good news, I hope?" he called out. He hoped to locate the missing lady and return to the keep before it got dark.

"Aye," she said. "It seems your bride didn't leave the keep after all."

"What?"

His knights grumbled in discontent, and he held his hand up for quiet.

The older woman, Sorcha, shook her head. "Curious how often a man searches far afield for what's right under his nose."

There was an odd glimmer in her eyes, as if she were speaking about something else. But he was too aggravated over the time he'd already wasted to try to decipher her meaning.

"So all this has been for nothing?" Warin complained, giving Ryland a smug look.

Ryland didn't completely agree. He'd gotten to see the lovely lady outlaw with the shimmering gray eyes again.

But aye, it was for nothing. His destiny and his bride—the woman with whom he was about to spend all the rest of his life—was waiting for him miles away at the castle.

"Thank you for the news." He dug in his satchel. The woodkerns may not have led him to his betrothed. But they had assisted him and saved him countless more hours of searching.

"That won't be necessary," Gray said. "I'll have two of the men lead you back." She gave a nod of confirmation to the woodkerns. "Nock? Mark?"

If he'd been listening closer, he might have taken notice of the strange names. He might have realized they weren't names, but commands. But he was too busy being a gentleman.

"I'm a man of honor," he insisted. "I told you I'd pay you for your help. You've given it to me." He gave her a lopsided grin and a wink as he held out a small velvet bag of silver. "You can buy your hounds a proper meal."

But Gray didn't smile at the jest. In fact, she looked tense. And guilty as hell. A sudden foreboding settled over him like a shadow.

Then she changed everything with a single command. "Draw."

Before any of his knights could unsheathe, the outlaws turned on them with loaded and drawn bows.

CHAPTER 14

"**S**hite!" Warin spat.

Laurence bit out a much worse oath.

Ryland ground his teeth. "What is the meaning of this?"

"Lay down your weapons," Gray said.

"The hell we will!" Ryland raged.

The gentleman outlaw reasoned with him. "Ye're outnumbered. We could fire a bolt through all your hearts ere ye could lift your blades. Ye know that."

Aye, he did know that. But Ryland felt he'd completely failed his men today. And the last thing he wanted to do was to make them surrender their arms.

"We mean ye no harm," Gray assured him.

The treacherous woman's words were unconvincing, considering there were almost a dozen deadly arrows trained on them.

"Surrender your blades," she said, "and I'll explain."

For a long moment, he only glared at her, venting his fury on her with a piercing, smoldering gaze. How he'd ever imagined she was a desirable, tempting sweetmeat of a woman he didn't know.

At last, he stared her down. She averted her eyes, as if she recognized hers was a betrayal of the worst kind.

With an angry growl, he commanded his men, "Lay down your blades."

With palpable fury, they did as they were ordered.

"Your daggers as well," Gray said, "and any other weapons ye're carryin'."

They tossed their remaining weapons to the ground.

"Your men are free to go..." she said.

"My men?"

"But ye'll be stayin' with us."

"What?" Warin exploded.

Laurence barked, "Impossible."

"We don't go anywhere without Sir Ryland," said Osgood.

Godwin agreed. "That's right. If he's staying, we're staying as well."

They crossed their arms over their chests, stubborn to a man.

"Your loyalty is admirable," Gray told them. "But if ye want to keep your lord safe, ye must take a message to the *clann* chieftain."

"A message?" Ryland asked. "What message?"

Gray's eyes narrowed to smoky slits. "Tell him he can have the king's man back for five hundred pounds."

Everyone gasped. Five hundred pounds was an absurd amount.

"Five hun-..." Warin said, gaping. "What the bloody hell do you..." He shot a quick glance at Ryland, who glowered back at him. "Not that you're not absolutely worth that much, m'lord, but..."

Warin was right to be astounded. Five hundred pounds could feed his entire household for ten years. What were the woodkerns thinking? There was no way Cormac O'Keeffe could raise that kind of coin.

Osgood tried diplomacy. "'Tis a rather large sum, my lady. Are you sure you won't reconsider? You know, the Bible says silver is the root of all evil."

Godwin mumbled, "I'm not sure this lot have read the Bible, Os."

Ryland skewered Gray with a dark stare. "What happens if O'Keeffe doesn't have it?"

"He does," she assured him with a grim sneer. "His coffers are overflowin' with the fines he's collected."

"What makes you so sure he'll pay?"

"He's been kissin' the feet o' your king for years now," Gray said, the bitterness in her words at odds with her sweet face. "The last thing he wants is for word to get back that Irish outlaws have abducted the king's man. He promised his daughter to an English knight. I very much doubt the king will send a second knight if the chieftain can't keep track o' the first one."

Ryland had to admit that made sense. It had never occurred to him that he might be a valuable commodity to the woodkerns. He cursed his shortsightedness. He should have foreseen the outlaws could hold him for ransom.

"What will you do with five hundred pounds?" There were a dozen woodkerns. That was enough silver to keep them all in comfort for the rest of their lives.

"'Tisn't your concern," Gray said. Then she turned to her men. "I think we've prattled on long enough. Bind their arms, lads. Conall and Niall, ye should leave before it grows dark."

"I'm not leaving," Warin insisted.

"Warin." Ryland shook his head. He knew Warin was troubled about leaving him alone with the outlaws. It was true that Ryland seldom went anywhere without his trusty friend. But if he was going to come out of this situation with any hope of victory, he needed Warin to do something for him on the outside.

As the friar bound his arms behind him, Ryland realized he was powerless here. He'd be sitting like a stabled ox, not knowing whether he was to be bred or slaughtered...

There was only one thing to do.

While his men reluctantly set off with two of the outlaws, he called out to Warin. "If you're unable to raise the ransom," he said carefully, "my brother's jeweled sword might be of value. Bring it on your return."

Warin's brow furrowed in puzzlement for a moment, and then recognition lit up his eyes. "Aye, that we will, m'lord."

And then his valiant knights vanished into the woods.

Temair busied herself with watering the hounds. She couldn't bear to look at Ryland right now, bound and helpless, with bitter accusation in his eyes.

She deserved every bit of his condemnation. She'd lured him here on the pretense of helping him, all the while intending to foil his plans.

As she bent down to put the basin of water before them, even Bran and Flann eyed her with suspicion. They sniffed at the water, as if they feared their traitorous mistress might have put hemlock in it.

"What?" she hissed at them. "Ye too?"

Maelan and Domnall collected up the weapons and took them inside the cave. She supposed they'd give them back to the knights when they returned with the ransom. After all, the woodkerns only took what poor folk could use. Farmers and cowherds had no use for swords.

Friar Brian, with his usual overabundance of courtesy, apologized to Ryland for the inconvenience of his bonds and assured him his ordeal would be over shortly.

Meanwhile, Sorcha, Lady Mor, and Aife secretly explained the plan to the remaining woodkerns.

Temair sighed. She regretted having to use the unwitting English knight as a pawn in the game of draughts with her father.

He didn't seem like a bad person.

He'd been kind to her hounds.

He'd shown true concern for his missing bride.

He'd even offered to pay the woodkerns for their help.

It wasn't his fault his stupid king had sent him to wed an imposter heiress.

But in war, there were no rules. Temair had to reclaim her legacy by any means possible.

Anyway, his part in this would be over in a few days, she thought as she patted the slurping dogs' heads. Once the knights returned, he'd be free to go.

She imagined he'd return to England. Like most Englishmen, he probably thought Eire was savage and unruly. Especially now.

As for his marriage, no doubt the king would arrange another suitable alliance for Ryland. His assets wouldn't go to waste. Indeed, prospective brides probably vied fiercely for such a prize as Sir Ryland de Ware.

A man in his prime.
Strong.
Handsome.
Clever.

Her gaze slipped over to where he sat on a stump. He was frowning at the ground between his knees, lost in thought.

She had to admit, he really was a fine specimen of a man. If circumstances had been different...if he weren't English...and if he weren't betrothed to her by command of the king, but rather by virtue of affection...

As if she'd spoken aloud, he suddenly glanced up at her.

Rattled, she looked away.

It was going to be a long couple of days—waiting for the ransom while dodging Ryland's damning stares, battling her sense of guilt, and trying to forget that she'd once let him kiss her.

"Gray," Domnall called out.

She looked up.

"He's your hostage," Domnall said. "What do ye want to do with him?"

The breath caught in her throat, especially when Ryland and the rest of the woodkerns leveled sharp questioning glares at her.

What did Domnall mean? What was there to do with him? He was a hostage, that was all. Shouldn't he just...sit...and wait?

At her silence, Domnall prodded. "He won't be worth a farthin' if he runs off into the woods."

Young Fergus offered, "Do ye want me to tie him to a tree?"

"Ye could chain him with the dogs," Ronan said.

"Or shackle his ankles so he can't walk," Domnall suggested.

Temair creased her brows in indecision. Was that really necessary? Surely he wouldn't leave the safety of the camp for the danger of an unfamiliar forest.

"Or," Ryland chimed in with dark humor, "I could just give you my solemn oath that I won't leave."

Domnall scoffed at that.

But noble Cambeal asked, "On your honor as a knight?"

"Aye."

That was enough for Cambeal.

Domnall thought otherwise. "Ye'd trust an Englishman?"

"A noble knight?" Cambeal asked, drawing himself up to his full height. "Absolutely."

Lady Mor agreed. "There's nothin' more sacred than a knight's vow."

Cambeal asked, "Is this agreeable to ye, Gray?"

Temair felt her face growing hot. Did no one sense the awkward paradox of that? Ryland had trusted her, and she'd promptly betrayed his trust. Why would he feel any compunction whatsoever to keep a promise made to her?

At her delay, Ryland spoke, his voice heavy with sarcasm. "I could give you a blood oath if you prefer."

"That won't be necessary," she decided. "Oath or no, if ye run off into the woods, my hounds will track ye down."

He gave a mock shudder, which infuriated her. He wasn't afraid of her dogs. The rogue had tamed the disloyal beasts with little more than salted pork and a few scratches.

Then he sobered. "I vow on my honor as a knight," he

said solemnly, "I won't leave the camp without your consent."

She should have doubted him. But she didn't. Even without Cambeal's confirmation, she got the sense that Sir Ryland was a man of his word.

So she acknowledged his promise with a nod. "Fine. I hope I don't live to regret it. Ye can untie him, Cambeal." Then, eager to get past the awkward situation, she called out, "What's for supper tonight, Friar?"

Brian hoisted up two rabbits someone had snared. "Rabbit pottage."

"And I've made oat bread," Sorcha announced.

There would have been blackberries as well, but in her hurry, Temair had left the basket behind.

Ronan waggled his bushy black brows and pulled out a wineskin. "A bit o' refreshment from a passin' jurist. He insisted we have it."

Young Fergus chortled at that, and the tense atmosphere in the camp began to dissolve.

Meanwhile, Sorcha laid out a cloth on the ground where the spoils of the day could be deposited.

There wasn't much.

Aife had nipped a few cloak pins from a jeweler. She'd exchanged one of them for information from the maidservant.

Cambeal had lifted a heavy silver pendant from the same jurist who'd donated the wine.

Young Fergus and Lady Mor dropped handfuls of coins they'd taken from a trio of passing nobles.

The woodkerns then went about their work as usual. Domnall gathered wood for the fire. Aife skinned the rabbits. Young Fergus took out a whetstone and sharpened blades. Old Sorcha, who knew how to read and write, recorded the take for the day. Friar Brian would distribute the gifts to needy families on the Sabbath.

Temair had watered the hounds, and they'd fed well already. There was nothing for her to do.

Sir Ryland was idle as well. He sat, staring morosely at the fire ring.

Even though holding him hostage had been *her* plan, she couldn't help but feel sorry for him. His king had used him to make an alliance, forcing him to move to a foreign country, to wed a woman he'd never met. Now Temair was using him to pay for an army to get her *tuath* back.

None of it was his fault. He'd just been in the wrong place at the wrong time.

He crossed his arms over his chest. His shoulders rose and fell as he let out a heavy sigh.

Domnall tossed a log onto the fire and grunted, "Were ye in the Crusades then, fightin' under Richard?"

"Aye," Ryland said. "I fought in the Battle of Arsuf."

Domnall's heavy brows went up. Then he nodded. "Was it as savage as they say?"

"'Twas a waste of good warriors," Ryland replied, surprising Temair with his insight. "Religious wars always are."

Their conversation caught the attention of Maelan, the other old soldier. "I fought at Acre. And ye're right. What a bloody massacre 'twas. And for what? Because one man didn't like what the other was thinkin'." He shook his head.

Cambeal approached with a frown. *"Ubi solitudinem faciunt, pacem appellant.* They make a wasteland and call it peace."

All four nodded sagely, staring into the flames that Fergus had stirred to life, sharing the sad brotherhood of warfare.

Temair watched them, half amazed and half irritated. The same way he'd tamed her hounds, Ryland was befriending the seasoned warriors of the woodkerns. There was something about him that drew both men and beasts to him.

That might be a problem.

"What about ye?" Ryland asked Cambeal. "Ye're from a noble family, aye?"

"Aye."

"Then why are ye…" He glanced around the clearing.

Cambeal smiled. "Livin' in the woods with a band of outlaws?"

Ryland shrugged. "Aye."

"I was cursed with a whole host o' brothers," Cambeal explained, "and I'm the youngest."

Ronan quipped, "His father has an heir and four spares."

"The eldest got our father's land," Cambeal said. "One fought for the High King and was rewarded with a holdin'. The other two made political marriages. All that was left for me was the church."

From behind the great black cauldron he was filling with leeks and barley, Brian said, "Ye'd have made a good monk."

"I'm afraid not," Cambeal replied. "I'd rather wear a cuirass than a cassock. Besides, the church hasn't been so good to ye, Friar."

"The church, perhaps not," Brian agreed, "but the Lord has been good to me."

Ryland turned to the friar. "How did a man of the church come to live among thieves?"

Friar Brian scolded the knight with the point of his knife. "We prefer 'outlaws' or 'woodkerns.' We're not strictly thieves."

"I see," Ryland said, obviously not seeing at all.

Temair explained. "We don't keep what we take."

Ronan raised the wineskin. "Well, except for this. This we're keepin'."

Ryland furrowed his brows. "If ye don't keep it, what do ye do with it?"

"We distribute it to those in need," she said.

"Aye. See that?" Brian said, gesturing with his knife to the goods piled on the cloth. "Sorcha will divide it up and decide who needs it most. Then on the Sabbath, I'll make my rounds, handin' it out to the crofters."

Ryland chuckled at that. "You must have the wealthiest crofters in all Ireland."

Nobody laughed with him.

Brian said, "Half o' them are starvin'."

"Starving? But they're crofters. They can grow their own food."

"So ye would think, wouldn't ye?" Temair said, biting back the rage that always burned in her when she thought about it. "But the chieftain doesn't see it that way. He takes most o' their crops. The bastard would rather feast with fine English lords than—"

"Gray!" Sorcha chided, "'Tis the man's father-to-be ye're speakin' of."

Temair froze. She'd forgotten. She'd also forgotten that Sir Ryland was probably one of the fine English lords her father had fed.

Ryland was scowling now. She'd hoped to make him understand that the woodkerns did what they did for good reason. Instead, it appeared she'd only made him angry.

CHAPTER 15

Ryland was appalled. He could well believe Cormac O'Keeffe was not well-liked. He'd seen how the man treated his servants.

But it had never occurred to him that a chieftain would allow his *clann* to starve for the sake of enriching his own coffers.

To think that good folk like these—a ragtag group that included a pair of battle-weary warriors, a noble knight, a matron who could read and write, an impressionable young lad, a goodhearted friar—had banded together, not out of greed, but to help their suffering neighbors...

He felt humbled.

And he silently swore that when he was lord here, he would make things right.

The jolly, black-bearded fellow, Ronan, cracked the uncomfortable silence by exclaiming, "Who's for a thimble o' wine, compliments o' the jurist?"

Considering there was one wineskin and over a dozen of them, a thimble-full was likely about all they'd get.

"I'll have a taste," the red-headed lad called Fergus said.

"One for me." Friar Brian stirred the pot. "The cook always gets a sip."

"Ryland?" Ronan asked, lifting a brow. "As our guest, ye should have the first taste. Ye can tell us if the wine of a jurist is lawful...or awful."

Ryland couldn't help but smile. The rhyme was almost as amusing as the fact that Ronan had called him a guest.

The woodkerns were unique. Noble knights and friars exiled to the woods. Thieves who gave their take to the poor. Abductors who treated hostages like honored visitors. They were unlike any outlaws he'd ever encountered.

He still didn't know what to make of Gray. She was both fierce and fun-loving. She possessed the earthiness of a crofter, but the regal bearing of a queen. She spoke of justice in strong terms. Yet she seemed to have no qualms about violating his trust.

What was a woman like her doing in a band of woodkerns?

He peered sidelong at the breathtaking maid. A lady so attractive should be wed by now. She shouldn't have to sleep outdoors. Or fret over starving crofters. Or wage war for her right of way on a fallen log. She should have a husband to protect her. She should have dozens of beautiful children with gray eyes.

Before he could ask her for her story, Ronan handed him the wineskin.

The wine was sweet and strong. After they'd all taken a swig, Ronan slipped into the cave and rolled out a wooden barrel.

"On to the good brew," Ronan announced, rubbing his palms together.

The ale, which they said was brewed every week by

Sorcha, flowed freely as the woodkerns settled down to supper. The rabbit pottage was tasty, considering it had been made from whatever was at hand. And the auburn-haired woman's oat bread soaked up every last delicious drop of the broth.

As they supped by the fire, the woodkerns regaled Ryland with stories. Most were humorous accounts of their thievery. Some were sad tales of *clann* folk who'd died in years past. And some gave glimpses of the outlaws' lives before they were outlaws.

It didn't take long before Ryland began to feel as if he were not a hostage, but indeed a welcome guest. There was no animosity or ill will toward him, even though he was English and one of the wealthy nobles they were supposed to despise. In this setting, they were all equals. It was curious.

Through all the storytelling, Gray was silent. She absently stroked the fur of the wolfhounds, who sat on either side of her now, like two tall pillars shielding her from harm.

"What about you, Gray?" he finally asked. "How did you come to live in the forest?"

Her fists tightened in the dogs' fur. He could almost see her mind flitting through possible answers.

In the end, she shrugged. "There isn't much to it. I lost my ma when I was young. My da had no use for me. So I ran away."

It was as vague an answer as she could have given him. But he didn't want to press her.

What was the point, after all? In another few days, he'd leave the outlaws, return to the keep, and wed his betrothed. He'd forget all about the woman named Gray.

Her shimmering silver eyes would fade from his thoughts. Her soft pink lips would seem like a dream he'd once had. The incredible kiss they'd shared would be only a hazy memory.

Only that memory wasn't so hazy at the moment. He remembered every intimate detail.

Her mouth opening in pleased surprise.

The fresh scent of water on her hair.

The welcome pressure of her body against his.

He hadn't realized he was staring at her until Ronan cleared his throat. "How about a bit of entertainment? Lady Mor can bring out her harp." He winked at Ryland. "Gray tells us ye're quite the minstrel."

"Nay, you don't want to hear me sing," he scoffed.

"We do," Ronan argued, waving his arms to get all the others to egg him on.

"Sing! Sing! Sing!" they chanted, ignoring his protests, until his resistance was worn down.

"All right, fine. But I'll warn you, I don't know many songs."

"What do ye know?" Lady Mor asked.

"*Le Lai du Chaitivel?*"

"One o' my favorites," she said, leaving to fetch her harp from the cave.

The song was a tragic one, about a vain lady who couldn't choose between four suitors and so encouraged them to compete for her affections. Three of the knights died, and the fourth was left impotent from his wounds. In the end, even though he won the lady, the surviving knight considered himself the unluckiest of all, for the other three had met quick deaths, while he endured prolonged suffering the rest of his life.

Ryland had forgotten how long the piece was. Halfway through, he thought perhaps he should cut it short. He didn't want to bore his audience.

But then he glanced over at Gray.

She seemed captivated by the music. Her eyes were closed, and she was swaying gently back and forth.

So he continued through the rest of the lines, finally finishing to the cheers of the camp.

"By Tuan's beard," Maelan declared, "I reckon 'tis the finest singin' I've e'er heard."

"Aye, me as well," Fergus gushed.

"Well done," Sorcha said.

The rest of the woodkerns agreed.

All but mischievous Ronan.

"Hold on now! Wait a moment," Ronan protested, holding up his hands to halt the praise. "I beg to differ." When the other woodkerns protested, he shook his head. "Nay, nay. 'Twas a pretty enough tune, and ye served it up fairly, Sir Ryland, to be sure. But I've heard better...indeed, among our own members." At the perplexed pause from the outlaws, Ronan gave a nod. "Gray?"

Gray stared back at Ronan, puzzled. Then her face blossomed into a smile, and her eyes danced merrily in the firelight.

"Is this true?" Ryland asked her. "Do you sing?"

"Well..."

Ronan answered for her. "Oh, sir, ye've never heard anythin' quite like it."

"I'd love to hear," Ryland said.

She gave him a sly look. "Are ye sure?"

"I insist."

"He insists," Ronan echoed.

Gray grinned and shook her head. Then she got up and trotted her hounds out with her to the middle of the clearing. The rest of the woodkerns started snickering.

"Sit," she told the hounds.

They did.

With exaggerated ceremony, she cleared her throat and said primly, "Lord Bran, how nice to see ye. How are ye this fine evenin'?"

She extended her right hand. Bran placed his paw atop it, then licked the back of her hand.

Ryland chuckled in approval.

"And Lord Flann, ye're lookin' quite handsome."

She repeated the trick with Flann, who sat back down with a bark.

"What's that?" she asked. "Ye'd like to perform a song? Well, by all means. Sing. Go on. Sing."

Ryland shook his head. He'd been gulled. The hounds raised their noses and made soft and miserable howls.

"Oh, isn't that beautiful?" Gray cooed. "But can ye sing a bit louder? Come on, sing."

They howled again, this time in an atrocious interval that grated on the ears and the nerves. Ryland simultaneously laughed and winced in pain.

"Exquisite!" Gray praised them. "But can ye put more heart into it this time? Sing, lads, sing."

Once more the hounds bayed at the sky, as if in horrible mourning. This time, the entire camp roared with laughter, which changed the dogs' howls into confused barks.

"All right," Gray told them, soothing them with a pat. "Ye can hush now."

Ryland clapped. "Brilliant. I fear you're right, Ronan. I've been *soundly* defeated."

"Ha!" Ronan exclaimed, appreciating the jest.

Inspired by the lively atmosphere, some of the others volunteered their talents.

Young Fergus juggled three pine cones with great dexterity, tossing them into the fire at the end, where the pitch snapped and crackled as they went up in flames.

Maelan played a quick tune on a wooden flute while Aife spun around in a gleeful dance that left her in giggles.

Cambeal and Lady Mor followed with a more stately dance.

Domnall was coerced into dragging out his bagpipes and playing a battle song, though the sound made the hounds howl in complaint. When he stopped, Bran laid his head down in relief, and Flann yawned as if bored.

When Conall and Niall returned from delivering the Englishmen to the main road, Gray rose. "We have an early morn and a busy day. We should all get a good night's rest."

Ryland watched while the others banked the fire and staggered off to their beds under the stars. To his amusement, most of them slept in the trees.

Just about the time he was going to ask where he should retire, Gray said, "Ye'll sleep out here, with the hounds and me."

Clearly, despite his vow, she meant to keep a close watch on him to prevent his escape. But Ryland couldn't say the idea upset him.

He liked the gangly, howling wolfhounds.

He liked their mistress even better.

Temair knew the wolfhounds were excellent guard dogs. They'd chuff and nudge her awake if Sir Ryland tried to steal away.

But the idea of spending the night so close to the handsome knight was unnerving.

It shouldn't have been. For the last six years, she'd been living with men. She'd seen them in every stage of dress and undress. Certainly, Sir Ryland was no different from any of the woodkerns.

But she felt strangely vulnerable as she spread her woolen cloak on the ground before the mouth of the cave. Even when she purposely lay down on her side, facing away from him, she felt as edgy as a fly at the perimeter of a spider's web.

He flapped out his own great cloak on the ground with an annoying whoosh, ruffling her hair—and her calm. Then, with audible grunting and groaning, he stretched out his long frame, far too close for her comfort, and let out a heavy sigh.

She stiffened.

Bloody hell, she could feel his breath on the back of her neck. He was so close, she could sense the warmth of his body beside her. So close she could smell him.

At least his scent—a masculine combination of spice, smoke, and leather—was not unpleasant.

Still, she wished she'd thought to make a barricade between them out of her hounds. Instead, Bran and Flann were curled up at their usual post at her feet.

Then, as if she weren't already too aware of his indecent proximity, he spoke.

"I hope you don't snore," he murmured.

"What?"

Incensed, she flipped over to confront him. How dared he suggest such an ignoble thing?

But by the light of the dying coals, she saw that he was grinning. She sighed.

"Good night, my lady," he said with a wink.

She frowned, mumbling, "G'night, English."

Then she turned back over. It was not going to be a good night. It was going to be a sleepless night. She could tell already.

She'd only glanced at him for a moment. But she couldn't get the image of his devilishly handsome face—inches away from hers—out of her mind...

The lock of dark hair that fell over his forehead with a rakish flair.

His heavy brows that descended together like storm clouds when he was angry and arched over his bright, merry eyes when he laughed.

The angles of his face—his square jaw, his strong chin, his broad cheekbones—accented by a manly dusting of stubble.

The saucy wink that made her heart flutter.

It wasn't right. She should despise him. He represented everything undesirable to her. The loss of her freedom. The wishes of her father. The will of the foreign king.

She'd spent six years as an independent woman, making her own decisions, fending for herself, living the way she chose. To go back to living under the control of a man was unthinkable.

No matter how handsome he was.

She flounced onto her back, disturbing the hounds, who grunted in annoyance.

She had to stop thinking about the English knight and start focusing on her plans to reclaim her *tuath*.

Taking back the holding wouldn't be easy.

Once she got the ransom money, she'd have to act fast, before her father found another imposter for Sir Ryland to marry. She'd need to assemble an army great enough to launch an attack on the tower house.

To be honest, she didn't even know exactly how to do it. She'd never witnessed a siege before. She hoped Cambeal and the soldiers could help her come up with a strategy.

She chewed at her lip.

Something old Sorcha had said was troubling her. Was it possible to take command of the *tuath* without bloodshed?

She knew force was the only way to control her father. But the last thing she wanted was to hurt her *clannsmen*. Cormac would no doubt send every man, woman, and child into battle against her to save *Tuath O'Keeffe*. Even Sir Ryland and his knights would be obligated to fight on Cormac's side.

She had trouble imagining firing an arrow into Sir Ryland's heart.

Then there was the English king to consider. Traditionally, coming from a long line of chieftains, Temair commanded the highest honor price in her *clann* and was most likely to be elected. Though women could not hold the chieftain position, she might choose her own husband and confer chieftain status upon him.

But times were changing. Rules were changing. The arrival of the English meant that chieftains were just as often appointed as elected. If she refused to wed the man of the king's choosing, he could conceivably send an army to take the holding by force.

It was a difficult situation. But unless she wanted her birthright handed over to an English knight and his counterfeit bride, she had no choice but to take action. Now. Even if it wasn't the most convenient time. Even if she wasn't fully prepared.

She flopped back onto her side with a sigh.

"You may not snore," Ryland murmured in the darkness, startling her, "but you certainly toss and turn like a tempest."

"I'm not accustomed to sleepin' in close quarters with strange men," she hissed pointedly.

"I can see why. They wouldn't get a moment's rest."

Her temper flared, and her voice dripped with sarcasm. "Well, I'm sorry if I'm keepin' ye awake."

"Oh, don't feel sorry for me." She could hear the humor in his voice. "'Tis the hounds I'm worried about."

She snorted. "At least my hounds have the good sense to sleep at my feet instead o' breathin' down my neck."

"Bloody hell, will ye two keep it down?" Conall suddenly called out from a nearby tree. "Some of us are tryin' to get a good night's rest."

Temair's face went hot.

"See what I mean?" Ryland whispered.

She shoved him.

He snickered.

She managed to fume in silence then. But that didn't stop the noisy workings of her brain. How Ryland could be so infuriating and amusing at the same time, she couldn't fathom. But one thing was clear. She couldn't be less inclined to fall asleep.

CHAPTER 16

The moon was high overhead when Ryland awoke to the sound of heavy snoring. It took him a moment to recall where he was. Another moment to realize that the furry head smashed up next to his belonged to a wolfhound.

He grimaced. He loved dogs as much as anyone. But he didn't particularly like their wet noses in his face. Especially when they were snoring loud enough to wake the dead.

He gave the hound's body a jiggle to stir him from sleep, intending to prod him back down to his mistress' feet, where he belonged. But when the dog lifted his head, the snoring continued.

It must be the other hound.

Ryland sat up on an elbow.

But the second dog was awake, staring at him.

Then Ryland peered down at the woman beside him.

The woman with lovely moonlit skin.

The woman with lashes that kissed her cheeks like black snowflakes.

The woman whose lips looked like the soft petals of a rose.

That beastly snoring was coming from *her*.

He grinned. Somehow that was incredibly endearing.

He swept the hair back from her face and gave her shoulder a gentle shake, stirring her just enough to stop her sawing. She sighed and snuggled deeper into her cloak.

When he pulled back his arm, his smile faded. He realized he probably shouldn't have done that.

Ryland was as good as married. He shouldn't be finding anything about Gray endearing. He should be faithful to his bride. Succumbing to the temptations of other women was a sign of moral weakness.

The hounds were both staring at him now, as if asking him what he intended to do about it.

He didn't have the answer.

What he needed to do most right now was relieve himself of the ale he'd drunk earlier.

For safety, he'd take one of the hounds with him. The dog would warn him of any danger. And if the woodkerns suspected their hostage meant to escape, they'd see he was well-guarded.

Careful not to disturb Gray, Ryland eased up from the ground and gestured to Flann to come with him.

Bran wanted to come as well, but Ryland didn't want to leave Gray unguarded. He held out his palm and whispered, "Stay."

Bran dutifully lay back down, lowering his head onto his paws.

Taking Flann by the collar, Ryland stole across the clearing and into the trees. He hoped he wasn't choosing a tree that was occupied by one of the outlaws. It was hard to tell in the milky moonlight.

Selecting a tree he hoped was sufficiently remote from the camp, he untied his *braies*. Flann obediently stood guard.

He was just finishing when he heard a twig snap behind him.

"Just where do ye think ye're goin'?"

It was Gray. He didn't dare turn around. His *braies* were still undone.

He started to tie them up, but she barked, "Raise your hands where I can see them. I've got an arrow trained at your back."

He raised his hands cautiously and cast a disappointed glance toward Flann. The damned hound had given him no warning whatsoever.

"Flann," she called. "Here."

The hound hesitated.

"Here!" she demanded.

Flann guiltily lowered his head and trotted back to her.

"Now," she said, "where were ye goin'?"

"Nowhere."

"Ye were tryin' to escape, weren't ye?"

"What? Nay."

"Then why did ye steal my dog?"

"I didn't steal him. I only...borrowed him."

"So ye could flee."

"If I'd wanted to flee," he reasoned, "I'd have taken *both* dogs."

"Then why did ye take him?"

He couldn't keep the sardonic edge from his voice. "I

was hoping the beast would warn me of approaching danger. Apparently, I was wrong."

"Turn around."

He hesitated. "I don't think you want me to do that."

"And I don't think ye're in a position to be disobeyin' my commands," she bit out, "since I've got my arrow aimed at..."

He turned around slowly. She *did* have an arrow aimed at him. Or she *had*, until her gaze lowered to his *braies*. Then her mouth fell open, and her bowstring went flaccid.

"May I?" he asked, indicating his ties.

Her discomfiture was quite entertaining. She nodded and averted her eyes, clearing her throat and fumbling with the bow.

He shook his head and tied up his *braies*. "You know, I swore on my honor I wouldn't try to escape. Didn't you trust me?"

She muttered something that sounded like an outlaw's creed. "Trust is for fools."

He clucked his tongue. "Only those without honor themselves are afraid to trust."

That got her hackles up. "What are ye sayin'? That I have no honor?"

From the branches overhead, someone suddenly spoke, startling the bloody hell out of them both. "Ye know, this is all very fascinatin', but some of us are tryin' to sleep." It was Ronan. He added, "And I'll thank ye not to piss on the tree where I slumber next time."

Gray marched off in a huff with her hounds, forcing Ryland to try to keep up as he tossed a "sorry" over his shoulder at the outlaw he'd offended.

Gray was already feigning sleep by the time he returned. Her hounds were now strategically positioned to form a curtain wall between him and their mistress. Their heads resting atop their paws, they looked up at him with doleful eyes, as if they knew he didn't deserve such punishment.

But perhaps it was for the best. Lovely Gray—with her fascinating fury and her becoming blushes—was doing strange things to his heart, making it beat faster and filling it with laughter. He needed to tame his passions before they got him into trouble.

Unfortunately, waking at dawn several hours later to a woman's alluring buttocks pressed against his groin didn't help.

Ryland winced. The sun was rising. So was something else.

Sometime in the night, the hounds had migrated back down to the foot of their cloaks. And Gray, seeking warmth or something more carnal, had nestled close to him until she now lay cradled in his arms.

Of course, she was completely oblivious to this fact. And he'd just as soon she didn't find out. But if he tried to extricate himself from their position, she'd no doubt accuse him of making advances. And if he didn't...

He grimaced. At the rate he was swelling against her, it would only be a matter of time before she awakened in horror.

Closing his eyes, he carefully inhaled. Her hair smelled like summer. It wasn't difficult to imagine waking like this every morn. With the touch of sunlight on his skin. The sound of birdsong on the air. The comfort of a woman in his arms.

He smiled. She really *did* feel heavenly against him. The warm pressure of her body against his was driving him mad with longing.

When he opened his eyes, he saw the rest of the camp was stirring.

Fortunately, Domnall the soldier suddenly growled out, "Up, everyone! The sun's high! The day's a-wastin'!"

In the noisy confusion as Gray struggled to wake up, Ryland was able to pull away inconspicuously. He yawned as if he'd only just wakened as well. She'd never know how close they'd been a moment ago.

Of course, his body was cursing him for leaving such a pleasurable situation, and it would be a while before it calmed enough to be presentable. But such were the harsh realities of being a loyal husband. He had to learn to curb his desires, even when temptation in the form of an irresistible outlaw lass pursued him with a vengeance.

Temair was still shaken from her encounter in the middle of the night.

It was silly, she supposed. It wasn't the first time she'd seen a man naked. It wouldn't be the last.

But somehow seeing Sir Ryland had been different.

Maybe it was different because his vulnerable state was so unexpected. She'd truly believed he'd been trying to escape. Not once did it occur to her that he might be innocent. The fact that she'd forced him to turn around under threat of death, only to discover that not only was he blameless, but she'd caught him with his *trius* down, made her feel like a brutish fool.

Maybe it was different because Sir Ryland was more

than just another man. They'd shared a kiss. They'd forged an undeniable connection. Something had happened between the two of them, some manifest spark that she felt lingering inside her like a coal, banked and waiting to burst into flame.

Maybe it was different because Ryland was dangerous, more menacing in a way than her father. He threatened her independence, her claim to the O'Keeffe land, her future. And seeing him standing there, unabashed, in all his manly glory, had made that threat all the more real.

To make matters worse, she didn't dare leave the camp—not with the roads crowded with fair-goers and the ransom demand delivered to her father. Cormac had a formidable temper. When it was roused, he was capable of seeking revenge with a single-minded drive that was terrifying to behold. Now, more than ever, Temair had to be cautious, for her father would definitely have placed a target on her back.

But remaining behind, Temair wasn't sure she could bear to look Ryland in the eyes. She was ashamed of what she'd done to him, embarrassed by her lack of trust, and humiliated that she'd been caught by Ronan, who was bound to spread the news around the camp faster than wildfire.

Temair pulled her hood over her head, wishing she could hide.

As she turned aside, she almost smacked into Ronan. Prepared for the worst sort of teasing after last night's mishap, she was surprised when he only nodded his head in greeting and continued on. She stared after him in wonder.

One by one, the woodkerns left on their missions. Fair days were always lucrative for outlaws. From far afield, the rich came with full purses, intent on spoiling their sweethearts with trinkets.

As a matter of tradition, the woodkerns stole only half of what they found on fair days. After all, they didn't wish to deprive anyone of an enjoyable day at the fair. But they figured most could afford to part with a sizable share of what they carried and still impress their mistresses.

The fewer outlaws that remained behind in the camp, the more tense Temair grew. So far she'd managed to avoid confronting Ryland. But soon it would be unavoidable.

It was Lady Mor who managed to keep Ryland busy, chatting with him beside the cave while Temair threw sticks for Flann and Bran to fetch.

Mor's bubbling laughter rang out, and Temair stiffened. Obviously, he'd said something to amuse her. Temair wondered if he was revealing how Gray had caught him in the middle of pissing.

But Mor never once looked her way, so maybe he was only telling her a jest.

Temair tossed a pine cone for Flann.

While he bounded after it, she looked sidelong at Ryland. He was leaning back against the rock with his arms across his chest, looking devastatingly masculine. There was a relaxed smile on his face as he watched Mor fluttering her graceful hands, making gestures to accompany whatever she was telling him.

Flann nudged Temair's palm with his wet nose. He'd already dropped the pine cone at her feet. Bran sat beside Flann and gave a single bark. He wanted to play too.

Temair picked up two pine cones and threw them in different directions, sending the hounds racing off.

Now Ryland was facing Mor, telling some story that required grand sweeps of his arms. Mor seemed spellbound. Her eyes were glowing, and she had one hand clasped to her breast as if his story was leaving her breathless.

Temair bit the inside of her cheek. Why hadn't Mor gone with the others today? She almost always went out on fair days.

It didn't matter, she told herself. As long as her hostage remained in camp, that was all that mattered. And if Mor's giddy giggling and limpid gazes kept him from leaving, it was for the best.

Flann and Bran nudged her thigh.

She frowned at Mor, whose auburn hair was shining like copper in the morning sunlight.

The dogs bumped her leg again.

She clenched her jaw. For a man about to meet his bride, it seemed Ryland was becoming a bit too friendly with Mor.

Flann barked. Bran barked.

"Shh!" she hissed.

CHAPTER 17

hen Temair glanced up again, Mor and Ryland were looking at her. She pretended not to notice, crouching down beside the dogs to give their chests a good scrubbing. When she peered out over Flann's back, the two were prattling away again.

She sighed in disgust. Bored with sticks and pine cones and the hounds in general, she decided she'd practice with her *bata*. After all, if war was coming, she'd best be prepared.

Cambeal had made a practice dummy out of wood. It had a straw-stuffed cloth head and held aloft a wooden sword and shield. Ronan had stitched Xs into the head for eyes, along with a downturned mouth, and added twigs at the top to make a comical thatch of hair.

She lugged the dummy from behind the mountain of rock into the clearing.

Bran and Flann ambled away to nap under the trees. They'd learned about the perils of getting too close to a swinging *bata* early on.

The most important thing about fighting with the *bata* was focus. Cambeal had drilled that into Temair, using every distraction possible to test her—from startling her with shouts to making young Fergus streak past naked. She'd learned to block out all outside influences and pay heed to her opponent alone.

She warmed up with a few lunges and, gripping the *bata*, stretched her arms up over her head, loosening her shoulders. Then, tossing her hair back, she faced the dummy.

Beyond the stuffed head, she could see Ryland was grinning over something Mor was telling him.

With a dismissive grunt, she started with the *bata* held horizontally in front of her in both hands. She began alternating hands, releasing one and using the other to flick the stick forward, hitting the dummy on the sides, where its ribs would be.

Lady Mor had never learned to use the *bata*. She always claimed it was not a weapon for a lady. She said she preferred to use her womanly wiles.

It looked like she was using those wiles on Ryland. He seemed to be quite amused by whatever drivel she was feeding him.

Temair frowned and moved on to two hits on one side, one on the other. Cambeal had taught her that switching up rhythms made a *bata* fighter unpredictable and hard to defend against.

That had certainly been the case when she'd fought with Ryland, she thought smugly. Even armed with a sword, he'd been unable to anticipate her moves.

Next she gripped the *bata* in both hands, swaying swiftly left and right with forward circles, hitting the dummy high and low, from shoulder to hip.

She wondered if Mor was clucking her tongue at Ryland now, exclaiming over how unladylike Gray was.

Temair shoved forward with full force against the dummy's chest, and then let her hands slide together to deliver a hard wallop to the side of its neck.

She sniffed with satisfaction. Though Ryland didn't realize it, she'd held back with him. A good *bata* fighter could maim and even kill a man with a well-placed blow.

The sound of Mor's high-pitched titters made Temair grind her teeth.

She poked forward with the end of the *bata*, jabbing the dummy hard in the stomach, finishing with a violent, two-fisted overhead hack that knocked the stuffed head right off of its wooden body.

It rolled across the ground, landing at Ryland's feet.

Lady Mor gave a feminine gasp and clasped both hands to her bosom.

Temair felt her face go hot with embarrassment.

The expression on Ryland's face, however, wasn't one of ridicule, but of amusement and interest.

"Mind if I give it a try?" he asked with enthusiasm.

Temair blinked in surprise.

Mor made a choking sound. "Silly Gray. Why would Sir Ryland want to learn to fight with a stick when he's got a big, long sword made o' steel?"

There was no mistaking her insinuation. But Ryland either didn't seem to notice or ignored it if he did.

"Do you have a spare weapon?" he asked.

"Aye." There were several more in the cave.

Lady Mor could see Ryland wasn't going to be distracted, so she tossed off one last tempting line. "Well,

I can't bear to watch such violence, m'lord. I think I'll take advantage o' the good weather and go down to the *lough* for a bath."

Temair wondered if coy Mor would linger there all day, waiting for Ryland to appear. Why it bothered her, she didn't know. After all, Ryland was promised to another—to *her* actually. And since that wedding wasn't going to take place, it didn't matter what romantic entanglements he pursued.

That's what she told herself. It wasn't how she felt. Mor's open flirtation nagged at her, almost as much as Ryland's apparent enjoyment of it.

Temair was glad Mor had left. Fighting with the *bata* required concentration, and Ryland clearly couldn't concentrate with a beautiful redhead nearby.

Once she moved the dummy out of the way and gave Ryland a *bata*, she showed him how to warm up. He picked it up very quickly. She supposed that made sense. He was a trained swordsman. The techniques couldn't be too different.

Soon they were lunging in unison, moving the *batas* slowly forward and back.

"Like this?" he asked, swinging the *bata* around to his side.

"Aye, only more..."

She showed him. He copied her movements. He actually was a very adept student.

When she tried to show him how to close the distance rapidly between his hands in order to flip the *bata*'s end around, he kept letting go of the stick. She moved closer in to show him. Putting her hands atop his, she slid them closely together so he could see how it felt.

It felt seductive. His hands dwarfed hers. His knuckles were warm. She could feel his battle scars under her palms. And the motion they made together, sliding slowly along the *bata*, made her face burn.

"Do ye have it now?" she asked breathlessly, stepping away.

"I think so. 'Tis a twist of the body at the same time, right?" He slid his hands together, twisted, and whipped the *bata* forward.

She nodded. She'd never realized how alluring a man could look, expertly wielding a *bata*.

After several repetitions, he asked, "What else?"

She showed him how to feint back with one arm and jab forward with the other. He showed particular enthusiasm for that.

"'Tis almost like using a sword and shield," he realized.

"But instead o' defense, the shield arm is meant to distract," she told him.

"Exactly!"

He repeated the motion, changing arms, until he was proficient. She was truly impressed by his progress.

"Ye're the fastest learner I've seen," she remarked. "It took me a month to learn all o' that."

"Well, to be fair," he said as he continued to feint and jab, feint and jab, "I've had a whole lifetime of learning to fight. I doubt you, Lady Gray, were born with a blade in your hands."

She joined him in feinting and jabbing. "True."

"How long *have* you trained?" he asked.

"Since I came here six years ago."

He nodded. "You're very accomplished."

His words made her glow inside. She wasn't sure how to respond.

After a long silence, broken only by their sharp exhales as they thrust forward, she finally worked up the courage to murmur, "I'd like to apologize for last night."

He nodded. "For the snoring, you mean?"

"What?" She stopped, turning on him. "Snorin'? I don't snore."

He stopped too. "The hell you don't."

"I don't!"

"Like to wake the dead."

She stared at him with her mouth agape. Then she muttered, "I'm certain 'twas one o' the hounds."

"That's what I thought at first too." He shook his head. "But nay. Your hounds were just as surprised as I was." While her mouth was still open, he added, "Don't let it trouble you. I'm sure you couldn't help it. There's really no need to apologize."

She finally closed her jaw, compressed her lips, and gave him a scolding poke with her *bata*. "That's not what I meant, and ye know it. I meant I apologize for doubtin' ye."

His slow, heart-melting smile told her he'd been teasing her. "I know. And I accept your apology."

She nodded, still bristling from his accusation.

Then she returned to the subject at hand, raising her *bata* vertically and showing him how to slide his hands together for overhead and underhand strikes.

Once he could do that smoothly, she said, "I'm just glad Ronan didn't share it with all the woodkerns."

"Oh, I threatened to throttle him if he breathed a word," Ryland confessed.

She stopped. "Ye did?"

He stopped as well and shrugged. "Of course."

She thought that was terribly chivalrous of him.

Until he returned to practicing with the *bata* and said, "I couldn't have him crowing all over the camp about how well-endowed English knights are."

That made her laugh. She swatted his backside with her *bata*.

He yelped in protest. "Why are you laughing? Do you doubt it?"

"That ye're well-endowed? I don't know. I didn't look," she lied.

"The hell you didn't."

"I didn't," she insisted, although her giggles gave her away.

"That's a lovely sound," he told her.

"Stop it."

"*'Tis* a lovely sound. You should laugh more."

She shook her head. He was only flattering her.

"Enough o' your nonsense. Try this," she said, eager to change the subject. She demonstrated a two-handed swinging blow.

"Now *that's* like swordplay," he said, instantly mastering the technique. After a dozen downward swings that whistled forcefully through the air, he smiled. "Is this how yonder friend lost his head?" He nodded toward the practice dummy.

"Aye," she said sheepishly.

His grin widened. "Maybe I should count my blessings you didn't lop off my head when you had the chance."

"Indeed," she replied.

"Would you like another chance?" He turned to face her and gave her a wink.

The light in her eyes was answer enough.

Now that she'd mastered the *bata*, Cambeal didn't train much with her anymore, which was why he'd made the dummy. Since she didn't often tangle with victims skilled at arms, she was seldom required to engage in physical confrontations.

Sparring with a real live opponent, as she had when they'd first met across the stream, was a rare pleasure.

With a nod of her head, she swept the *bata* diagonally before her in a salute.

He returned the greeting.

Then she began the battle.

Of course, he withheld his strength to make it a fair fight. Likewise, she withheld her speed to keep him engaged. They battled back and forth, scrabbling across the clearing and kicking up dust, whacking the occasional tree, both as gleeful as the hounds chasing after sticks.

Then he began to taunt her. "Is that the best you can do?" He grinned as he blocked her overhand blow. "Shall I tie one hand behind my back to make it a more fair fight?" He dodged a jab aimed at his side. "Or if you're too worn out," he said, forcing her back with a few annoying pokes, "I can always wander down to the *lough* to see what Lady Mor's up to."

The mention of Mor pricked Temair's temper. And the fact that it bothered her made her even more furious. She replied with a ferocious attack that backed him up against the wall of the mountain. "Ha!"

But then he surprised her with a return assault that sent her scrabbling back to the middle of the clearing. "Oho!" he retorted.

It was time to summon up her most devious tricks, the ones she hadn't shown him.

Taking a deep breath of preparation, she began her onslaught. Twirling her *bata*, she caught him unawares with a sharp rap on his shoulder. Then she spun halfway around, jabbing unexpectedly backwards to catch him in the belly. While he was recovering, she whipped the *bata* around by its end, where it smacked him on the hip, knocking him off-balance. Using the tip of the stick, she tangled his legs and made him stumble back. Before he could regain his balance, she stepped toward him, placed the *bata* flat against his chest, and shoved him against the trunk of a tree. Finally, she brought the *bata* up swiftly to press against the vulnerable spot between his legs.

The effect was instantaneous.

With a ragged gasp, Ryland stiffened. Effectively at her mercy, he dropped his weapon.

Temair gave him a smug, smoldering smirk. That move never failed to take all the fight out of a man.

She expected to see a glimmer of amusement in his eyes now.

She expected his lips to stretch in a good-natured grin.

She expected to hear his warm chuckles of surrender any moment.

But he wasn't smiling.

CHAPTER 18

As Temair gazed into Ryland's hooded eyes, her smile faded.

He wasn't afraid she'd actually do him harm, was he?

Nay.

It wasn't fear veiling his eyes.

Nor danger flaring his nostrils.

Nor apprehension leaving him breathless.

The gaze he lowered to her mouth was full of raw need.

Suddenly aware of the pressure of her *bata* against his groin, Temair couldn't help but remember what she'd glimpsed last night. Flashing through her mind's eye was the compelling image of his naked flesh nestled in dark curls. The memory alone triggered a brilliant shock and a lusty tension between her own legs. The intense sensation made her knees weak.

Her breath caught. She lowered her gaze, trying to conceal her sudden powerlessness, fixing her eyes instead on Ryland's mouth. His delicious, tantalizing, irresistible mouth.

Damning the consequences, she followed her instincts. Leaning closer, she slowly let the *bata* slide down. She watched as he sucked a breath of anticipation and pleasure between his teeth.

But when the backs of her knuckles chanced to brush his hard and eager swelling, it was all Temair could do not to gasp in wonder.

His eyes were shut tight now. But she still saw longing in the furrow between his brows and in the way the corner of his lip was caught under his teeth.

She let go of the *bata* and let it fall to the ground. Closing her eyes, she angled her wrist to capture him in her palm. Even through his clothing, she could feel the heat of him, full and firm and demanding.

It took her breath away.

She managed to lift her lust-heavy lids just enough to see his thirsty tongue trace the rim of his bottom lip.

And she was undone.

Bunching the front of his tabard in her free fist, she surged forward with a soft cry and claimed his mouth.

His kiss was even sweeter than she remembered. Hot and searching, his lips drank from hers as if she harbored the most amazing ambrosia. His tongue made soft trespasses to bathe her in liquid passion. And when he groaned against her, her blood shot through her veins with the force of a winter flood.

The longer they kissed, the more she desired to kiss him. Time and place vanished. Reason deserted her. The world melted away until there were only the two of them.

Lost in a haze of seductive pleasure, Temair vaguely wished it would last forever.

Ryland was drowning in a sea of lust, as helpless as a storm-wrecked ship. And yet he had no desire to claw his way back up to the surface.

He'd never been kissed with such fervor. He'd never been so quickly aroused. Nor so completely enchanted.

It came as no surprise then that he was in no hurry for it to end.

But chivalry was at the very core of his being. And guilt was a cruel master to a man of honor. What they were doing wasn't right. He was promised to another. He must be faithful to his bride.

Besides, he was doing Gray no favors, leading her on in this way when nothing would come of it. Even if she *was* as sultry and tempting as a Saracen concubine.

So it was with great regret and a good deal of physical torment that he slowly pulled away from the kiss, taking Gray gently but firmly by the shoulders and setting her at arm's length.

She blinked as if waking up and raised trembling fingers to her blushing lips.

"I'm sorry," he whispered. "I just..."

She stepped abruptly backwards, obviously embarrassed. "Nay, 'tis my—"

"I can't do this. 'Tisn't—"

"O' course not," she muttered. "I shouldn't have—"

"'Tisn't that it wasn't pleasant and—"

"Nay, ye're absolutely right." She looked away and tucked her hair behind her ear. "I had no call to—"

"If I didn't have a bride…"

She nodded rapidly, but wouldn't meet his eyes. "'Twill not happen again."

His heart sank at her words. But she was right. Nothing good could come of kissing Gray, no matter how pleasurable it was.

He picked up their discarded *batas* and handed hers back to her. Neither of them wished to engage at the moment, not even in battle.

As it happened, they'd been wise to stop when they did. In the next moment, old Sorcha arrived at the camp, carrying a great basket of peas. She would have been livid, he was sure, to find Gray dallying with the man who was supposed to be her hostage.

Sorcha eyed the *batas*. "Are ye still fightin'?" She shook her head. "I'd have thought ye'd made peace by now." She looked around the clearing. "Have ye seen Mor?"

"She's gone to bathe in the *lough*," Ryland told her.

Sorcha raised a suspicious brow but made no comment. She set down the basket and dusted off her hands. "Well, then, here. Perhaps ye can put away your weapons and see if ye can stop brawlin' long enough to make yourselves useful by shellin' these peas for supper."

Ryland was not in the habit of shelling peas. In the de Ware household, the servants did such things. But he supposed in an outlaw camp, everyone had to do their share in order to survive. Anyway, he could use the distraction.

It wasn't difficult work, especially once he watched Gray do it a half dozen times. The only challenge was keeping his fingers from tangling with hers as they reached for peas. And keeping his eyes from straying to her rosy lips.

Their conversation was stilted and aloof. They chatted about the weather, the hounds, the fair, the forest. He learned that the weather was pleasant for summer. The hounds were good for hunting and protection, less good for jobs requiring stealth. The fair brought visitors from all the nearby towns. And the forest was full of birds, squirrels, rabbits, and an occasional wolf.

Gone was the flirtatious, charming sprite he'd sparred with all morn. In her place was a serious and dutiful maid who answered with as few words as possible and didn't spare him a glance.

He couldn't help but be disappointed. Even though it was his own fault. Even if he'd done the right thing.

Hell. He hoped his bride-to-be was half as attractive to him as Gray.

Part of him wished he'd never met the beautiful lady outlaw.

And part of him hoped he'd never be ransomed.

By the time they finished shelling the peas, the woodkerns began returning to camp. It looked like they were carrying enough treasure to live like lords for the next year.

But that wasn't what they intended. As before, they deposited their goods on the cloth that Sorcha spread on the ground. She catalogued every coin, every jewel, every weapon, assessing its value and assigning it to one of the family names scrawled in her ledger.

Their generosity was inspiring. He'd never seen such charity before, not even from the priests where he lived. When it came to the accounting of alms, the church in England was lax. Ryland suspected the well-fed, well-read priests took a considerable portion for themselves.

What they did donate, they gave with a great deal of that deadly sin of pride.

But the woodkerns seemed genuinely concerned with fairness and anonymity.

As Mor had explained earlier, what they stole from the rich was not the nobles' hard-earned silver, but wages earned on the backs of the poor.

Ryland would have to look into this more when he was lord. There were kings and paupers in any society, but when the kings feasted while the paupers starved, something was amiss.

Gray delivered the bowl of shelled peas to the friar, who poured them into his cauldron of bubbling broth.

Ryland nodded toward the day's take, asking Gray, "Do the families know from whence these gifts come?"

"You mean that they come from outlaws?" she asked. "Nay."

"They might turn down the gifts if they knew," the friar said, adding a pinch of pepper to the pot. "Some o' them think we're angels." He laughed about that.

"We're neither outlaws nor angels," Gray said. "We're tax collectors, keepin' the accounts balanced."

Ryland arched a brow. Cormac O'Keeffe was definitely neglecting things if outlaws were keeping the accounts balanced. It seemed he was going to have his hands full, once he was in charge.

Gazing out the tower window, Cormac figured it was just as well the simpering harlot he'd hired was dead. Like his real daughter, she'd been too mouthy for her own good. He wasn't about to let her extort silver from him to ensure her silence about carrying his bastard. Not when there were easier ways to shut her up.

Now that she was at the bottom of the bog, she'd give him no grief.

And now that Sir Ryland de Ware and his knights were chasing after his ghost of a daughter, he had time to change his plans.

He looked below to the busy road which passed by the tower house.

The fair would bring fresh faces. Perhaps, among the traveling merchants and entertainers, he'd find a more malleable lass, one amenable to taking on the role of the chieftain's daughter. Then he could begin again.

As before, he'd have to keep the lass secreted away at the castle. Soon, Sir Ryland and his knights would return empty-handed. They'd be forced to go back to England in shame, where the ungovernable Sir Ryland would likely be wed to someone else.

Then Cormac would execute the second part of his scheme. He'd announce that, by some miracle, his long-lost daughter had wandered out of the wood and returned home.

King John would naturally send a new bridegroom. This time, Cormac would insist upon a gentle knight worthy of his daughter, rather than one like the last, who'd frightened her into running away.

Meanwhile, of course, he'd get the imposter pregnant.

He tapped on the stone sill, studying the prospects winding their way along the road toward the fair. Some lugged wheelbarrows. Some walked beside carts. Some rode on hobbies. Surely there was a small, dark lass among them who could pass for his daughter. And bear his child.

CHAPTER 19

Temair filled her cup with ale for the second time, slugging down half of it at once.

The woodkerns, arriving full of treasure and tales, had had a profitable day. Gathering around the fire, they boasted of their adventures and the fruits of their labor.

But Temair's day had left her as prickly as a cat in a thunderstorm.

Not only had she felt frustrated by being restricted to the camp while the others were out looting, but her head was still spinning over her situation with Ryland.

First of all, she should never have kissed him again. No matter how tempting and inevitable and right it had felt at the time, she shouldn't have done it.

It wasn't right. Not at all. As far as Ryland was aware, he was promised to another. He was practically a married man.

And yet, the bride he was promised to was *her*. So it wasn't as if that indiscretion could legitimately be considered cheating.

The fact that Ryland had put a stop to the kiss said much about his honor. She respected him for that.

On the other hand, perhaps he'd only stopped her because he'd found he wasn't attracted to her, not in the way she was attracted to him. And that hurt her pride.

And now, unsure whether she admired or begrudged him for his actions, she ended up vexed at herself for even caring what he thought.

She wasn't going to marry him.

She'd already decided that.

So what did it matter whether he was a cheat?

Why should she care if he did or didn't like her?

What difference did it make if freshly bathed Lady Mor was sitting on the other side of him, fluttering her lashes?

Temair pounded down the rest of her ale.

At the sound of Mor's giggles, she winced and got up to refill her cup...again.

Friar Brian had just begun to serve up the pea pottage when Conall and young Fergus strode into the camp with two strangers.

Sorcha exchanged a quick glance with Temair. Any other day, entertaining the nobles they'd robbed was commonplace. But with a hostage on the line and Temair's identity at stake, it was a bold and risky proposition—one that Conall and Fergus probably shouldn't have undertaken.

She trusted Ryland would say nothing to divulge his identity that might threaten the safe transfer of his ransom. Meanwhile, the woodkerns would have to do nothing to arouse suspicion.

"Welcome to our lovely camp!" Conall announced.

Although the noble visitors looked irritated at being inconvenienced, they were civil enough.

Fergus introduced them. "These are Sir William and Sir Robert."

Cambeal and Niall introduced themselves and invited the two gentlemen to sit by the fire. The friar prepared to fill bread crusts with pottage for the guests.

As was customary, Sorcha explained. "Sir William, Sir Robert, we may be outlaws, but we never take more than we need. And if ye're willin' enough to hand it over without a fuss, we're glad to give ye sustenance for your journey home."

Sir William laughed. "Generous outlaws—ha!" He elbowed his companion, who wasn't quite as jolly.

Sir Robert made a sour face. "The last thing we need is more sustenance."

"True enough," William agreed. "We've just come from Chieftain O'Keeffe's table." With one hand, he patted his broad belly. With the other, he fended off Brian's offer of pottage. "I doubt I'll need sustenance for another week."

Temair dug her fingernail into her wooden cup. They'd just eaten at her father's table? Had Cormac mentioned her? Had he talked about the ransom?

As casually as she could, she asked them, "Did ye happen to see any other English knights there?" She ignored Sorcha's sharp look of warning.

"Maybe we did," Robert said evasively. "Maybe we didn't."

William gave his companion a chiding cuff. "There were a few Irish nobles at supper," he volunteered, "but no English knights."

"Why are you telling them?" Robert bit out.

"Because they asked," William replied.

"But they're outlaws!"

"What's the harm?" William shrugged. "They're going to rob us either way."

"Precisely," Robert said. "I would think you'd know better than to barter with their kind."

"And I would think you'd know better than to goad them into doing us further harm."

Robert frowned suspiciously at the woodkerns around him, as if wondering if they might chop off his fingers or poke out his eyes.

"At any rate," William continued, "we may as well enjoy the evening and be sent safely on our way, aye?"

Cambeal, ever the diplomat, intervened smoothly. "Sir William is right. We have no wish to do ye harm, as long as ye give us no reason to do so. We only hunger for news o' the outside world."

"Aye," Temair chimed in, eager to find out what the hostage situation was. "Can ye give us the latest blather from O'Keeffe?"

"What Gray means," Sorcha said with a tight, forced smile, "is we'd all love to hear news about our dear *clann* chieftain."

Temair bristled at that. She didn't give a piss what happened to Cormac O'Keeffe. She did, however, want to know what was going on at the tower, so she remained silent.

William hesitated. "You know, on second thought, I wouldn't mind a cup of your ale to wet my tongue after such a long journey."

Temair pressed at the ache growing between her eyes.

Couldn't he just spit out his news and be gone?

Aife brought ales for both of them. William raised his ale and took a healthy swig. Robert peered down at his cup as if he feared it might be poisoned.

Temair grew impatient, waiting for them to quench their thirst and begin their story. Beside her, Ryland seemed uneasy as well. Then she realized why. He probably wanted to know what had become of his knights as much as she did. If William and Robert hadn't seen them, where had they gone?

Finally, William, his tongue loosened by two cups of ale, started recounting the details of the banquet they'd been served.

Temair wasn't much interested in that. It was a cruel reminder that her father had a habit of snatching the suckling pigs from his starving tenants' sties and roasting them for the pleasure of a few foreign guests.

Her head was buzzing from her third ale when she rose to get a fourth. William, already nursing his fourth cup, sat forward and motioned the outlaws closer with a drunken gesture of conspiracy.

"Did you know," he confided, "that King John himself has sent an Englishman to wed the daughter of the O'Keeffe?"

She sensed Ryland stiffen beside her. But Temair was accustomed to hiding secrets, so she continued to sip blithely at her ale. Meanwhile, she was hanging on the nobleman's every word.

Robert, trying to keep up with William's consumption of ale, was now drunk enough to blurt out a few important details.

Though the two hadn't seen Ryland's knights, they'd

heard a lot of gossip from the servants, who were eager to share what they knew.

"Some say they can hear her in the middle of the night," William said.

"Who?" Ronan asked.

"The chieftain's daughter," he said.

Robert added, "'Tis said he keeps her in a cell at the tower."

"And no one's laid eyes on her in six years," said William.

"Not since that fateful night she murdered her sister," said Robert.

Temair squeezed the wooden cup in her fingers until her knuckles were white.

The whole camp had gone quiet. William and Robert probably presumed it was due to their suspenseful storytelling. But nobody dared breathe a word, lest they reveal Temair's identity.

The last person she expected to speak on her behalf was Ryland.

"Ballocks!" he spat. "'Tis an unfounded rumor. There's no evidence Temair O'Keeffe had anything to do with her sister's death."

Temair was stunned. That Ryland was aware of the local rumors surprised her. But even more surprising was the way he was standing up for her. Nobody had ever sounded so sure of her innocence.

Not even the woodkerns defended her with such trust. Indeed, not all of them believed that Temair was completely blameless in her sister's demise. They might not think Temair intentionally pushed her sister off the tower. But some of them assumed it was an unfortunate accident caused by Temair's temper or carelessness or neglect. Even Temair felt she might be partly responsible.

Ryland's touching words—combined with the fact that she was on her fourth ale—made tears well in her eyes.

William held up his palms in protest. "I'm not saying she did it. I'm just passing along what the servants said."

"I pity the bridegroom," Robert snickered. "The poor fool is walking into a trap. He'll be lucky to survive a fortnight if O'Keeffe is marrying off his murderous daughter to the king's man."

Ryland's face was grim. "I'm sure the king's man is not one to give much credit to the prattling of maidservants."

Temair's heart swelled. Ryland was defending her.

Then she furrowed her brows. She supposed he wasn't actually defending *her.* He didn't even know she was the chieftain's daughter. It was more about him defending his *own* reputation as a man who knew the difference between fact and fiction.

But Robert wasn't listening. "I wonder how long he'll last before the monstrous she-devil does him in."

"God's wounds!" Ryland exclaimed. "How dare you disparage a woman you've never met?"

Temair could feel the heat of righteous indignation rising off of him. It was thrilling. And flattering. And seductive.

William nervously licked his lips as he gripped Robert's arm, keeping his companion under control. "Oh, I'm certain that's not what he meant. You didn't mean that, did you, Robert? Of course he didn't. What would we know of the wench, after all? We only just arrived at the keep."

"You should guard your tongue," Ryland warned.

"Oh, absolutely," William agreed.

Robert yanked his arm out of William's grip with a snort.

Before a brawl could ensue, Temair changed the subject. "It grows late, gentlemen. Have ye finished your ales? 'Tis best ye were on your way before the wolves start prowlin'."

Robert gulped down the last of his ale. "Aye, fine."

William looked mildly disappointed. He probably would have enjoyed spending the night with the woodkerns. "Ah. Right. Thank you for the ale."

"Thank *ye* for the silver," Temair said pointedly.

"Oh, aye," William said with a sigh, untying his leather purse and handing it to her.

"And yours?" Temair urged, nodding at Robert.

He scowled, but did likewise.

Temair counted out half of the coins from each purse and handed them back.

"You don't want all of it?" Robert asked.

William swatted him for asking such a stupid question.

Temair smiled. "We take what we need and what ye can afford, no more. Niall and Maelan, see them to the road, will ye, and turn them in the right direction?"

Obviously, Temair didn't want them returning to the keep with information about the woodkerns.

The visitors left then, and the outlaws breathed a sigh of relief.

But Temair couldn't stop staring at Ryland.

He'd stood up for her. Despite the nasty rumors, despite what everyone else maintained was the truth, he wasn't convinced. And he was giving the bride he'd never met the benefit of the doubt.

She decided it meant even more that he *didn't* know she was the chieftain's daughter. It meant he was giving his blind trust. It meant he believed a person was innocent until they were proven guilty.

What an amazing man he was, she thought. So honorable. And chivalrous. Charitable. And forthright. He was everything a knight should be. Everything a *man* should be.

She knew she was a bit tipsy from the ale, which always bared her heart and loosened her tongue. But Temair knew she was right about Ryland. Her vision blurred with tears as she resisted the urge to sob out how she felt about him.

Instead, lowering her voice, she leaned toward him in confidence…and almost tipped over. Indeed, she might have landed on her nose if he hadn't caught her. She supposed she shouldn't have drunk that fifth ale. Or was it sixth?

"Careful," he warned.

"Do ye truly believe that, Ryland?" she gushed.

"Believe what?" he said. "Hold on. Are you drunk?"

"Maybe."

His lips twitched. "Believe what?"

"That she's innocent?" she whispered.

"Who, my bride?"

She nodded.

"Aye, I do."

A lump clogged her throat. "Ye don't think she's a murderer?"

He shook his head.

"Or…or a monstrous she-devil?"

CHAPTER 20

Ryland couldn't be sure about that.

No one had seen the woman in six years.

She might not have had a bath in all that time. Hell, if she *had* been kept in a cellar in the dark as some claimed, she could be as gray and pasty as a toadstool. And if the only person she had contact with was her wretched father, she might even be mentally damaged—suffering from anxiety, loneliness, trauma.

He answered honestly. "I hope not."

Lady Mor had apparently overheard their conversation. "And what if she *is* a monstrous she-devil?" she asked with a wicked glint in her eye. "Will ye wed her anyway?"

"Of course." There was no question. It was his responsibility and obligation. "But...you've seen her before, haven't you? In fact..." He turned to the remaining woodkerns as a whole. "You all knew my bride from before, did you not? What was she like? Do you remember?"

Everyone spoke at once.

"Short," blurted Domnall. "Fair-haired."

"Small and dark," corrected Aife, "just as the chieftain described her."

"She was always a good lass," the friar said.

"Ye'd like her," Ronan said with a wink.

"A bit too tall, if ye ask me," said Lady Mor.

"Difficult to say," Cambeal said with smooth nobility, "though a well-loved woman is always beautiful."

"She doesn't look like any of us," young Fergus said, licking his lips. "That's for certain."

Wise Sorcha held up her hand to silence them all. "Temair is lovely. I don't think ye'll be disappointed."

Ryland smiled and thanked them for their opinions, though he was thinking it was a good thing his bride had returned to the keep when she had. Considering the wide variations in her description—tall, short, fair-haired, dark-haired—Temair would have been nearly impossible to find.

Once the woodkerns returned to their own conversations, he whispered to Gray, "What do *you* think? Honestly. Do you remember her?" If anyone would tell him the unflattering truth about his bride, it was Gray. She seemed to prefer to speak plainly.

But when he turned to her, she was staring at him with a besotted smile on her face. He couldn't help but grin back. She'd been staring at him for some time now. Clearly, she'd overindulged this evening.

Her cheeks were flushed. Her eyes were half-closed with sleepy languor. Though she sat on an anchored log, she swayed unsteadily.

Even drunk, she looked adorable. Her eyes softly glistened. Her hair shone like black silk in the firelight. Her rosy lips looked vulnerable and inviting.

It was difficult thinking about his prospective bride without instinctively comparing her to the breathtaking beauty beside him.

But at his question, Gray's expression grew troubled.

"What do *I* think?" Emotions battled back and forth on her face until he almost wished he hadn't asked the question. At last she gave him a careful answer. "I think she's no better or worse than ye'd expect...considerin'."

"Considering?"

"Considerin' her...history."

That was something Ryland had been wanting to know. "Do you think 'tis possible the chieftain...mistreated Temair?" he asked.

Lady Mor volunteered her opinion, loudly enough for the rest of the camp to hear. "Cormac O'Keeffe mistreats everyone."

The woodkerns' silence was damning. Not that he expected anything else. They were understandably wary of speaking ill of Ryland's future father-in-law. But apparently they weren't in a rush to defend him either.

"He's not known for his kindness," Gray finally admitted.

Once she'd uncorked that keg, the rest of the woodkerns' opinions began to flow freely.

"He's got a temper."

"Not many o' the crofters have a good word to say about him."

"He's a spare-the-rod-spoil-the-child kind o' man."

"Folk at the tower house *did* say he kept her locked in a cell."

"'Tis a well-known fact he beats his servants. There's no tellin' what he did to his daughters."

"There's some who know," Gray interjected, her voice bitter. "Is it any surprise Temair left? Bloody hell, if she hadn't run away all those years ago, there's no tellin' what might have—"

"All those years?" Ryland asked.

The camp went suddenly still.

"Days," Gray corrected. "All those days ago."

Ronan forced a laugh. "Maybe ye'd better lighten up on that ale, Gray. I fear your mind's a bit muddled."

"Aye, lass," Cambeal said. "'Twould seem your tongue has a will of its own."

Sorcha stood up suddenly. "Perhaps 'twould be best if we all retired. We don't want to say things we may regret. And we'll have clearer heads in the morn."

Everyone was quick to agree. But Ryland couldn't shake the notion that something strange had just happened. The outlaws were hiding something. They had a secret. And he didn't like secrets.

Ryland de Ware had one rule of battle. Never go in unprepared. Secrets were counter to that philosophy. And the sooner he uncovered them, the better.

The twilight moon was just cresting the treetops as the woodkerns banked the fire and sought their beds.

Fortunately, the woodkerns hadn't questioned their "guests," William and Robert, too closely about the four English knights who were supposed to be at the castle, negotiating a ransom payment. Otherwise, they would have discovered that Ryland's men hadn't returned to the keep at all. As far as Cormac O'Keeffe knew, Ryland was still hunting for Temair. He was unaware that his daughter's bridegroom was a hostage.

God willing, he'd never find out.

In the meantime, Ryland would have to learn everything he could about the O'Keeffe clan, their allies, their enemies.

He'd been able to classify Cormac O'Keeffe within an hour of meeting him. The chieftain was a bold, boastful, selfish bully, disliked and feared by his own people. If the chieftain had any allies, they were made by bribery or at the point of a sword. Cormac had no doubt expected the king to send a peaceable bridegroom who'd inherit the title upon his death. That had been the king's intent and Ryland's plan as well.

But now that he'd seen the extent of Cormac's villainy, he knew that plan would have to change. Ryland needed to claim the title as soon as he was wedded to the chieftain's daughter. He was confident there would be little resistance from the *clann*, who would doubtless welcome the fall of their corrupt chieftain.

Temair O'Keeffe, however, was a mystery. Even those who purported to know her seemed to disagree about who she was, what she looked like, and what her intentions might be.

Then there were the woodkerns. At the moment, since they believed they were holding Ryland hostage, awaiting his ransom, they thought they had leverage. But Ryland would soon turn the tables on them. When he did, would they then view him as a foe who'd betrayed them? Or would they embrace him as their champion?

Beside him, Gray struggled up from her seat, staggering to her feet. He rose and reached out to steady her, taking her by the elbow.

She looked up at him with grateful eyes and blurted out, "I wish ye didn't have to go. Ever."

He grinned. On the morrow, poor Gray would no doubt regret much of what she was confessing tonight. But as befuddled as she was, he still found her irresistible.

And he knew what she meant. Part of him didn't want to go either. Taking Temair O'Keeffe for a wife, he was heading into uncharted waters. But he knew a woman like Gray could make him happy for the rest of his life.

Of course, he couldn't say that.

"If I don't go, you'll never get your ransom," he pointed out.

"I don't care. 'Tisn't about the coin anyway. Not really," she confided.

He furrowed his brows and checked to make sure no one else had heard. "What do you mean?"

She stood on her toes and pulled him down by his shirt so she could whisper in his ear. "'Tis about...gettin' back what's mine."

Her breath tickled.

"What do you mean? What's yours?"

Gray blinked a few times, as if she'd forgotten. She was obviously still under the influence of the ale. "Oh." She shook her head. "I'm not s'posed to tell ye that."

Now she had his interest. "You can tell me."

"Nay," she said, "I can't."

"I won't tell a soul."

She hesitated then, weaving on her feet in indecision as she gazed up at him with eyes full of worship. "Ye're the most beautiful man I've e'er seen. I swear it."

It was hard not to chuckle at her infatuated proclamation. "A warty frog is beautiful when you've drunk as much ale as you have, Lady Gray."

She giggled, and the sound poured over him like water over a fall, clear and bubbly and refreshing.

But as soon as it trickled to a stop, her eyes grew sad again.

"Can't ye just stay here?" She clutched his tabard in both hands now, like a desperate beggar. "Ye could join our band of outlaws."

He snickered at the idea.

"Nay, truly," she insisted. "I can teach ye how to use the *bata*, and we can stay here in the forest. Ye wouldn't like that drafty old tower anyway. Stay with me here."

A tiny part of him actually found that appealing. To dwell out here among the trees, beneath the stars, with very few possessions and very few ties was adventurous and romantic. To spend his days in the company of friendly folk and his nights in the arms of a woman as beautiful as Gray...

"Stay with me," she purred.

But he'd made a vow—to his king, to the chieftain, to his bride. Above all else, he was a man of his word.

"Come," he said. "We'll talk about it on the morrow."

Giving a short, low whistle to summon the hounds, he walked with her to their sleeping spot in front of the cave, letting her lean on him when her knees wobbled. He spread both of their cloaks on the ground and helped her to lie down.

He couldn't help but smile as she sprawled across both cloaks with graceless abandon. Her eyes were closed before he could even snap his fingers to make the hounds lie at her feet.

He nudged her over to make room for himself. Then he stretched out beside her, gazing up at the heavens.

The stars were beginning to appear, like bright raindrops against the violet sky.

He thought she was asleep.

She wasn't.

"Ryland?" she murmured.

"Aye?"

"What were ye like as a lad?"

"A lad?" He crossed his arms over his chest and thought about it. "I don't know. I suppose I was like any lad. My father taught me how to fight when I was young. My mother taught me how to be courteous." He chuckled. "My older brothers taught me how to run very fast."

She giggled.

"Ah, you're laughing," he said. "Did you have older brothers as well?"

"Nay, just an older sister. She never chased me."

"Where is she now—your sister?"

There was a hesitation in Gray's voice. "She's...she's gone. I don't know where. The last time I saw her was the night...the night I joined the woodkerns."

"Six years ago?"

"Aye."

Ryland wondered if she realized what a strange coincidence that was. It was six years ago that Temair O'Keeffe's older sister had fallen from the tower.

As he stared up at the night sky, the stars began to shift as his eyes rearranged them into different patterns, altering his perceptions. A curious tingling began at the back of his neck as his thoughts likewise coalesced into a shifted reality.

Questions crept in to tease at the edges of his mind.

Questions that made his breath catch.

Questions that created new patterns like the stars in the sky.

They were wildly improbable questions. And yet...

He tried to keep the tension from his voice as he asked her, "Is Gray your real name?"

"What do ye mean?" Was that panic he heard?

"Is it the name you were born with?"

"'Tis...the only name I go by." It was an evasive answer. "Because o' my gray eyes," she explained.

"What about your last name?"

"I...don't have one."

"You don't have one?"

"Not that I can remember." She yawned.

He didn't believe that for an instant. If she'd only left home six years ago, she could certainly remember her last name.

On the other hand, maybe it was common among outlaws to discard their last names. Cambeal had done so with his, saying he didn't wish to bring shame to his family.

"What about your sister?" he asked. "What's her name?"

Gray was silent.

When he glanced over at her, she was asleep.

He was half-tempted to shake her awake and interrogate her further. But he supposed the outlaws wouldn't look kindly on that. Her wolfhounds would look even less kindly.

Hope and the unimaginable battled in his brain.

Was it possible Gray was actually Temair?

Part of him was sure it couldn't be true. Cormac claimed his daughter had run away only a few days before. Certainly the chieftain wouldn't lie about that. What possible reason could he have for deceiving Ryland?

Still, it was curious that no one else had seen Temair in all that time, that, according to rumor, she'd been locked away for six years.

It was difficult to argue with the evidence staring him in the face, even if it was only guesses and fragments.

And the part of him that believed it might just be true that Gray *was* Temair couldn't begin to fathom why she would keep that secret.

All night long, between bouts of sleep, he wrestled with doubt.

Were the woodkerns protecting Temair from Ryland?

Were they trying to foil the king's plans?

Had they kidnapped Temair to use her as leverage against her father, the same way they were demanding ransom for Ryland?

Had Cormac hidden the disappearance of his daughter six years ago? And if so, what game was he playing now?

Was Gray part of some twisted plot to deceive the English invaders?

Or could she be telling the truth—that she didn't remember anything?

Sometime, long past midnight, Ryland finally got to sleep. He began to dream.

He was with his beautiful gray-eyed bride, and they were standing on a bed, laughing and fighting with *batas*. Every time he thought he was getting close to winning the battle, she'd block his advance and dance out of his way.

Eventually, he gave up trying. They tossed their weapons—and their clothing—aside. Then they collapsed together onto the pallet.

Lying with her was like visiting heaven. He reveled in her naked body, closing his eyes. He caressed every inch of her, savoring her velvety flesh. He pressed his mouth to hers, drinking the passion from her lips. Tenderly, he slipped his fingers over her silken shoulder and across her bosom until her gently rounded breast filled his hand. Aroused and enchanted, he sighed with pleasure...

Suddenly, he was awakened by Bran's wet nose nudging his arm. Yanked from the dream, Ryland cracked open his eyes to a sharp sliver of morning sunlight. The dog was staring sheepishly at him.

Then he realized the position he was in and froze.

It had only been half a dream. His body was wrapped around Gray like a cloak. A slip of parchment wouldn't have fit between her lovely back and his chest. Their legs were tangled together like fronds of seaweed. Her warm buttocks pressed against him intimately, making his blood surge, and he grew instantly hard.

His arm was draped over her shoulder. Somehow, his hand had managed to find its way inside her garments to her soft, supple breast.

He didn't dare move. He hardly dared breathe.

To be fair, her hand was clasped over the top of his. It appeared she'd guided him there in her sleep. But that didn't make him feel any less guilty. And it didn't make him feel any less aroused.

He couldn't stay like this. She'd wake up. The rest of the camp would wake up.

Moving as little as possible, he lifted his eyes to take inventory of the camp. At first, he thought everyone was sleeping.

Then he saw her. Sorcha. Leaning against a yew tree with her arms crossed over her bosom, watching him.

CHAPTER 21

Ryland felt the blood drain from his face. There was no way to explain this situation.

But as he continued to stare back at her, he realized Sorcha wasn't angry. She was amused. She found his predicament entertaining.

He didn't think that was right either. Shouldn't she be protecting one of her own?

But before he could scowl at her in disapproval, she came to his rescue.

"Wake up, ye pagan sluggards!" she cried, clapping her hands loudly. "'Tis the Sabbath."

In the chaos of her shouting and clapping, Ryland was able to extricate himself from Gray without her notice.

She groaned as she slowly rolled onto her back.

Ryland sat up on his elbow. His palm was still warm where it had caressed her flesh. His heart was still pounding. And his loins still ached.

His voice came out as a ragged croak. "Good morn."

Temair recoiled in pain. Why was he talking so loudly? And why was her mouth so dry?

She'd just been having the most lovely dream. But Sorcha's shrill announcement had shredded it. Now her head was throbbing, and she couldn't even remember what she'd been dreaming.

"Morn," she whispered back. Even that hurt.

"Too much ale?" he murmured.

She nodded. She didn't dare open her eyes. Even through her lids, the brightness of the sun was blinding.

Bloody hell. Why had she drunk so much? She knew better.

One of the hounds licked her face, and she pulled away with a disgusted sneer.

"Nay," Ryland hissed. With a snap of his fingers, the dog retreated.

She rose up on her elbows and tried to clear the fog from her brain. What had happened last night?

She remembered two English knights had come to supper. Then she remembered why she'd refilled her cup so many times. The knights had been talking about Temair being a murderer.

Had she said anything? Had she revealed any secrets? It had been a long time since she'd gotten that drunk.

Ryland asked her softly, "Would you like water?"

She nodded. Her mouth felt as dry as dust. And something was poking at the back of her brain, trying to remind her of something she'd said or done that she shouldn't have.

What was it?

She could hear the other woodkerns coming slowly to life with yawns and muttering. The fire started to crackle.

The sparrows chirped in the yews—little piercing chirps that drilled into her aching temples.

"Here." Ryland returned, placing the cup into her hands.

She sipped at it until she felt restored enough to pry open her eyes. "Thank ye."

He was watching her expectantly.

"What?" she asked.

He shook his head and lowered his gaze. "Nothing."

She *had* done something. He was acting strangely. What the hell had happened?

She racked her brain. She remembered stating her frank opinion of Cormac O'Keeffe. But so had the rest of the outlaws. And he hadn't seemed to be offended by it.

"Did I..." she began.

"What?"

"If I did...or said anythin'...untoward..."

He rubbed at his chin in consideration. "Well, you *did* promise that when I'm ransomed, I can take Flann with me."

That coaxed a smile from her. "Ye're full o' shite. That I'd never promise...no matter how much ale I drank."

He laughed. "What about Bran?"

She shook her head, then pressed fingers to her temple. Even that small movement hurt.

"How did you get these fine lads anyway?" he asked, bristling Bran's fur with his fingers.

She told him the truth. "I don't know where they came from. After my ma died, the two pups just trotted up to me and ne'er left."

He scratched Flann under the chin so he wouldn't get jealous. "You're good lads to look after a lost little maid."

His touching words caught her off-guard and choked her up. Quickly, before he could notice, she gulped down the rest of the water and returned the cup to him.

"Six years ago?" he asked.

"Aye."

"So your mother died when you were..." he prompted.

Temair narrowed her eyes. Ryland had asked one too many questions. What was he trying to find out? He was a kind man, an honorable man. But he was also a very clever man. She had to be careful what she revealed.

"Just a young lass," she said, being as vague as possible.

"Well, I'm glad these lads were there for you."

She nodded. Maybe she was being overly cautious. Whatever she'd said or done last night, it didn't seem to have changed anything between the two of them.

"I should get up," she decided. But when she sat forward, the blood pounded in her head. She grimaced.

"Raw eel," he said.

"What?" she moaned, burying her face in her hands.

"Raw eel. 'Tis the English cure for too much ale. Would you like me to pull one out o' the stream for you?"

She peered at him between her fingers. He had to be jesting. Indeed, his sober expression couldn't hide the twinkle of mischief in his eyes.

Two could play that game.

"Aye," she told him, "and while ye're doin' that, I'll be buryin' myself neck-deep in river sand." At his quizzical look, she said, "'Tis the *Irish* cure for too much ale."

His laughter should have grated on her ears, but it didn't. Instead, it felt like a warm, comforting cloak wrapped around her.

"Since 'tis the Sabbath," he murmured, "perhaps I'll just pray for your recovery."

Temair wondered who he'd be praying to. The woodkerns worshipped an assortment of gods, from the *Tuatha De Danann* to Odin to the Holy Spirit. The friar had never tried to convert any of them. They practiced good will, and that was all that mattered. But at the behest of the friar, though they couldn't afford to be completely idle on the Sabbath, they did abstain from thieving.

Ryland hopped up to his feet and held out a hand to assist her. Temair didn't much feel like getting up, but his outstretched hand and his bright smile were impossible to resist.

She glanced around the camp. The Sabbath was often the busiest day of the week for the woodkerns. Friar Brian and young Fergus were packing up satchels full of goods to distribute to the various households. Lady Mor served up bread to break everyone's fast and began grinding grain for the supper loaves. Six of the men took off for the *lough* with fishing poles. Sorcha started brewing a new batch of ale. And Aife slung a basket of dried herbs over her arm, preparing to spy upon the *tuath,* which had now become a daily task.

Ryland noticed the activity as well. "What can I do?" At Temair's astonished blink, he shrugged and explained. "I may as well be of some use."

"'Tis my turn for laundry. You could come along and help." She was hesitant to leave him behind in the camp, not because she didn't trust him, but because she didn't trust Lady Mor with him.

"Laundry?" She could see he was surprised by that.

"Livin' in the wood doesn't make us savages." She arched a brow. "Besides, 'tis a skill everyone should learn, noblemen and paupers."

She loaded him up with bedding and bundled all the spare clothing and odd rags that needed washing. Then she grabbed her laundry bat and led him to the stream and the spot where they'd first met.

The basket she'd forgotten was still there, though some opportunistic animal had tipped it over and eaten all the blackberries.

She untied the bundle and dumped the clothing by the streamside. "The most important thing is not to lose the laundry in the current."

She showed him how to separate the smaller items like stockings and rags and to wash them first, scrubbing them by hand on a stone and setting them to dry on bushes. To her amusement, he was an apt student, hanging on her every word as if she were teaching him the finer points of swordplay.

When they got to the *léines*, she demonstrated the laundry bat. Soon he was beating the dust from the garments, stirring them in the current, and draping them over hazel branches to dry as if he'd done it all his life.

"Ye keep this up and ye'll make someone a good wife," she teased.

He grinned back. "I'm fairly sure my bride-to-be has a staff of laundresses to wash her clothing."

That had been true at one time. Temair had even had a maid to help dress her. But living with the woodkerns, she'd quickly learned to be self-sufficient.

"What about you?" he asked. "Are you ever going to make someone a good wife?"

He'd said it casually, but it startled her enough to make her lose her grip on the *léine* she'd been washing. The linen garment dropped into the water and started to float away. She made a successful grab for it, but she had to step into the stream, soaking her *brogs*.

"Shite."

"I didn't mean to upset you." She didn't believe him. His eyes were dancing, and he sounded very insincere.

She *was* upset. She wasn't sure how to answer that question. Until the events of the last few days, marriage had seemed like a distant possibility. But with a bridegroom appointed to the O'Keeffe heiress, her father setting up an imposter, and Temair mustering funds for an army to battle for her legacy, a wedding seemed imminent.

Of course, he knew none of that. His question was perfectly innocent.

"I'm not upset," she lied, giving the last stocking a final swish in the water and hanging it over the long branch of a hazel. "I'm just in no hurry to get married."

That part was true.

Ryland considered her answer. If Gray *was* Temair, he could see why she would say that. Cormac O'Keeffe wasn't exactly a shining example of a good husband and wedded bliss.

But if she was Temair, she would also know that *Ryland* was her betrothed. Did she really find the prospect of being married to him so revolting?

Ryland didn't. Not at all. Though it surprised him to admit he was attracted to an outlaw, it was true. He was quite fond of the wayward lass.

He wished there was some way to discover for certain whether Gray was in fact Temair.

As soon as he'd realized where she was leading him, it occurred to him that he was in a position to escape. For a wild moment, he'd considered it. He wouldn't even have had to break his oath, for she'd given him permission to leave the camp. Since she'd taken him to the log bridge where they'd first met, he was close enough to the road to find his way back to O'Keeffe.

But the niggling doubt about Gray's identity and his certainty that his men would save the day made Ryland decide to leave things as they were. If she didn't want to reveal who she was, she must have a reason. The last thing he wanted to do was to spook her into doing something unpredictable that would endanger the whole plan.

He leaned against the hazel trunk and crossed his arms. "Surely you'll want to marry eventually."

"Why should I?" She dunked the last *léine* in the stream, stirring it with the laundry bat.

He frowned. Why indeed? He supposed, living with several men, she could satisfy her carnal appetites any time she wished, a thought that left a sour taste in his mouth. But didn't she long for more?

"Don't you dream of sharing your life with one special man? Having his children?" he asked. "Doing his laundry?"

Laughing, she tossed the laundered *léine* at him, smacking him in the face.

With a grin, he peeled the wet linen away and dutifully draped the thing over the hazel branch, next to four stockings and a couple of rags. Unfortunately, it proved too heavy for the thin limb, and the branch snapped. The *léine* dropped into the mud, and the end of the branch landed in the water. He watched in horror as the stockings and rags floated off the end of the branch in the current.

"Oh, nay!" she cried, slogging forward in the stream.

He charged in after them as well, snagging two stockings. Then he slipped on the algae-slick rocks, stumbling into the water.

Swimming after the rest of the escaped laundry, Gray managed to catch the two remaining stockings. But the rags had already floated too far downstream to recover.

From midstream, Ryland threw his pair of wet stockings onto a flat rock beside the stream, where they thankfully stuck. He raked back his hair with both hands and prepared to apologize to Gray for his carelessness.

But when he turned toward her, he saw she'd drifted downstream. She was up to her neck in the cold water, clutching one stocking in each fist above her head, and fighting the current.

"Let go of the stockings!" he cried.

But she still held them aloft.

"Let them go! You'll—"

Her head dipped under.

His heart pounding with fear, he immediately dove into the water and swam toward her. She was nearly submerged, barely gurgling above the waves with her arms still over her head, when he intercepted her. He swiftly wrapped his arms around her body and lifted her face clear of the water.

She blinked and sputtered as he swam with her, making his way toward the shallows. When she started shaking and gasping, he peered at her in concern, afraid she might be choking.

But to his amazement, the minx was laughing.

"Your face!" she cried with glee, as if it were the funniest thing she'd ever seen.

"My face?" he asked, incredulous. "You almost drowned."

"Drowned?" She burst out in giggles. "Is that what ye thought?"

"What else was I to think?"

"Sorry." She sounded anything but sorry.

She might think it was amusing. He did not. Still, it was hard to be angry when her gray eyes were sparkling like that.

She tried again. "Truly, Sir Ryland. I'm sorry."

This time her eyes softened. He half believed her.

They were close enough to the shore to stand up now. Still disgruntled, he asked, "Why didn't you just let go of the damned stockings?"

"Because they're Lady Mor's," Gray said, "and she would snatch me bald if I lost them."

Now that Gray was safe, he began to see the humor of the situation. But seeing her in peril had affected him more than he cared to admit. He took Lady Mor's stockings from her, slogged toward the shore, and laid them out over a rowan bush.

When he turned back, Gray was wading out of the water. But unlike the first time they'd met at this stream, she wasn't wearing her leather armor. Instead, she was dressed in only her linen *léine*. And she was soaked to the skin.

Her long, loose black hair flowed over her shoulders, falling away where her breasts emerged. Beneath the cold, clinging cloth, the tips were outlined in sharp relief. Lower, he could see the hollow of her navel. Lower still, he could make out the curves and recesses of her hips and the defined angle where her legs intersected.

He felt the air desert his lungs.

She might as well have been naked.

CHAPTER 22

The water was still up to Temair's knees when she stopped. Ryland was looking at her strangely. No one had ever looked at her like that before. His glance flickered down over her body and then back up. When his eyes returned to hers, they reflected a solemn, intense hunger, like that of a starving wolf about to devour her.

She should have been frightened. She was alone. Weaponless. With a man who could easily overpower her. A man who saw her as his captor.

Worse, it suddenly occurred to her that she'd led him to a place where he could escape and easily find his way back to the tower house. She'd been weak and foolish.

Yet that was not how his gaze made her feel. It made her feel desirable, powerful, irresistible.

Her eyes lingered on his mouth. She remembered the flavor of him. She wanted that again—to taste the water on his lips, to thaw at the heat of his tongue, to feel the pressure of his hips and the urging of his fingers.

In her mind, she came to him.

In truth, it was Ryland who crossed the space between them. Throwing caution aside, he walked boldly into the water, caught her head between his hands, and sealed the desire burning between them with a kiss that singed her senses and melted her into a helpless puddle.

Enraptured, she plunged her fingers into his wet hair. She gasped against his mouth as his tongue touched hers, and it seemed a flame licked at her soul, branding her.

His fingers drifted down, sweeping her face, grazing her chin, wrapping around her throat. She gulped. His hands were large enough to strangle her or snap her neck.

But he didn't. He let his thumbs slide down past the racing pulse of her throat to delve into the shallow crevice between her breasts. She sighed, arching her back in invitation.

Flattening his palms, he moved his hands with eager tenderness over her breasts, rasping against the sensitive crests. She groaned at the lovely sensation. His answering groan incited her to more erotic heights.

Breaking from the kiss, she let her head fall back, offering her bosom to him. He leaned forward, lowering his lips to her throat, licking the droplets from her skin.

Slowly he worked his way down, bestowing kisses on her bosom, gently peeling back the edges of her *léine* as she begged wordlessly to be bared for his touch.

His thumb at last slipped beneath her *léine* to brush across her breast, to the peak where her desire was centered. Her gasp turned into a moan as he lowered his head to envelop her between his warm, searching lips.

The tips of her fingers dug into the tense muscles of his upper arms as he moved to give the same sweet attention to her other breast.

When his mouth returned to hers, she clawed his wet shirt from his shoulders, wanting, *needing* to feel his hot flesh against hers.

With frantic fingers, she pushed down the top of her *léine*, freeing her breasts. Then she surged forward in a lusty collision with his muscled chest.

The sensation was more divine than she'd imagined. Though he was strong and solid, his flesh was warm and yielding. A sensual comfort surrounded her, as if she were bathing in rich, heavy cream.

Yet within that comfort throbbed a new longing. An itch betwixt her thighs. A yearning deep in her womb.

As if he sensed her pain, he grunted and moved his hand down her stomach toward the source of her distress. Even through the linen, his fingers found and pressed that aching part of her with unerring precision.

Resting her brow on his shoulder, she squeezed her eyes shut and buried a sob of delight against his chest.

He growled and hefted her up by her waist.

She instinctively wrapped her legs around his hips. But even as she rejoiced at his bold advance and the intimate contact, she cursed the hindrance of her skirts. To her dismay, she found that simultaneously clinging to him, kissing him, and moving her sopping garments out of the way proved impossible. She writhed in passionate frustration...and accidentally threw him off-balance.

He staggered on the rocks. At that same instant, she heard the unmistakable sounds of someone coming through the forest. She stiffened and tried to scramble down.

Burdened by her extra weight and thrown off-kilter by her movement, Ryland lost his footing a second time.

This time, he couldn't regain his balance. Together, they tumbled into the water with a loud splash.

It was probably for the best. The intruder was Aife, returning from the tower house. Spotting Ryland and Temair as soon as she started across the log bridge, she stopped with a gasp. As the two of them scrambled up to the shallow streambed, struggling to put their clothes back in order, Aife looked from one to the other, unsure what to say.

Ryland made a valiant attempt to put things to rights. Unfortunately, so did Temair. And they spoke at the same time.

"I feared she was drowning," he said.

"I've been teachin' him how to swim," she said.

Aife obviously wasn't convinced by either story. She glanced at the laundry strewn over the bushes, cleared her throat, and finished crossing the log bridge. "I have news from the keep," she said to Temair, blushing as she added, "when ye're done with all the...launderin'."

Even after Aife departed, leaving them alone, Temair knew it was too late to continue where they'd left off. The mood had been spoiled.

"I'm sorry," Ryland muttered. "I should never have done that."

"Nay, 'tis my fault," she replied. "I know better."

Temair *did* know better. She had to accept the truth. She wasn't going to wed Ryland.

Even if he was her betrothed.

Even if she was growing very fond of him.

Even if she craved the handsome knight with every ounce of her being.

Not if it meant ceding control to the English king. And

especially not if it meant living in the household and under the thumb of her father until he saw fit to die.

So if she didn't intend to wed Ryland, she had no right to seduce him. It wasn't only a form of self-torture. It was irresponsible and cruel to him.

"I can't fall prey to my desires," Ryland murmured, as if to himself, "no matter how desirable I find you."

Temair's heart leaped at his words. He found her desirable?

Then he added, "I owe my fealty to my bride."

He gave her a sideways glance then, as if waiting for her opinion on that. But she could say nothing. It was a frustrating and bittersweet paradox that he both desired Temair and wished to be faithful to his bride.

Suffering in silence and unrequited lust as she waited for the laundry to dry, Temair couldn't make up her mind if Ryland's integrity made her love him or hate him.

Hours later, while Ryland and the rest of the woodkerns supped by the fire, Temair and Aife conferred privately in the cave.

"Ye're sure?" Temair whispered.

"The chieftain was seen speakin' at length to a lass at the fair," Aife murmured, adding pointedly, "a small, dark lass."

Temair felt a chill go through her. "A new imposter." It was stunning how quickly her father could replace her.

"There's more."

"More?"

"I spoke to everyone I know in the *tuath*," she said. "No one has heard a thing about a ransom."

"What?" Temair exploded in disbelief. The sound bounced off the cave wall, startling Aife. Temair glanced toward the vines at the mouth of the cave and lowered her voice. "How can that be? Are ye sure?"

"Aye. And no one's laid eyes on the knights o' de Ware since they first headed into the wood."

"But that's im-... What about..." Temair furrowed her brows and chewed at her thumbnail. "If they didn't return to the tower house...where did they go?"

She knew Conall and Niell had led the knights back to the main road. And since their esteemed commander, Sir Ryland, was a hostage, his men would naturally wish to make all haste to negotiate his release with O'Keeffe. Wouldn't they?

Bloody hell. If her father wasn't even aware that Sir Ryland de Ware was her hostage, she'd never collect that ransom. And if she didn't get the ransom, she'd never muster an army to take back the *tuath*.

Like the rags she'd watched float away downstream, it seemed her plans were rapidly drifting out of reach.

But she wasn't ready to give up. She still held Sir Ryland de Ware captive. Even if her father had managed to find an imposter, he couldn't very well marry off the bride without the bridegroom. For the moment, at least, things were at a standstill.

It didn't make sense. How could Ryland's men simply disappear? She'd seen how loyal they were to him. Surely they would do everything in their power to see him safely returned.

So what was going on?

What was she missing?

"They can't have just vanished," she said.

"Maybe they were waylaid by murderers," Aife suggested, "or devoured by wolves."

It was possible, but highly unlikely. "Ye travel that road all the time with no incident."

"Aye, true."

Nay, the more Temair thought about it, the more she was convinced that something more devious was afoot.

For one thing, even though he'd had the opportunity, Ryland hadn't attempted to flee. To her chagrin, she'd led him straight to the log bridge, steps away from freedom, forgetting that he could find his way back from that place. Yet he hadn't even tried. Why?

Temair paled, afraid to consider the reason. Her mind filled with dark possibilities. She felt her heart crack slowly into a hundred pieces.

Had she been so blind? Had she been too distracted by Ryland's seduction to see what was right in front of her?

A powerful knight like Sir Ryland de Ware hadn't earned his spurs by sitting back and allowing others to fight his battles. For a man like that, the only course of action was to take matters into his own hands. He would take charge, act with aggression, and secure his release on his own terms.

He meant to betray her. Of course he did. He hadn't sent his men to collect the ransom at all. He'd instructed them to do something else. But what?

How long had he been carrying on this deception? From that very first kiss he'd given her with his lying lips? When he and his men had followed her back to the camp? She wasn't sure. But somehow the tempting villain had managed to gain her confidence. She flushed with shame to think of how vulnerable she'd left herself to his charms.

It was only a matter of time before he turned on her like a rogue hound and snapped at her trusting fingers. She swallowed down the nasty taste of betrayal, which sank into a hard lump in her stomach.

But she couldn't afford to dwell on her own humiliation or the hurt that squeezed her heart. For the sake of her legacy and her *clann*, she needed to find out where his men had gone.

"Send him to me," she said.

"Who?"

"Sir Ryland." She whipped out her dagger, flipped it through her fingers with a flourish, and leaned back against the shadowy wall to wait. "I need to have a word with him."

Standing before the vine-covered entrance of the cave, Ryland hesitated. He didn't have to wonder what Gray wanted with him in this dark and private place. But that way lay madness. He could hardly control himself around the tempting lass.

It had been only a few hours, but already he missed the stream-wet taste of her, the soft, yielding pillows of her breasts, the welcome strength of her legs around his hips.

His blood grew hot.

His breath grew shallow.

His pulse raced.

His loins tightened.

Hell.

Would it be so terrible after all to tryst with the lass before he had to bid her farewell? He might be promised to another, but he wasn't yet wed. Besides, the married men in his company had bedded far more wenches than he before shackling themselves to a wife. Since he'd probably be leaving on the morrow, surely it wasn't so unforgiveable to indulge in one last night of wild abandon before he marched away to bind himself to one woman. Forever.

Was he a fool to tempt fate this way? Or was he more of a fool to turn down a beautiful and willing lass?

In the end, his knightly honor won the battle of conscience. He knew he would regret it if he succumbed to his animal instincts. He was betrothed to another. And even though he'd not yet met the lass, chivalry required that he preserve his body for her. His body. His heart. His honor.

With a decisive sigh, he swept the vines aside and entered the cave. The interior was almost completely dark, lit only by the firelight filtering through the leafy curtain.

"Gray?" he called out, narrowing his eyes into the shadows.

"Here." Her voice, coming from the left side of the cave, was soft and inviting. For a torturous moment, he wondered what she was wearing. Or not wearing.

"I can't see you."

"This way," she purred.

He grimaced. She obviously expected him to feel his way to her. He ventured carefully forward with outstretched hands, lowering them when he realized they were breast-height.

He'd taken four steps when a sudden hard shove in the middle of his chest knocked him back against the cave wall. His head struck rock, and in that dazed instant, he felt the sharp point of a blade slip under his chin.

"Where are your men?" she bit out.

Her voice was no longer soft.

No longer inviting.

And her words sobered him as fast as a slap.

She wasn't inviting him to a tryst. She was conducting an interrogation.

She knew. She knew his men hadn't returned to Cormac O'Keeffe. That spy, Aife, must have brought her the news.

He had to think fast. Which wasn't easy when his head was spinning and there was a dagger at his throat.

"Answer me," she hissed, giving his chin a painful jab.

He sucked a breath between his teeth. She'd probably drive that blade into his throat if he told her the truth. Besides, it was too late for her to stop anything. The wheels were already in motion.

His best option was to feign ignorance. "What do you mean?"

"They didn't go to the tower house," she said. "So where did they go?"

He pretended surprise. "They're not at the tower house?"

"Nay." She gave him another jab. "And I think ye know where they are."

"How would I know that?" he said tightly. "I've been your prisoner this entire time."

"Where...are...they?" she demanded.

"I swear I don't know." That much was true. He wasn't exactly sure where they were at this moment, only where they were headed.

"If they don't bring me the ransom, ye'll never see your bride." She pressed the point of her dagger against the vein pulsing in his neck, not hard enough to break the skin, just enough to make him nervous.

"Wait. Are you sure?" he said. "They have to be there. You saw how loyal they were to me. They would have gone with all haste to collect my ransom."

"If they were in such haste, then why have they not returned?"

"Perhaps Cormac didn't have the coin yet," he suggested. "Five hundred pounds is a great sum. Perhaps he needed more time."

"Then your men should be waiting for it there... impatiently. But they're not."

Gray was a clever lass and an expert interrogator. It was a challenge to outwit her quick mind. He'd have to switch tactics then and prey upon her soft heart.

"They're not?" He let his shoulders sink. "But if they're not there... Oh, god."

"What?"

"You don't think they..." He was glad she couldn't see the deceit in his eyes. "Nay, 'tisn't possible. They're loyal to me. I know they are. They'd never do such a thing."

"What?"

"'Tis too underhanded to consider."

"What?" she ground out, punctuating her impatience by poking his jaw with her blade.

"Could they have...betrayed me?" His voice cracked over the words. "Do you think they might have... confiscated the ransom?"

"Shite." Clearly, this would not be good news for Temair.

"It doesn't seem possible," he said. "And yet... What other explanation could there be?"

CHAPTER 23

"**S**hite," Temair said again. The possibility that Ryland's men had crossed him had never occurred to her.

"And if they took the coin," Ryland said woodenly, "then they may already be on their way back to England."

"Shite!"

Enraged, Temair punched the cave wall with her free fist, wincing as she bruised her knuckles.

"My own men," Ryland said, stunned. "How could they? I trusted them. Damn it, I *trusted* them."

Bloody bastards! Most English knights she'd met seemed chivalrous to a fault—fond of their fealty oaths, their sworn honor, and their brotherhood. She expected they'd die before they'd stab a fellow in the back.

Apparently that wasn't true. Apparently Ryland's men were traitors.

It made perfect sense that they'd escaped with the ransom. That much coin would make a generous prize, split between the four of them. And they could be certain Ryland would never be able to exact revenge upon them, for without the ransom, he'd remain a captive of the woodkerns.

Abarta's ballocks! Her dreams of reclaiming her land shattered like thin ice. She'd counted on that coin to finance the battle for her legacy. To have it stolen—and by foreigners, no less—was a travesty.

Now her only leverage was holding on to Ryland de Ware. Still, once Cormac learned both his bridegroom and his ransom had gone missing, he'd pursue their return with a vengeance. He held a grudge like no other, and his vindictive doggedness knew no bounds. Indeed, it wouldn't surprise her if the chieftain set the whole bloody forest afire to flush out the prospective groom.

She ground her teeth, enraged and frustrated by the way her vicious father always seemed to be able to seize the upper hand.

Yet at the same time, she felt sorry for Sir Ryland. The forthright, noble knight hadn't invited any of this. He'd done nothing to earn such disloyalty. His only failing seemed to be trusting in men he shouldn't.

He'd believed King John when he'd said there was an heiress waiting to be his wife.

He'd believed Cormac O'Keeffe when he'd said Ryland's bride was lost in the forest.

He'd believed his men when they said they would ransom him.

But, without mercy and without remorse, they'd all betrayed him.

Temair thought he deserved better than that. She'd met enough dishonorable nobles in her outlaw pursuits to tell that Sir Ryland was a rare gentleman with an honest heart.

She decided that she, at least, wouldn't join the ranks of those willing to stab him in the back. She lowered her blade and stepped away.

In the dim light, she could see him lift a hand to check his throat. He'd find nothing. She'd been careful not to injure him. She might be unyielding, but she wasn't cruel.

"I'm sorry I doubted ye," she murmured, sheathing her dagger.

"'Tisn't your fault," he said, hanging his head. "I would have done the same."

He sounded so despondent, so disappointed. He probably realized that she couldn't let him go now. And that meant that he'd not only lost his men. He'd also lost his bride.

She tucked her lip under her teeth. Maybe she could ease at least part of his pain on that score.

"There's somethin' ye should know," she said. There was a long silence as she mustered the courage to tell him.

Finally, he prompted her. "Aye?"

She swallowed and braced herself for his reply. "Ye never truly had a bride."

He froze. "What do you mean?"

She furrowed her brow, unsure how much she should reveal. "I mean, Temair hasn't been seen in the *tuath* since the night her sister died."

"So I've heard." He shook his head. "Are the rumors true then—that she's been kept...in chains...locked in a cell?"

"Nay."

"Nay?" He puzzled over that. "Then how..."

"She didn't just disappear that night. She *ran away.* She ran away and never returned."

He fell silent.

Indeed, it was so long before he spoke that she began to wonder if he'd heard her. When he finally found his voice, his manner had changed. He seemed to be choosing his words carefully, as if he were afraid of breaking them.

"I see," he said. "So the chieftain—he lied about her disappearing just days ago?"

"Aye. I'm afraid Cormac O'Keeffe sent ye to chase a ghost."

"But why? He signed an agreement with the king, promising his daughter in marriage."

"A daughter he didn't possess."

"Surely he wouldn't make a promise he couldn't keep. Violating an agreement with the king? He might as well sign his own death warrant."

"Oh, he planned to uphold the agreement," she said, "with an imposter."

"An imposter?" he scoffed. "How would he manage that?"

"Ye forget. Temair hasn't been seen there—by anyone—in six years. Her looks could have changed a great deal." She lowered her voice to a bitter whisper. "And even if someone suspects the imposter is not his daughter, Cormac has ways o' frightenin' the *clann* into silence and submission."

He nodded. He must have seen enough of Cormac to believe her. "How can you be so sure this woman is *not* the real Temair?"

Part of her wanted to end the farce and tell him, *Because* I'm *the real Temair*. But she would gain nothing by it, only a return to living under her father's rule. So instead she said, "Aife has seen the woman claimin' to be Temair with her own eyes. There are...differences."

"Still," he argued, "it makes no sense. Why would he use an imposter? 'Twould be surrendering his bloodline. He might as well simply hand over his holding to the crown."

She hesitated. She was reluctant to share so much with the man who was meant to usurp her claim.

On the other hand, betrayed by his men, Ryland was stuck with the woodkerns now. Since he wasn't going to reign over O'Keeffe, she might as well tell him.

"He planned to get her with child himself."

After a shocked silence, he exploded with, "What?" Then he spat out a curse. "He meant to bed my bride and make me believe the babe was mine?"

She nodded.

"But surely the lass would never stand for that," he argued. "Sooner or later, the truth would come out."

"So ye would think, wouldn't ye? But that's not always the way o' things. I've seen it before. Lasses who suffered in silence. Who wouldn't speak up for themselves." The hatred Temair harbored for her abusive father made her blood boil. As she spoke, she felt her tongue getting away from her. But she couldn't seem to stop it. "Out o' fear, they wouldn't lift a finger in their own defense. Or confide in anyone who could help them. Or take the hand that was offered to her, even when I..."

She broke off. Unexpectedly, her words had conjured up the haunting image of her sister. Beautiful, innocent Aillenn. At the mercy of their vile father. Violated. Damaged. So broken and suffering that she was compelled to take her own life.

In her mind's eye, Temair saw her sister falling. Over and over. And there was nothing she could do about it. Nothing but feel remorse for not *somehow* saving her.

She felt suddenly overwhelmed, sick with sorrow. She staggered, and a sob escaped her at the horrible memory.

"Are you all right?" Ryland clasped her shoulder in concern.

All at once, she couldn't breathe. Her throat ached with unspent tears.

What was wrong with her? She'd thought she was past everything. She'd thought her feelings were shut away, locked safely deep inside, behind that wall of stone.

But now the horror lurking in her soul surged like a river threatening to burst through the wall.

Ryland, with a few gentle words, removed a single rock.

The wall shuddered.

He drew her into his arms.

She felt the foundation dissolving into dust.

She buried a sob against his shoulder, appalled at her lack of control.

"That's all right," he murmured. "'Tis all right, m'lady." One reassuring hand went around her waist. One cradled her head. "I'm here."

His tender gestures of compassion were too great to withstand. The wall collapsed all at once, releasing an enormous river of raw grief.

Temair keened softly against his chest for her sister. For her lost innocence. For her helplessness. At last, she surrendered to heartfelt sobs of pure anguish.

Through it all, Ryland held her tenderly, rocking her, stroking her hair, murmuring reassurances.

"'Tis all right, m'lady. I'm here for you. Cry all you wish."

She clenched her fists in his shirt, drenching it with her tears. She mourned her mother, her sister, her *clann*, and the precious years of her youth. She mourned for all she had lost and all she would never recover. She mourned the unfairness of life and the way evil men could triumph while good ones languished.

All the while, Ryland never wavered in his sympathy, holding her until her weeping finally subsided to an occasional hitching breath.

"I'm sorry," she whispered.

"Hush," he said. "There's no need to be sorry."

"I don't know what's wrong with me."

"There's nothing wrong with you."

"I've ruined your tunic."

He chuckled softly. "Tossing me in the stream ruined my tunic. This is nothing."

She gave him a weak smile.

He was such a good man. So kind. So good-humored. So understanding. It was a bittersweet reality that if things had been different, she might have enjoyed being his bride.

She lowered her eyes to his mouth. His lips were still curved in a smile, and she couldn't help but recall the compelling pressure and release of his kiss. She longed to feel that heavenly sensation again, to taste the desire on his tongue, to feast upon his delicious flesh, to rain kisses over every inch of him...and more.

She gulped. She could do it now. She could tryst with Ryland.

No bride awaited him. So he was no longer bound by

fidelity. He could make love to her without guilt. They were free to...

Before she could finish the thought, he cupped her chin in his hands and swept down to claim her with a forceful and lingering kiss.

Ryland could no longer resist her—the fresh scent of her hair...the soft silk of her skin...her sweet, sad smile...the way her trusting hand curled upon his chest...how perfectly she fit into the crook of his shoulder...the way she warmed him where their bodies met—nor did he feel compelled to.

The temptation to kiss her was beyond his endurance.

And there was something else.

Something he'd never expected.

He was in love with her.

How it had happened, he didn't know. But seeing her lead the woodkerns, listening to her passion for the poor, watching her play with her wolfhounds, sharing laughter and tears with her, he had fallen in love. Deeply. Desperately. Hopelessly.

Which made falling into an embrace with her as easy as tumbling into the stream.

And once in the currents of their shared yearning, he found that love growing stronger and stronger, pulling him down in pleasure, threatening to drown him in joy.

Their lips collided again and again as they feasted on earthly delights. Holding her face between his hands, he teased her mouth open with his. He tasted her fully, reveling in her awe as their tongues met and mingled.

He moved his palms out then to bury his fingers in her hair. She moaned and leaned into his kiss.

Her hands, once placed innocently on his chest, now roved over his shoulders and slipped around his neck, pulling him even closer.

Desire poured like warm honey over his body. And like a bee to a flower, he fed upon her sweet nectar again and again.

Soon he felt the familiar ache of lust between his thighs. Caught up in the seductive moment, he nudged that part of him against her, hoping to ease his pain.

She gasped against his lips, and he backed off, afraid he had hurt her.

But she ground her hips against his again with a reassuring groan of need, pressing him back until he was pinned against the cave wall.

There was no mistake. She wanted him.

CHAPTER 24

emair wasn't sure whether it was rabid lust or a hunger for power that coursed through her veins as she held Ryland prisoner against the wall. All she knew was that she was burning with need, craving his touch, and she meant to have her way with him.

Which luckily seemed to coincide with his wishes.

He withdrew his hands from her hair, exploring her with unbound eagerness, letting his fingers trace her throat, her shoulder, her bosom, cupping the leather armor that shielded her breasts.

His caress was heavenly. But she was still unsatisfied. She released him long enough to drag the top of her *léine* down, baring herself to his touch.

"Oh, m'lady," he sighed, gazing down at her. His tongue slipped out to lick his lips, and he closed his eyes in yearning.

She shivered with desire as his palms grazed her flesh, kneading her tenderly. He nuzzled her neck, kissing the place beneath her ear that sent lightning coursing through her. Her hands closed into fists as she sipped a breath between her teeth.

He licked his way down her throat, and she turned her head aside to grant him access. He moved lower, tickling her with his thick curls. Then he lavished attention on her breasts, lifting them up to kiss her responsive flesh, bathing them with his tantalizing tongue, sucking gently there until she felt like sobbing in hunger.

She burrowed her fingers in his hair and tipped back her head, reveling in the hot vibrations traveling through her body.

The craving between her legs was strong now. It would not be denied. There was nothing to stop him taking what he wanted. She only had to make him want her.

When he had laved her thoroughly, she pushed him back against the wall and unbuckled his belt. He made no protest, not even when she cast the belt aside and boldly reached inside his *braies* for the treasure within.

He let out a ragged breath as she enclosed his firm, smooth warmth in her hand. Drunk on her own dominance, she rubbed against him, delighting at the way he shuddered in response.

"I want ye," she whispered.

"I can see that," he growled back.

"Do ye want me?"

He chuckled once. "You can't tell?"

Her smile was smug.

But not for long.

In the next instant, he wrapped an arm around her waist, picked her up, and turned to pin *her* against the wall.

Her outrage was quickly replaced by naked lust as he pressed the heel of his hand against the throbbing place between her legs. When he circled slowly, grinding against the bone there, she cried out in pleasure.

"Hush," he whispered. "They'll hear you."

"Don't hush me," she hissed. "'Tis your fault."

"What?" He circled over her again. "This?"

She clamped her lips against another outcry.

He chuckled as he reached under the hem of her *léine*. She squeezed her eyes shut with anticipation. His hands glided over her naked buttocks. Then he slid one hand to the front of her, caressing the curls guarding her womanhood. While she held her breath, he slipped a fingertip between her curls to delve into her most secret place.

"Oh!" She clenched the top of his shoulders. "Faith...what are ye doin' to me?"

"Don't you like it?"

At first she couldn't decide. She liked it. But it felt...forbidden.

At her lack of a reply, he withdrew his hand. "You don't like it?"

"Nay, I..." She felt strangely bereft without his touch. "Aye, I like it."

"Are you sure?"

"Aye."

"Because I can—"

"Aye!" She groaned in relief when he replaced his hand.

"Shh," he said on a laugh. "They'll all come running in, thinking I've molested you."

"Ye *are* molestin' me."

"Aye, that I am."

As he continued to rub across her—sometimes in long, fluid motions, sometimes in flurries that made her tighten and swell as if she might burst—she felt an increasing ache deep inside, a yearning for something more.

Still, a tiny voice of reason spoke to her in the haze of passion. She knew she should pay heed to it.

"I should tell ye," she gasped out. "I'm a virgin."

"I should tell you," he replied. "I'm not." Then he smiled, kissed her tenderly on the brow, and promised, "On my honor as a knight, I vow I'll be gentle."

She shuddered as a particularly strong wave of desire surged inside her. "I can't make ye the same promise."

He must have sensed something then, for he slipped his hand away and murmured against her hair, "Let's find a softer place."

There was a stack of straw-stuffed pallets beside the cave wall. He quickly pulled one down and threw one of the winter coverlets over it to form a makeshift bed. He helped her onto the mattress.

For a moment, she felt too vulnerable, too exposed. Without her armor, on her back, she was at his mercy. He loomed over her—a massive, rutting beast that could smother her with the coverlet or throttle her with one hand.

But in the next instant, her fears were put to rest. With exquisite tenderness, he cradled the back of her head in one hand, brushing the hair from her brow with the other. By the faint firelight flickering through the vines, she could see him gazing down at her with such adoration that it took her breath away.

He bestowed upon her a sweet kiss, not of lust, but of cherishing...a kiss so full of love and wonder that it made her feel like a precious jewel in his hands.

Slowly, he reached beneath his long linen shirt to untie his *chausses*, removing them and his *braies*, and freeing his staff. Then he stretched out beside her, propped on one forearm.

"You're so beautiful," he murmured.

His words moved her.

"May I?" he asked, lifting the hem of her *léine*.

Amused by his polite request, she took the *léine* off over her head herself.

To her satisfaction, his gaze turned smoky. He used his free hand to trace her contours, leaving ripples of desire everywhere his fingertips touched, until she was quivering with need.

"May I?" she asked him, snagging the hem of his shirt.

His smile twisted, and he bent down to let her do the deed.

She was unprepared for the effect the sight of his broad shoulders and naked chest would have upon her. While it was true he possessed nothing that not every man possessed, somehow he was different—more powerful, more magnificent, more commanding.

And the quick glimpse she'd had that night of what nestled in his black curls hadn't prepared her for the bold manifestation of his hunger for her.

Her eyes widened. Her heart throbbed. Her breath quickened.

"Are you afraid, m'lady?" he whispered.

She shook her head. She wasn't afraid. She was aroused.

He leaned down to murmur in her ear. "I'll take care. But it may hurt the first time."

She knew that. The woodkerns could be quite forthcoming with the details of their sexual exploits.

"I'll take revenge later," she vowed.

Her humor took him by surprise. "I believe you will."

Then he moved above her until their bodies were mere inches apart. She could feel the heat between them as if it were a living thing. Supporting himself on one brawny arm, he nudged her knees apart until she opened to him like a flower.

When he lowered his body, and their skin made contact, the sensation was so divine that she let out a drawn-out sigh of bliss. It felt as if they melted together like candle wax. His body was warm and vital, firm yet yielding. She arched up against him, delighting in how the muscles of his chest compressed her breasts.

He kissed her then, and this time it was a slow, deep, intense kiss that seemed to draw her soul from her body. When his hand moved betwixt her thighs, it was with a leisure that belied the raging lust he displayed.

Simultaneously possessed of both the need to pursue and the desire to surrender, she floated in a curious enthrallment, captive and captivated by her own emotions.

Again, he intruded upon her most secret spaces, coaxing her with his fingers to yield. Again, she soared upward to a heavenly realm until she was gasping against his mouth and liquid need filled every vein.

Then, just as she thought she could fly no higher, he surged forward with a groan, embedding himself inside her like a dagger.

She rasped in a gasp of shock.

He froze, but didn't withdraw.

"Oh, god, I'm so sorry," he whispered, his voice laced with a strange mixture of regret and ecstasy. "I didn't mean to injure you."

Injure her? He hadn't injured her. Not really. She had known far worse pain, growing up. This was but a sting.

He clasped her head between his hands. "'Twill get better, I promise. Try to relax."

She nodded.

It did get better. Much better.

Soon, as he glided smoothly within her, she began to ascend again. His beastly grunts and the sweat of restraint that glistened on his brow excited her almost as much as the seductive friction of their movement.

Together, they rode a wave of increasing passion until, breathless with yearning, they crested the wave to explode into a thousand droplets that scattered across a shimmering sea of release.

Ryland grimaced, fighting the need to bellow in rapturous relief.

But Temair cried out, and he had to quickly clap a hand over her mouth to stifle the sound.

As they struggled to catch their breath, he thought he'd never felt such a union before, such a perfect blending of body and spirit. She'd entrusted him with a precious gift, and he felt honored and completed and more in love with her than before.

He hoped he hadn't hurt her too much, for that was the last thing he wished to do. As he uncovered her mouth to press a worshipful kiss to her lips, he thought he must be the luckiest man alive.

"Are you all right?" he whispered.

"Nay," she croaked.

"Nay?" He furrowed his brow.

"Ye've won the battle," she said, gasping. "I've been soundly defeated."

"Indeed?"

"At least if I die from my wounds, Sir Ryland de Ware, I shall die content."

He grinned. She'd made him unimaginably happy. Exhausted with pleasure, as he gently rolled off of her onto his back, he admitted, "Then we shall both die content, for you've defeated me as well. I fear I shall ne'er rise again."

A lazy grin curved her lips as she looked over at him with shining eyes "So say ye *now*."

Then she turned away from him, snuggling back against him, her lovely backside teasing his loins. If she wasn't careful, he *would* rise again.

Still glowing in the aftermath of ecstasy, he enveloped her in his grateful arms. "Ah, lass, I love you." The words surprised even him as they dropped easily off his tongue.

In answer, she took a deep breath and exhaled a long sigh of contentment.

Ryland kissed the back of her head, marveling at the softness of her ebony tresses. But though his body was spent, his mind was wide awake, marveling over this extraordinary turn of events.

Everything was going to work out now. He was sure of it.

By a few slips of her tongue, Gray had given herself

away. And the confirmation that the beautiful, enchanting, spirited outlaw that he'd fallen in love with was in truth his bride Temair could not have pleased him more.

Even better, though she didn't know it, their salvation was on the way.

On the day his men had left the camp to collect the ransom, Ryland had given Warin a secret message.

To the woodkerns' ears, it would have sounded innocent. He'd simply asked Warin to bring his brother's sword.

What the outlaws didn't know was that his brother's sword was in his brother's hand—in faraway England. In Ryland's absence, his brother Adam had taken charge of Ryland's remaining knights—three dozen well-armed and well-trained soldiers. What Ryland had conveyed to Warin was that, rather than going to collect the ransom, they should return to England to summon the rest of his fighting forces.

He didn't expect there would be cause for battle. But he'd reasoned that if he was going to live in this country, he couldn't let common criminals believe they could abduct people and hold them hostage whenever they liked. A show of force in the form of a great company of magnificent knights marching through Ireland in full battle armor would rein in their unlawful habits.

Of course, now he understood that the woodkerns were a force for good. They were the sole champions for those victimized by the villainous chieftain.

Now he knew about the evil scheme Cormac had concocted to fool the king and fleece his *clann.*

Now he realized the depths of Temair's suffering.

He meant to right those wrongs. And it seemed to him

that a retinue of powerful English knights under his command might be the way to do that.

His only worry was—when it came time for Ryland to gather his knights and march on the tower—whether his bride-to-be would view them as a rescue force or an invading army.

He should explain everything to her before his men arrived.

He should tell her that he knew now who she was.

He should reveal his plans to overthrow Cormac O'Keeffe, to ensure prosperity for the *clann* and clemency for the woodkerns.

He should confess that he would be honored to be her husband.

And then he should ask her formally to marry him.

But before he could open his mouth to tell her all that, she began snoring—the long, loud, sawing snores of a woman at peace and well-satisfied.

He grinned. He supposed he'd have to learn to sleep through all that racket if they were to be man and wife. In any case, he supposed his news could wait till morning.

CHAPTER 25

"Gray!"

Temair awoke with a jolt, sitting straight up.

It was morning. She rattled her head, trying to clear the fog of sleep.

She was naked. Why was she naked?

"Gray! Quick!" It was Lady Mor's voice, just outside the cave entrance.

"Be right there!" she croaked back.

Beside her on the pallet, Ryland scrubbed at his eyes as he awakened.

It took a moment before she remembered what had happened. It took another moment for her to blush and cover her breasts.

"Hurry!" Lady Mor implored.

Now Ryland was alert. He scrambled to his feet in all his naked glory, donned his *braies,* and then began shoving his legs into his *chausses.*

Lady Mor sounded fretful. Temair supposed she ought to see what was wrong. But she'd much rather stay here and watch Ryland get dressed. Or get him undressed again.

"Are you coming?" Ryland asked, tying up his *chausses*.

"I suppose," she said on a sigh. "'Tis likely some silly quibble over whose turn 'tis to gather kindlin' or who took the last oatcake. And I'd much rather—"

"Gray!" Lady Mor cried.

He gave her a wink. "She sounds serious."

Against her better judgment, Temair quickly dressed in her armor to see what Lady Mor wanted.

The moment she swept the vines aside and stepped into the late morning sun, Lady Mor seized her forearm and confided, "There's an army on the road, Gray."

She blinked. "What?"

"There's a bloody army on the road," she hissed. "Fergus spotted them first. They're just waitin' there at the clearin'. The lads are watchin' from the trees."

"An army?" Temair murmured. "What kind of army?"

"English."

At that moment, Ryland emerged from the vines, and they silenced.

"Is everything all right?" he asked.

Lady Mor gave him a summary glance. It was clear she didn't approve of what she knew they'd been doing in the cave. But there were more important things at stake.

"Everythin's fine," Temair said. She wasn't sure what Lady Mor's news meant. But she didn't think the fact that outlaws were holding one of their noblemen captive would sit well with an English army. "Lady Mor wants me to help her...get a rabbit out of a snare."

"Aye, hurry," Lady Mor added. "'Twould be a shame if it escaped."

Temair hated to lie to him, especially after their intimacy last night. But it was for the best.

"Do me a favor," she bade him, already grabbing Lady Mor's arm and leading her forward. "Watch o'er the hounds while I'm gone?"

He glanced down at Bran and Flann, who were chained to the tree beside the cave, standing at attention. "Of course." He called after her, "Or I could help with the snare."

"Nay!" she yelled. "We'll be back in a bit."

Ryland watched them set off through the forest. Temair had taken her *bata*. He'd overheard what Lady Mor had said. English soldiers had been spotted on the road.

His men were here.

He couldn't risk an encounter between the knights of de Ware and the woodkerns. He'd never forgive himself if violence broke out and anyone on either side was injured.

But he'd sworn he wouldn't leave the camp without her permission.

He eyed Bran and Flann. Temair had asked him to look after them. If they happened to get loose...

A moment later, the dogs were leading Ryland through the woods, stealthily following the scent of their mistress. He strained to keep up with the hounds, clambering over mossy rocks, slogging through the leaves, snapping off branches in his haste.

Could he arrive in time to defuse the situation?

The woodkerns would probably assume an army of English knights meant an invasion by the enemy. They would do everything they could to defend their precious land.

And while his knights would never commit the first act of aggression, they wouldn't hesitate to reply with full force if they were threatened.

Ryland couldn't help but dread that he'd made a grievous error in inviting his company here. The last thing he wanted was to be responsible for starting a war.

His heart was pounding and his chest heaving with exertion when he crossed the log bridge at last. As he entered the daisy-studded clearing where his knights had first encountered the woodkerns, he finally glimpsed Temair through the trees, very near to the road. She'd donned her hood and pulled up her scarf to hide her face.

Before he could call out to her, he saw her leap out onto the road.

From the road, he heard his brother Adam cry, "Outlaw!"

Then he heard the unsheathing of three dozen swords.

Ryland's heart knifed sideways.

"Nay!" he bellowed back. But no one answered.

Bran and Flann, sensing their mistress was in danger, broke away and tore across the clearing like demons toward her.

"Nay!" Ryland cried again, bolting after them in desperation.

It was too late. The dogs had already darted out into the road.

Wolfhounds were strong enough to pull a knight from his saddle and tear him to pieces. It was what they were trained to do. If the woodkerns gave the command...

"Nay!" he heard Temair scream—a panicked scream that chilled his blood and made his heart jab his ribs. "Please! They won't hurt ye! I swear!"

Ryland charged forward, finally emerging from the trees. He burst onto the road just as his brother raised his sword to attack the hounds snarling at his horse's flank.

"Adam!" Ryland bellowed.

Startled, Adam stopped his blade. "Ryland?"

"Don't hurt them," he panted. "They're only protecting her." Then he snapped his fingers. "Flann! Bran! Here!"

The dogs gave one last chuff of aggression and came to him, sitting obediently on either side of him.

Then he turned to look at Temair.

She'd pulled down her scarf and was staring at him in dread. "Ye know these men?"

Before he could answer, Laurence reined in front of Adam. "He should," he sneered. "They're his own."

"Remember us, lass?" said Osgood, gesturing to his brother Godwin.

Warin smugly added, "Never try to get the best of a de Ware."

The woodkerns made their appearance then, materializing as if by magic from the trees, their bows drawn. Ryland gulped. If he'd arrived a split-second later, he was certain Adam would have gotten Cambeal's arrow through his heart. The knights froze, realizing they might no longer have the upper hand.

Ryland raised his hands in a gesture of calm. "Everyone, please. Put away your weapons. There's no need for fighting."

The woodkerns had no interest in obeying him. They were under Temair's command. And as long as the outlaws had loaded bows, his knights weren't going to put up their swords.

He looked at Temair for help. But she was studying him now with a horrified fascination.

"Ye never sent them for the ransom," she realized. "Ye sent them for reinforcements."

"I can explain," he said.

"Who is this woman?" his brother demanded.

"Ye betrayed me." She said the words under her breath, but they sounded as loud as a cannon to Ryland's ears, and they hit his heart with the same damaging impact. "I trusted ye and—"

"Who *is* this woman?" Adam repeated.

"This woman is my bride," Ryland declared, "Temair O'Keeffe."

Temair felt as if the world careened out from under her feet. For a moment, she couldn't breathe. Then she gasped—a long, rough, rasping breath of shock—and dropped her *bata*.

"How..." Her chest caved in, and she staggered back from him. "When..."

"Last night," he said. "I'm sorry, Temair. I meant to tell you, but..."

But he'd been too busy trysting with her.

One of his men called out, "You're betrothed to an *outlaw*, m'lord?"

Another said, "She's a *pretty* outlaw, I'll grant you that."

His fellows chuckled.

"Quiet!" Ryland barked.

Temair's brain churned as she remembered everything Ryland had ever said, wondering how much of it was untrue. Maybe all of it. And maybe the only reason he'd made love to her last night was to secure his marriage rights.

She felt her heart crack.

And then she felt dread creep over her like a black shadow.

Would Ryland drag her back to her father?

Her breath quickened with panic. Orlaith had promised her—the woodkerns had promised her—she'd always have a home with them. She couldn't go back to the tower house. She couldn't be subject to her father's abuse again.

She wouldn't.

Before anyone could stop her, she snatched up her *bata*, wheeled, and fled—back through the forest to the only home she knew.

"Temair!" Ryland cried.

She refused to answer. She didn't want to see him again. Ever.

Her throat clogged with grief, and tears streamed down her face as she crashed through the trees.

She told herself they were tears of fury and frustration.

The heavy ache in her chest said otherwise.

She was heartbroken.

"Shite!" Ryland spat, seizing the collars of the hounds, who wanted to run after her.

He hadn't wanted Temair to find out like this. He'd

wanted to break the happy news to her while she lay close to his heart, cradled in his arms.

"Go after her, m'lord," Warin urged him, narrowing his eyes at the woodkerns. "They dare not shoot us while you're in pursuit of their leader."

Ryland shook his head. Warin might be his best man, but he was more a man of quick impulse than measured judgment.

His brother Adam scoffed. "Their leader?"

Ryland sighed. What Adam knew about Ireland would fit in a thimble. There was much for him to learn.

"That's right," Ryland announced proudly. "And aye, she *is* my bride. So I'll thank all of you to watch your tongues."

Warin drew back as if he'd struck him.

"Now. Will ye not lower your weapons?" Ryland asked the woodkerns. "I can explain."

But they refused to stand down. He supposed they were right not to trust him. After all, in their eyes, he'd betrayed their mistress.

"Ye can explain while we have our bows drawn," Maelan replied with a scowl.

Ryland's men were sorely vexed—all but Warin, who looked as anxious as a priest in a brothel. Old Sorcha had him in her sights, and her bow kept wavering as her strength waned.

He'd have to make it fast.

First he addressed the woodkerns. "I meant to speak to her last night."

"But ye were too busy 'polishin' your dagger,' isn't that right?" Ronan sneered, still staring at his target, Osgood.

Ryland bit the inside of his cheek.

"If she's his bride," Adam sneered back at Ronan, "then he's entitled to 'polish his dagger' any time he wants. I don't see the problem with that."

Ronan's black beard quivered. "I'll tell ye the problem. She doesn't want to be wed to a kiss-arse o' Lackland."

His men took offense at that, and Ryland held up an arm to silence them.

The noble Cambeal, his arrow still trained on Adam, asked Ryland, "How long have ye known who she was?"

"Only since last night," he replied.

"And what do ye intend to do?" Cambeal pressed.

"What I came to do—marry her."

His men grumbled about that. So did the woodkerns.

Old Sorcha addressed him. "Listen to me well, m'lord. When Temair came here six years ago, she was broken and battered. I think ye know why. We took her in. And we made her a vow. We promised she'd always have a home here."

Menacing Domnall had his bolt aimed at Laurence. "That vow may not be the oath of a proper knight," he snarled, "but 'tis worthy, all the same."

Young Fergus jutted out his stubborn chin as he held his bow steady. "She's under our protection. Ye can't have her. She's ours."

Ryland knew Temair had run away the night her sister died. He could guess her father had mistreated her. But he didn't realize the woodkerns feared her husband might do the same.

"I would never hurt Temair," he told them. "You can be assured of that."

"And why should we believe ye?" blond Niall asked. "Ye lied to us about the ransom."

Ryland swallowed guiltily. "I did. But that was before I knew who she was, before I knew you were much more than just a band of common outlaws."

"And now?" Friar Brian arched a brow. "Why should we trust ye now?"

Ryland raised his head. "Because I love her." It was cathartic to say it aloud. "I love Temair."

"An *outlaw?*" Warin couldn't resist blurting out.

"That's right," Ryland said, "and I couldn't be more proud."

Then he decided he was done defending himself. These were his men, after all. They answered to him.

"Enough talk. I need to find Temair. Adam. Cambeal. You're in charge. Make peace. When you've done that...Friar, will you lead them all to the camp?"

Friar Brian nodded.

"Where are you going, m'lord?" Warin asked.

"I'm going to prove my worth to my bride."

With that, Ryland let go of the hounds' collars and loped after them as they followed Temair's scent.

CHAPTER 26

When Bran and Flann came nosing in to the cave through the vines, Temair figured they'd gotten loose and run after her through the woods. So, sitting against the cave wall with her knees drawn up to her chest and her head buried, she paid no special heed to the hounds when they began licking at her hands.

But the next intruder made her spring to her feet and grab her *bata*.

"Get out!" she shouted, brandishing her weapon before her.

Ryland held up his hands. "I just want to talk."

"I don't want to listen." She flipped the *bata* around and swung at him.

He blocked it with his forearm, grimacing as it struck bone. "I'm sorry, Temair. I meant to tell you last night."

"Was that before or after ye took my maidenhood?" she bit out. Then she jabbed the *bata* forward, catching him in the chest and making him stagger back a step. "What could ye possibly have to tell me?"

She hit him in the thigh, hard enough to leave a bruise, sneering, "That ye knew who I was all along?"

He retreated with a grunt, clutching his thigh with one hand and holding up the other to try to calm her. "Nay."

She advanced, clouting him on the opposite hip. "That ye plotted with my father to find me?"

"Nay."

He was backed against the wall now. She shoved the hard knob of the *bata* under his chin, pressing at his vulnerable throat. Her words were laced with bitter betrayal. "That ye stole my maidenhood to ensure your claim to my land?"

"What?" he choked.

Ryland's eyes narrowed into burning slits. He'd clearly had enough. With lightning speed, he seized the knobbed end of the *bata* and forced it aside, holding it away from his neck with brute strength.

"Nay, damn it! None of that is true," he snarled. "Until last night, I believed you were Gray, Queen of the Outlaws."

"Then why would ye summon all your knights?" Her arm trembled as she fought for control of the *bata*. "To drag me back to O'Keeffe? To force me to wed ye?"

"Drag you..." He scowled. "Well, now that you mention it, I have a question for *you*, Temair O'Keeffe."

He wrenched the weapon from her hand as easily as prying a twig from a child. While she gaped in surprise, he flung the *bata* out through the curtain of vines.

Flann and Bran, thinking he was playing a game, chased after it out of the cave.

Then he caught his fist in the front of her *brat* and pulled her close. So close she could see the glitter of menace in his eyes. So close she could hear the growl of rage in his throat. So close she could feel the sizzling heat of his words as he bit them out.

"*You* knew who *I* was from the very beginning. You knew I was your betrothed. You led me on. You encouraged me. You tempted me with glances and kisses and touches. You made me hunger for you." His gaze drifted down over her with lascivious need, and he leaned forward to whisper in her ear. "You shared your body with me, Temair." She shivered as her fury twisted into something very different. "All that time, you could have claimed me as your husband. And yet you didn't. Why?"

She gulped.

He answered for her. "I was just a pawn to you, wasn't I?"

"Nay," she breathed.

"A means of extorting silver from your father."

She blushed. At one time that had been true.

He pierced her with an accusing gaze. "You deceived me, Temair."

Her guilt didn't last long before her jaw dropped. "Hold on. *I* deceived *ye?*" She brought her fists up between them, freeing herself from his grip, and shoved him back against the wall. "*Ye* pretended ye didn't know where your knights had gone."

He scowled, but couldn't deny it.

She poked him in the chest with an accusing finger. "*Ye* claimed ye'd been betrayed." She poked him again for good measure.

He grabbed her by the shoulders and wheeled with her, pressing her back against the wall and holding her there by the throat with one massive hand.

He arched a brow at her. "*You* claimed no one had seen Temair in six years."

She gave him a smug smile. "I said no one in the *tuath* had seen her, which was true. But *ye...*" She knocked his arm away and shoved at his shoulder. "*Ye* swore on your 'knightly honor' that ye wouldn't leave the camp without my permission."

"You asked me to watch the hounds," he crowed. "Could I help it if they took off after you?"

She narrowed a smoldering gaze at him.

He crossed his arms in challenge. "But *your* betrayal is assuredly the most cruel, *Lady Gray*. You pretended you were not my bride."

She could think of only one worse betrayal. She crossed her arms in imitation of him. "And *ye* pretended to love me."

"I *did* love ye." He shook his head. "Curse me for a fool, I still do."

Her heart caught, and her arms slipped out of their fold. "Ye do?"

"Aye!" he snapped, irritated with himself. "Though god knows why, since you only wanted me for the ransom."

"That's not true." At least it didn't feel true now.

He looked glum as he kicked at the floor of the cave. "What were you going to do with all that coin anyway?"

She lowered her eyes. "I'd rather not say."

He lifted her chin with his knuckle and moved forward until he was only inches away, drilling into her with his dark, demanding eyes. "You'd rather sell me for five hundred pounds than marry me. I think I deserve to know."

She pulled her head away. It sounded awful when he

said it like that. But she supposed she did owe him an explanation. "Fine. If ye must know, I wanted it for an army."

He frowned, baffled. "An army?"

"Aye." She raised her chin, proud of her plan. "An army o' mercenaries."

"An army."

"That's right."

"For what purpose?"

"To lay siege to the tower house."

He cocked a brow at her. "*Your* tower house?"

"'Tis not mine. It belongs to my devil of a father," she bit out, "until he's deposed...or dead."

He lowered his brows. "So you planned to attack the tower house and remove the chieftain."

She hesitated. What she intended was treason. "Aye."

He stared at her a long while, saying nothing, showing no emotion. She wondered if he might turn her in as a traitor.

"I planned it. I didn't do it," she said defensively. "Ye can't turn me in for only *plannin'* to do a thing."

He stroked his stubbled chin thoughtfully and turned away from her. His silence was unnerving.

Finally he spoke. "Mercenaries are risky. They can't be trusted. Their loyalty is for sale to whoever pays them the most."

She scowled. Was he actually criticizing her plan? "I know that."

"What you'd need is an army of cohesive and seasoned knights."

She bristled at that. "I don't exactly have an army at my beck and call."

"Don't you?"

She opened her mouth to speak, but no words came out. She closed it again.

He turned back to her then. There was a curious spark of ambition in his eyes.

Her breath caught. His knights. *His* knights. Was he offering what she *thought* he was offering?

"Your men," she breathed, almost afraid to hope. "Ye would help me?"

"By all rights, the *tuath* belongs to you," he told her. "Cormac has betrayed the king. He's betrayed me. He's betrayed you. And he's betrayed his *clann*."

Temair couldn't believe what she was hearing. "Ye'd really help me get the *tuath* back?"

"On one condition."

"Aye?" She'd do anything.

"You'll consent to be my wife."

She didn't need words to give him her answer. With a soft cry of joy, she surged forward to embrace him.

Ryland knew they had to act quickly.

His men awaited his orders.

The woodkerns had to be placated.

There was a siege to plan.

Decisions had to be made about what to do with Cormac, with the Temair imposter, with the *clann*.

Hell, Ryland hadn't even had breakfast yet this morn.

But none of that mattered when Temair rushed into his arms, gratitude shining in her beautiful gray eyes. And when she pulled his head down, slanting her mouth across his, her kisses were enough to dull his hunger.

He buried his hands in her lush black hair, tipping her head to deepen the kiss. A moment ago, her lips had curled down in willful anger. Now they were pliant with affection and bliss.

He nudged her lips apart with his own, letting his tongue tease at the edges until her jaw loosened and she opened her mouth in welcome. He slipped his tongue into the wet, warm recesses of her mouth, and she responded, swirling her tongue around his, feasting on him.

Like starving beasts, they devoured each other— gasping, clawing, gnawing, groaning. Her passion was intoxicating, like an elixir of obsession poured from her lips into his mouth. One sip sent ripples of current through his loins. But as he drank her all in, he felt every nerve in his body come alive with yearning. They kissed and kissed, until he wondered if he'd ever get his fill of her.

At least now he knew he'd have a lifetime to try.

As Temair gazed up at Ryland from below lust-heavy lids, she felt drunk on his love.

All her worries vanished.

Her limbs felt as limp and malleable as custard.

Her head floated in a haze of pleasurable sensations.

And her body craved only one thing.

More.

In fact, now that she knew what ecstasy awaited her, she was even more eager to dash down the path of seduction to that final destination. Common sense and propriety deserted her as she acted on impulse and began raking at his clothes.

He helped her, unbuckling his belt, unlacing his *chausses*. She helped him as well, kicking off her *brogs*, loosening her *léine*.

They half-staggered, half-dragged themselves to the pallet, discarding garments as they went.

In the filtered light of day, Ryland was even more magnificent. Her heart thrummed as she ran fervent hands over the sculpted contours of his chest and shoulders, the flat expanse of his stomach, the solid bones of his hips.

She sighed as he aroused her with feather-light touches of his fingertips, grazing her ears, her throat, her nipples.

The rest of the world disappeared as she writhed in sensual need. He pressed her back gently onto the pallet, holding himself above her, and she arched up against him, her impatience clear.

"Slowly," he murmured with a rueful chuckle, "or 'twill be o'er too quick."

She frowned. She had no patience for his patience. She reached between them and stroked him with a brazen hand.

He groaned, but he caught her wrist and dragged it up, securing her hand beside her head. "Slowly," he repeated.

With a glimmer of mischief in her eyes, she used her other hand to capture him.

Again, he growled with pleasure. "Witch," he accused, shaking his head. Then he snared that hand as well, anchoring her by the wrists to the mattress. "I don't want to hurt you."

"Hurt me?" she breathed. *"Ye're* the one with all the *bata* bruises."

"Your vengeance?" he murmured.

"Aye."

To her dismay, he forced her to endure his leisure. As she lay helpless, he licked the delicate flesh of her eyelids, tugged her lower lip carefully between his teeth, explored the sensitive crevices of her ear with his tongue until she was squirming in sensuous torture.

Even when he released one of her wrists, she couldn't summon the strength to move it. And when his hand glided down her abdomen to nestle in her curls, she sobbed and rocked her hips upward.

He shivered as her motion brushed against that part of him that craved her most, and she suddenly realized, though she was pinned beneath him, she was far from powerless. She arced up again, grinding against him, and he inhaled sharply.

"You play a dangerous game, m'lady," he muttered.

"I like dangerous games."

"So I've noticed." He lowered his head, giving her ear a swipe of his tongue and then blowing gently across it, making her quiver. At the same time, his fingers slipped over the sensitive, vulnerable spot between her legs, creating an instant shock of lust. He whispered, "But you want to win this one, aye?"

"Aye," she begged.

His fingers worked magic upon her, sliding over her wet flesh, pulsing, pulling, drawing, inciting her until she could bear no more. Just as she thought she might scream, every muscle in her body stiffened while the sharpened point of her desire continued to rise. Then, when she thought she could endure no more, she cracked apart like a clay pot struck by a *bata*.

He pressed his palm against her as she cried out, bucking and trembling with relief. And then, even before she'd completely regained her senses, he pushed into her, making her moan with pleasure this time instead of pain and giving her a divine feeling of completion.

When she dared to crack her eyes open, the expression of tormented restraint on Ryland's face thrilled her. It seemed he was fighting his own desires. And as she'd discovered, it was a losing battle.

Intoxicated with wonder and power, she curved one leg around his buttocks, holding him deeply inside her. Then she pushed against his shoulder until he yielded, rolling onto his back.

With a grin of triumph, she sat astride him, seizing his wrists and pinning him to the pallet. "I win."

"I surrender."

CHAPTER 27

Ryland wondered, as the mischievous woman began moving instinctively against him, if she knew how difficult it was for him not to instantly explode. Everything about her aroused him.

Her ash-colored eyes like banked coals, flaring to life at a moment's notice.

Her scarlet lips, equally adept at cursing and kissing.

The insistent clench of her fists around his wrists as she took control.

The shining ebony locks of her hair, lashing his ribs.

The provocative sway of her small, rose-tipped breasts as she found a pleasing rhythm.

The erotic slap of her buttocks upon him when she began riding him with fevered haste.

But it was the awe in her face as she reached her pinnacle again that finally sent him over the edge into his own bellowing release.

On and on the waves of rapture continued until he was completely spent, as weak as a kitten.

She too must have been drained, for she collapsed

atop him, damp and panting, too weary to rise.

A long while afterward, when their breathing slowed and his heart returned to its quiet pulse, he suspected she'd drifted off. Until she spoke.

"Aye," she murmured against his shoulder.

"What?"

"Aye."

"Aye, what?"

"Aye, I *will* marry ye."

He grinned and placed a kiss on the top of her head. "I'm glad to hear it."

She raised her head to look into his eyes. "Ye know, I think I fell in love with ye the first day we met."

He lifted a dubious brow. "You had an odd way of showing it, knocking me into the water."

"I had to show ye who was in charge."

"Is that right?" With his remaining strength, he rolled her onto her back again, bracing himself on his forearms to look down at her. "And who would that be?"

She smiled up at him, a cocky smile without a hint of surrender. "Ye may think ye're in charge. But I know your weaknesses."

He gave her a wink. "I fear my biggest weakness is for Irish outlaws." He coiled a strand of her soft hair around his finger and gazed into her dreamy gray eyes. "I only pray you'll take pity on me and be merciful."

She wasn't merciful. Not in the least. Almost immediately she began to entice him with smoldering gazes and provocative kisses. She pressed her tempting breasts against his chest and locked her legs around his hindquarters to hold him within her.

It wasn't long before his weakness for Irish outlaws

got the best of him. He swelled and hardened, and when she squirmed under him, he obliged her by guiding her swiftly back to that exquisite realm of ecstasy.

Their fingers clasped, they crested together, crying out in glorious victory as their two bodies were forged into one.

When Ryland finally eased out of her, Temair made a small mew of protest. For one remarkable moment, they had seemed flawlessly joined—not only in body, but in spirit—and she didn't want to lose that.

As if he sensed her disquiet, he pulled her into his arms.

"I feel like the luckiest man alive," he murmured against her hair.

His words made her glow.

Until he added, "To think I was afraid to meet my bride."

She wrinkled her brow. "Afraid. Why?"

"Because o' the rumors."

She stiffened. The warmth of the moment turned icy with his words. He'd said he didn't believe the rumor that Temair had murdered her sister. He'd said it was unfounded. She was almost afraid to ask. "Ye believed the rumors?"

"I didn't know what to believe."

Her throat ached. But she wouldn't cry. She promised herself she wouldn't cry. Her voice was wooden. "So ye thought I was a murderer—"

"What? Nay!"

"That I'd killed my sister—"

"Nay!"

"And ye feared I might kill *ye*."

He turned her toward him. "Nay! Never!"

She stared at the ceiling of the cave, numb.

He explained. "I meant the rumor that Cormac had kept his daughter under lock and key for six years." He shook his head. "I couldn't imagine what the loneliness and isolation might have done to you, that's all."

She swallowed down the lump in her throat. "So ye don't think I killed her?"

"Nay, not for a moment."

His trust in her was sweet. It was touching. But she also realized, with a sort of tragic inevitability, that it was misplaced. She moved her gaze slowly toward him until their eyes met. "Well, ye're wrong about that."

For an instant, her admission startled him. But he continued to stare at her, so deeply it seemed he was peering into her soul. Then he shook his head. "Nay, I'm not. I know you now. I know you'd never do such a thing."

"Ye can't know that. Ye weren't there."

"Why don't you tell me then, Temair?" he coaxed. "Why don't you tell me what happened that night?"

She'd only told the story once aloud—when the woodkerns first took her in. But in the deep, dark, shadowy places of her mind, she'd recited it over and over, thousands of times, each telling more excruciating than the last. She didn't want to dredge up that pain again. She shook her head.

He gently persisted. "What happened to Aillenn?"

She blinked in surprise. It had been a long while since she'd heard her sister's name. Most people no longer spoke of her by name. Most people had forgotten her.

Still Temair didn't answer.

"If we are to be husband and wife," he said, "there should be no secrets between us."

She gulped. He was right. But it was one thing to share her body, another to open her soul.

He took her hand, clasping it between his two. "I know the memory is painful, Temair. I know you don't want to talk about it. But I vow I will love you, no matter what you tell me. For better or worse."

She looked at their joined hands. His words were earnest and kind and heartfelt. But she didn't know how he could possibly keep that promise. After all, how could he love her when she didn't love herself?

As Ryland watched Temair's eyes fill with silent tears, his heart ached. He wished he could take away her anguish.

Making love with her had bound the two of them together somehow, melded their souls so that he felt her pain as if it were his own. Now all he wanted to do was remove it.

"'Twas my fault." She said it so softly, he almost didn't hear it.

But how could anything have been her fault? "You were only a child."

She shook her head. "I could have saved her."

He gave her hand a squeeze. "Tell me everything from the beginning. Please, Temair. I want to hear it."

She closed her eyes. For a long while, she said nothing. He could see she was struggling to find the courage.

"Please," he asked tenderly.

When she finally spoke, her voice wavered as if she

were a young lass again, reliving her life, moment by moment. But she told him everything.

She told him about her childhood of bruised ribs and black eyes and a split lip.

She told him how she always fought back and how her sister did not.

She told him the terrible secret she didn't find out until later—that while Cormac used his fists on Temair, what he did to Aillenn was much worse.

She told him about hiding in the stable with Bran and Flann that night, about Aillenn coming to her, pale and shivering, a specter of herself.

She told him about her sister sending her away, telling her to flee and never look back.

Then she choked over her words, coming to the difficult part of the story.

Ryland realized he was clenching his jaw tightly enough to crack his teeth, so great was his hatred for Cormac. But uncontrolled rage would do Temair no good. So he forced himself to take a steadying breath and bade her continue. "Go on. 'Tis all right."

"I told her to come with me. I told her we could sleep in the woods with Bran and Flann. I told her we could hide together until the morn." She broke off suddenly with a sob.

"But she didn't listen," he guessed.

She shook her head. "I should have tried harder. I should have dragged her into the woods. I should never have left her." Her voice was raw and ragged. "If I hadn't left her, she wouldn't have leaped from the tower. She wouldn't be dead now. 'Twas my fault. 'Twas all my fault."

"Listen to me!" Ryland seized her by the shoulders, locking eyes with her. His own vehemence astonished him. "'Twas not your fault! You couldn't have done anything to save her. If she hadn't leaped to her death that night, she would have sliced her wrists the next or taken poison the night after. What your father did to her—she couldn't live with that. There was nothing you could do or say to change that. 'Twas not your fault. Do you understand? 'Twas the fault of that bloody monster, Cormac."

She looked as if she wanted to believe him. But he knew it would take time. She'd been living with the guilt over her sister's death for six years. Maybe one day she would accept the truth. Maybe one day she *would* believe him.

Until then, the least he could do was slay her demons.

He released her shoulders and then raised her hand to his lips, kissing her fingertips. "Come on. Let's go take back your *tuath*."

Temair felt as if a yoke had been lifted from her shoulders. The grief would never be gone, but at least she no longer felt burdened by guilt.

Ryland had helped her conquer one enemy. And now he offered to help her vanquish another.

They had just finished dressing when Bran and Flann came trotting back in through the vines. The hounds had apparently forgotten all about fetching her *bata*. They were probably hungry.

"Come on, lads," she said as she and Ryland emerged from the cave. "We'll see if there's any food left from break—"

She froze in her tracks. Ryland bumped into the back of her. Then he too froze.

The camp was packed with people. Woodkerns and English soldiers sat on every available rock and stump. Those without perches leaned against trees, sat on the ground, or stood. They were awkwardly silent. Most of them had ale. All of them were looking anywhere but at her.

How long had they been here?

Bloody hell! Long enough to have overheard them trysting, she was sure. She felt her face go hot.

Unconcerned by what they thought of him, Ryland was the first to find his voice. "Have you all made peace then?"

Noble Cambeal nodded. "Aye."

"Aye," Ryland's man, Adam, replied. Then a mischievous twinkle came into his eyes. "What about you two?" He swept an appreciative glance over Temair.

Temair would have bitten off his head, but Ryland intervened.

"Look at my bride like that again, brother," he said, "and I won't be responsible for her actions."

"What?" Adam said, puzzled.

Temair straightened with pride. So this was Ryland's brother? She doubted he was half the man Ryland was.

"Now," Ryland continued, "we have to work together. I'll need you all to cooperate."

Sorcha held up her hand. "Wait a moment, de Ware. Ye're not in charge o' the woodkerns."

Before Ryland could answer, one of his knights shot to his feet. "Hold your tongue, old woman. Do you know who you're addressing?"

"Wait a bloody moment!" Ronan pushed away from the tree he was leaning on. "Do ye know who *ye're* addressin'? That's the lovely woman who made the ale ye're drinkin'!" He muttered into his black beard, "Bloody bastard."

"I heard that!" the knight snarled.

"Ye'll hear more than that if ye don't show the proper respect," Ronan said.

"Respect?" spat another knight. "To a band of knaves and scoundrels?"

Young Fergus chimed in with passionate outrage. "How dare ye insult your hosts!"

"Hosts?" scoffed the first knight. "You're outlaws, for the love of god!"

Friar Brian bristled at that. "Don't be takin' the Lord's name in vain."

Chaos exploded then as the outlaws bickered with the knights. Even the hounds joined in with loud barking.

How would Temair ever get them to fight together? They couldn't even sit in camp and drink ale together.

Fortunately, Ryland didn't think it was a problem. Taking Temair by the hand, he strode into their midst and bellowed for their attention. "Silence!"

Everyone hushed, including the dogs.

"We have a challenging feat ahead of us," he said, "one that's going to require the courage, brains, and brawn of everyone here. We need you to set aside your differences, pledge your loyalty, and commit to working together."

Old Sorcha turned to Temair for her approval of this plan. "Gray?"

"Temair, Temair O'Keeffe," she corrected, straightening with pride. "Sir Ryland de Ware and his knights have promised to help me reclaim what is mine by rights. We're goin' to depose the chieftain and take back the *tuath*."

There was one breathless moment as they digested her words.

"Now?" Young Fergus squeaked.

Ryland nodded. "Before they have time to prepare a defense."

Aife timidly asked, "And will...*we*...have a place there...in your *tuath*?"

Temair nodded. "Ye will *always* have a place with me."

The woodkerns erupted into cheers.

CHAPTER 28

Many decisions had had to be made around the fire before they set out. But Ryland had listened carefully to her advice concerning the *clann*, and she'd respected his wisdom when it came to warfare.

Now, as they traveled along the road—Temair with her hounds and the woodkerns armed with bows at the fore, and the knights following in formation behind Ryland on horseback—Temair felt a moment of doubt.

She'd been concerned about fighting her kinsmen. But Ryland had assured her that a full-scale battle was unlikely. They could win the day without resorting to violence. After all, if the *clann* had little allegiance to Cormac, they would welcome Temair and take her side.

But she wasn't sure he was right. After all, the rumor persisted that Temair had killed her sister. If they believed that, she would lose her honor price and her claim to the *tuath.*

Then there was the imposter. What if they believed

she was the real Temair and that this vagrant outlaw living in the woods was the fake?

The entourage continued along the road in grim silence as everyone mentally prepared for the encounter ahead. But when they topped the ridge and Temair saw the tower house in the distant valley below, her step faltered.

For six years, she'd imagined what this moment would be like—how the keep would look, how triumphant she would feel.

But now that it loomed in the distance before her, fortified with palisades and plaster, it seemed unassailable. The sight of it reduced her to a child once again, helpless and fearful of the things that had happened within those walls.

She tightened her fist around the hounds' leashes, wondering if she had the strength to face her father after all these years.

At that moment, Ryland reined up beside her. "Will you ride with me? It will show solidarity."

Glad to have his support, she handed the hounds off to Ronan and let Ryland help her mount in front of him.

Almost at once, she felt more at ease. He literally had her back. And sitting proudly astride a noble steed, she felt like the entitled heiress she was.

The crofters couldn't fail to be impressed by the sight. It was probably the first time they'd seen such an imposing army of archers and horsemen. They stopped in the field to watch. A few broke and ran down the road ahead of them, no doubt to alert their neighbors that an English force was marching toward them.

As Temair sat tall and proud at the fore of the

magnificent army, people began to take notice of her. She saw them pointing at her and whispering behind their hands.

The cottages grew closer and closer together, and word traveled quickly. Soon people were rushing out their doors to watch the knights pass, staring in awe. Up ahead, a crowd gathered, filling the road, and the knights were forced to stop.

An old woman waddled through the crowd, narrowing her eyes at Temair. "I know ye!" she cackled. "Ye're the chieftain's daughter!"

The people around her gasped and began murmuring in speculation.

"Temair?"

"She's not dead?"

"Those are her hounds."

"But the chieftain said he locked her up."

"'Tis the lass. I'd know her anywhere."

"Look at her eyes. 'Tis her. 'Tis Temair."

Temair gulped. Would they welcome her or burn her at the stake?

"That's right," Ryland proclaimed. "This is Temair, bride of Sir Ryland de Ware and heiress to O'Keeffe, and she has come to claim her *tuath*."

His announcement was met with gasps and then silence. For an awful moment, Temair considered they might despise her as much as her father. If that was so, the *tuath* would have to be claimed by force. These people—the people frowning and whispering and casting dubious glances at her—might well die. They would never know that this foreign army was fighting—not for their defeat—but for their benefit.

But these were her *clannfolk*. These were her people. She couldn't have their blood on her hands. She couldn't wage war against them.

She gazed again at the tower, still a quarter-mile away. The tower where Aillenn had fallen to her death. The tower where, by some cruel trick of fate, Cormac still lived.

She couldn't let him continue unpunished. For her sister's sake, for the sake of all who suffered at the hands of a tyrant, she had to find the strength to be brave.

"My beloved *clannfolk*," she announced, "I've come to give ye aid, to improve your lives and restore your wealth." She shook her head. "For too long ye've been sufferin' under the rule o' my greedy father."

A few men nodded their heads.

"For too long ye've worked your fingers to the bone," she continued, "and for what? To have my father steal your hard-earned coin?"

The crowd voiced their agreement.

Encouraged, she went on. "Cormac lied about me. He lied about my sister. I didn't kill her. She threw herself from the tower." Her voice broke, and she felt Ryland's hand of reassurance on her shoulder. "I ran away the night she died. These good folk..." She gestured to the woodkerns. "These good folk took me in. They kept me safe, safe from Cormac's fists."

There were murmurs of sympathy. No doubt many of them remembered Temair's battered face.

"But now I'm grown. 'Tis time to take back what is rightfully ours. Time to free ourselves from the shackles of a villain. Time to give the *clann* the leadership it deserves."

There were cheers all around her, and she knew she was doing the right thing.

Behind her, Ryland cleared his throat.

She smiled. She wasn't going to forget him.

"But I cannot do it alone," she told the crowd. "King John has sent Sir Ryland de Ware to be my husband." Before the grumbling about foreign rule could begin, she hastily added, "And he has vowed that he and his army will help us take back the *tuath*."

"'Tis an invasion!" someone yelled, and others joined in.

"Nay!" she cried, trying to placate them. "Nay!"

Another man called out, "How do we know they won't just kill everyone in the *tuath* and hand it o'er to Lackland?"

Temair felt Ryland stiffen, and she knew his men were twitching in their saddles.

"Please!" She raised her hands to calm the crowd, and an impulsive thought popped into her head. It was a great risk. But she had faith in Ryland. And she wanted to show him she had faith in his men as well. "I'll make ye a promise. If even one o' the *clann* is killed by the Knights o' de Ware..." She licked her lips, hoping she wasn't making a mistake. "I'll give up my claim to the *tuath* and let ye choose anew."

She heard a strangling sound from Ryland and curses from his men, though none of them dared openly oppose her.

It wasn't until they continued their march toward the tower house, leaving the cheering *clannfolk* in their wake, that Ryland snarled under his breath, "God's hooks, Temair. What have you done?"

"I can't kill my own people."

"What you're asking is impossible. You've taken the teeth out of my army. Cormac has *some* loyal supporters. What if they attack? What if they give us no choice?"

She frowned. "Ye told me there would be no cause to kill anyone."

"I told ye I'd *try* not to kill anyone."

"I trust ye," she told him. "Ye're an excellent fighter, and ye know your own strength. I'm certain ye can do it. And I'm certain ye'd expect no less from your knights."

While Ryland appreciated her vote of confidence, the last thing he needed was more pressure going into this confrontation. He loathed going into battle blind, and he had no idea what kind of resistance he was up against.

He knew Cormac had fewer soldiers than he—a score at most—for the chieftain had shown off his fighting forces when they'd first met, hoping to impress Ryland.

But the *clann* had the advantage of defending their own home. Despite Aife's carefully drawn maps of the keep, Cormac's soldiers would know all the hiding places and secret passageways. The stairways would favor the defenders' sword arms, and they would be under no constraint to spare lives.

There were other things to consider. How loyal were Cormac's men? Had he mistreated them as well? Would they surrender willingly once they recognized Ryland had the advantage? Or would they fight to the death?

What if his knights killed someone and Temair was forced to surrender her rule?

That would complicate things. Ireland wasn't like

England—not yet anyway. Rule wasn't strictly hereditary. The people chose a chieftain by honor price, and Temair, coming from a long line of noble chieftains, held the highest honor price. By marrying Ryland, that worth would transfer to him.

If she gave up her claim to the *tuath*, the king would be displeased. He could rescind the marriage offer or decide to take the holding by force. Then there *would* be bloodshed.

One thing was certain. If they survived this and managed to hold on to the tower house after Temair's reckless promise, Ryland would take charge of the *clann's* army. Temair might excel at one-on-one combat and knocking rivals into the water. But she knew nothing about siege warfare. It was obvious she didn't have the stomach for it.

As they drew near the tower, everyone dismounted. Temair joined the ranks of the other archers. Of course, as soon as she was out of hearing, his men began attacking him with furious whispers.

"Are you mad, m'lord?" Warin hissed. "How can we fight them if we can't kill them?"

Laurence agreed. "It can't be done. We might as well go in unarmed."

His brother Adam clucked his tongue. "Not even wed, and she's already got your ballocks in a vise."

"Enough!" Ryland tensed his jaw, giving his brother a withering glower. "He has fewer men than we do, and they'll be expecting a negotiation, not a battle. If all goes well, it may not even come to blows."

Adam curled his lip. "Where's the fun in that?"

Ryland gave him a chiding shove.

"Listen," he said to his men, eyeing them in turn. "Temair is right. A good knight knows his own strength. A good knight can control that strength. You are the best knights I know. These people are not her vassals. They're her family. They will be *my* family. I'm trusting you to keep them safe."

"What?" Cormac exploded. His shout bounced around the great hall, making the messenger flinch in fear. "That's not possible!"

Of course, it was completely possible. He hadn't seen his wayward daughter in—what was it—five, six, seven years? But it was unthinkable that she could be alive. He'd been so certain she'd been killed by the elements, ravaged by outlaws, or eaten by wolves.

"Ye're sure?" He seized the quivering youth by the front of his *brat*. "Ye're not even old enough to have known her."

The lad's throat bobbed up and down. Finally he replied, "The...the other *clannfolk*...they said 'twas her. They knew her by her...her wolfhounds...and...and her gray eyes."

Cormac felt fury rising in him, felt it burning its way up his throat, his ears, his eyes. With a fierce growl, he shook the youth like a rat and tossed him away. The lad squeaked like a rat too as he hit the floor, then scrambled away as if the devil were after him.

Cormac pulled at his beard as he paced the hall, ignoring the maidservants cowering in the corners. This was unfortunate news.

That Temair was still alive was bad enough.

That she'd found her way here was worse.

That she was in the company of the Knights of de Ware was a disaster.

The wily wench knew things about him, things that would rob him of his honor price and maybe even his life.

Now the entire *clann* would know that the lass he was keeping in the tower was not his real daughter.

But how much else had the vixen revealed? What had she told de Ware? And what would the swaggering knight pass on to the king?

He hawked up the bitter taste of dread, rolled the spittle around in his mouth, and spat into the fire as he passed. It sizzled like a brand.

How could he salvage the situation?

Temair had to die.

She was too dangerous to leave alive.

Once she was dead, his secret would be safe. And he could figure out the rest later.

"Goffraid!" he barked to his best bowman, posted at the door of the hall.

"Aye, m'lord?" The man snapped to attention.

"Grab your quiver and follow me."

They mounted the steps to the top of the tower, where he could spy upon the visitors. Though he blamed it on the difficult five-floor climb, what Cormac saw when he peered down from the tower left him struggling for breath.

De Ware had brought a veritable army, complete with horses, swordsmen, and archers. If this wasn't a siege, it was a damned good imitation of one.

Then, as Cormac squinted against the sunlight flashing off of their helms, he saw her.

Temair.

He almost didn't recognize her. She was no longer the ugly, wild, flat-chested urchin he remembered. She'd grown into a woman. She was almost beautiful. Like her mother. Yet nothing like her mother.

She was dressed like a soldier, covered in leather armor and *trius*. She had a bow slung over her shoulder. And she was holding on to those two infernal wolfhounds that had always snapped at him.

Then she turned her face toward him, and he remembered the insolent mouth that was always begging for a clout, the sly eyes that needed blacking, the stubborn jaw that made him long to crack it.

"Shoot her," he bit out to his archer.

"What?" Goffraid asked.

"Shoot her. Now."

"A woman?"

"Shoot her, or I'll shoot *ye*."

Goffraid's eyes widened. He pulled an arrow from his quiver and nocked it into his bowstring.

Cormac's nostrils flared as he waited impatiently for the archer. "Through the heart," he growled. "No need to make her suffer." In truth, he wanted her to die fast to be sure she couldn't blurt out some unfortunate confession with her last breath.

Goffraid's arm wavered as he drew back the bow and took aim.

"Hurry up!" Cormac hissed.

Goffraid licked his lips and blinked as if trying to clear his vision. The longer he waited, the more his arm shook.

"Do it!" Cormac snapped.

Goffraid, startled, let go of the string, and the arrow

flew wildly off its mark, arcing over the treetops and disappearing into the woods.

"Fool!" Cormac barked, backhanding the bowman, who staggered back and fell on his hip. "Must I do everythin' myself?"

Cormac snatched the bow from him and set an arrow into it. Closing his eyes down to vengeful slits, he aimed at Temair's wicked, conniving heart, drew back, and let the bolt fly.

CHAPTER 29

Beside Temair, Bran gave a sudden yelp of pain and limped onto his side. Temair gaped in horror at the arrow protruding from the hound's haunch. But before she could go to him, Ryland dove toward her, shielding her with his body and rolling on the ground with her in his arms.

He looked up at the tower. She followed his gaze.

Her heart gave a hitch.

Cormac, vexed and red-faced, stood glaring down at her, his beard quivering.

To her amazement, after being at his mercy for so long and suffering at his hands, his countenance didn't inspire fear in her, only hate. And if he'd remained there any longer, she would have burned a hole in him with her gaze.

Friar Brian was already tending to Bran. The poor hound was whimpering while Flann sniffed at him. "He'll be fine. 'Tis just a shallow wound."

She nodded in relief.

Ryland's men needed no orders. Once they witnessed his hostile act, they sprang into action. They charged the door of the keep, battering it with their shoulders until, by brute force, they broke the bolt and the door swung open.

Ryland murmured, "Stay here."

Then he leaped up, drew his blade, and headed into the keep.

"Not on your life," she muttered to herself, jumping to her feet.

The fall had cracked her bow, so she cast it aside. But clever old Sorcha had brought Temair's *bata*, and she pressed it into her hands with a grim look.

"Ye make him pay, lass. He owes ye for your sister."

With a determined nod, Temair whipped the *bata* through the air with a violent sweep of her arm and stormed through the door.

For a moment when she entered the great hall, she was overwhelmed by memories. There were more trinkets around the room than she recalled and more tapestries on the wall, but the same oppressive stink of stale ale and peat smoke lingered in the air.

The Knights of de Ware stood in the center of the hall, their weapons out. But they faced no adversaries. A half-dozen maidservants clung together in a tearful knot. Three kitchen lads sat with their hands between their knees and their eyes wide with awe. Five men in leather armor had already tossed their weapons to the ground and had their hands up in surrender.

Ryland spotted her. "Temair, I asked you to wait outside."

She would have told him exactly what she thought of his orders, but just then, an oblivious young lady came trotting down the stairs. "I'm comin'."

She froze with a gasp when she saw all the soldiers in the great hall. "Who are ye?"

Temair narrowed her gaze at the dark-haired lass. She was dressed in a fine white *léine* and a *brat* embroidered in blue and saffron that Temair recognized as Aillenn's. The silver and pearl pendant around her neck had once belonged to Temair's mother.

"Who are *ye?*" Temair demanded, though she already knew what the lass would say.

The lass pulled herself up to her full height, which was a head shorter than Temair. "I'll have ye know I'm the chieftain's daughter, Tem—"

Before she could finish, Temair charged toward her, *bata* raised.

The lass gave a terrified shriek and tried to flee upstairs.

But Temair hooked her ankles with her *bata*, tripping her. The lass fell hard at the bottom of the steps. Temair hauled her upright by the back of her *brat* and planted the lass on her feet before her.

The lass glowered at her as she licked her bloodied lip. "Ye'll be sorry for this," she threatened. "Cormac will—"

Temair reached out and snagged her mother's pendant. She gave it a hard jerk, and the chain broke.

"How dare ye!" the lass shouted. Her eyes closed to angry green slits.

Temair dropped the pendant down the front of her leather armor.

"That's mine!" the lass sneered.

"Not anymore." With rage born of despair for all she'd lost, Temair used one hand to wrench her sister's *brat* off of the lass's shoulders.

The lass gasped, clutching her *léine*, which had slipped low over her bosom. "Unhand me!"

One more tug freed the *brat.*

The lass drew in a shocked breath, holding her *léine* tightly for fear Temair would rip that from her as well. "Cormac! Cormac! Help!"

The mention of her father's name stirred Ryland's knights, who, Temair saw, had been watching the exchange with great amusement. Now they sobered and stood with their swords at the ready.

"Where is he?" Temair asked the lass, brandishing her *bata.*

"Cormac!" she screamed.

When Temair let her go, the lass ran back up the stairs. Temair followed her. The lass would lead her to Cormac.

Cormac cursed under his breath as the arrow missed its mark. The devil child was completely unharmed. He shook with rage.

Then her rescuing knight glared up at him with vengeance burning in his eyes, and Cormac knew he was doomed.

They were coming for him. He could hear the knights bashing in his door. Turning swiftly away, he threw the useless bow at Goffraid and hurtled down the stairs.

It was too late to save his keep. He knew that now. That cursed Sir Ryland de Ware had seen him with the bow. Cormac would never be able to explain that away.

But he could still save himself. There was another way out of the tower house. He could escape while his guards were battling the knights in the great hall.

First, however, he had to collect his treasure. He couldn't leave it behind. He might have to abandon his jeweled sword, his platters of gold, and his embroidered finery. But he could save his coffer of gems and coins. He'd worked for years to amass it, planning to one day purchase an honor price that would make him equal to an overlord in the English king's eyes.

He scrabbled beneath his bed, digging out the wooden chest concealed there. As big as his belly and filled to the brim with precious metal, it was heavier than he remembered and hard to carry. But desperation gave him strength.

Sweat beaded his brow as he struggled with the coffer. As he emerged in the passageway, he could hear a skirmish downstairs. He quickly shuffled to the far side of the tower to descend there.

The secondary escape was just two floors down from his chamber, one floor above the great hall. He stole down the steps, huffing and straining with the extra weight of the chest.

Just before he pushed open the door, he heard the voice of the lass—the one he'd hired to be his daughter—screaming his name.

Cursing her and all her sex, Cormac shoved his way outside. Momentarily blinded by the brightness and the sweat dripping into his eyes, he closed the door behind him and started down the rickety wooden stairs.

The way was clear when he reached the ground. All he had to do was disappear. He could follow the river to the sea. He had enough wealth on him to pay for food, lodging, whatever he needed to make his way to Cork or Waterford, somewhere he could gather his thoughts and come up with a new plan.

Staying in the shadow of the tower, he scuttled through the coarse grass, wheezing from the effort, heading for the river.

It was then he heard the dog.

As she'd guessed, when Temair burst into her father's chamber on the fourth floor, dogged by Ryland and two of his knights, the imposter was there. Her father, however, was not.

"Where is he?" Temair demanded. "Where is Cormac?"

Shrinking away from the knights, the lass retreated into a frightened huddle in the corner and mewled, "I don't know."

Where could he have gone? Was he still at the top of the tower?

"I'll check the chambers on this floor," Ryland said, nodding to his knights. "You two check the floors below."

"I'm goin' up," Temair said, swallowing back dread. There were too many bad memories at the top of the tower.

She closed her eyes, willing away the image of her sister falling. Over and over.

"Are you sure?" Ryland asked. Then, before she could answer, he decided, "I don't want you going up there alone."

"I have to." She had to confront Cormac—and her fears. She flashed him a cocky grin to cover her apprehension. "Don't worry. He's old. And slow. And unwieldy. Hell, he can't even shoot straight."

Ryland conceded. Nonetheless, he didn't look pleased when he left to search the rooms.

Still trembling in the corner, the imposter lass murmured, "Ye're her, aren't ye? Ye're the real Temair."

"I am."

"He told me ye were dead." She wrinkled her brow. "Why would he do that?"

"Because he wishes I were," she said with a grim smile. "Now more than ever."

With her heart pounding in her breast, Temair left the room and mounted the steps of the tower.

Her legs shook like custard as she emerged at the top and ventured toward the edge of the wall where Aillenn had fallen all those years ago. She held her *bata* aloft in one tightly clenched fist, ready to confront the villain who had caused her sister's death.

Then a movement caught her eye from the field behind the tower. Cormac. He was there, fleeing the keep, thrashing awkwardly through the weeds like a hound through snow.

"Nay," she bit out. She wasn't going to let him escape. He had a debt to pay. "Nay!" she cried.

She tore back down the stairs as fast as she could, knocking knights aside on her way through the great hall.

By the time she burst out the front of the tower house, Friar Brian had taken the arrow out of Bran's haunch and stanched the blood. The poor beast was licking his wound, and when he tried to rise to greet her, he limped.

"Good lad, Bran," she said, giving him a quick pat. "Go lie down now." To the friar she said, "Will ye keep him here? I need Flann."

Brian held Bran's collar.

"Stay, Bran, stay," she said. Then she patted her thigh for Flann to come. Flann whined, reluctant to leave his brother. "Come on, lad. Let's get the brute who did this."

As if he understood, Flann trotted up and made a single impatient spin, eager to go.

Temair raced with him along the perimeter of the tower to the back side, where Cormac was visible in the distance. Then she knelt by Flann and pointed to the small figure.

"Ye see that? Ye see him? That's the man who killed my sister. That's the man who shot Bran. Bring him to me."

Then she rose and flung out her arm. "Get him!"

Flann obeyed at once, running at breakneck speed, barking and baying at his target. Temair followed him, loping across the field.

She saw Cormac turn. One glimpse of the beast that pursued him made him stumble forward in panic. He tripped and fell to the ground, disappearing in the tall grass.

Scrambling up, he lifted something heavy in his hands and lumbered forward again. What the devil was he carrying?

When Flann got close, Cormac dropped his burden, picked up a stone, and threw it at the hound. He missed.

He tried another. It came closer this time. Temair ground her teeth and picked up her pace. If that bloody bastard hit Flann...

Cormac didn't try a third stone. He bent to retrieve what he was carrying. She recognized it now. It was the chest he used to keep his coin.

She suddenly noticed how close he was to the river. If he jumped in before Flann reached him, there would be no way to catch him. He'd float away as easily as the laundry in the stream.

She bolted forward, closing the distance. Flann had almost reached the riverbank, where the fertile earth turned to silt. But Cormac was already dragging the chest across the sandy soil.

"Nay," she murmured as he lifted the chest up and waded into the water.

"Nay," she said as the water reached his knees.

"Nay!" she cried as he staggered forward into waist-high water.

Flann didn't hesitate. He loved to swim. He bounded into the river and began paddling toward Cormac.

Then Temair remembered. Cormac hated the water. He didn't know how to swim.

Even as she had that thought, she reached the riverbank and saw him go under. And despite how much she loathed him, despite how many times he had wronged her, despite how often she'd wished he were dead, she couldn't let him drown.

Near to where Flann was swimming, Cormac popped up once, flailing at the water with one hand while his other gripped the chest.

"Let it go!" she yelled. "'Tisn't worth it!"

But he wouldn't. He clung stubbornly to the chest, and he went under again.

Now she knew how Ryland had felt, watching her with Lady Mor's stockings. Temair, however, would have dropped them in an instant if she were drowning.

Tearing off her armor and kicking off her *brogs*, she dove in. The current was strong, but so was she.

She swam up just as Cormac surfaced again with a gasp. Flann barked, and she reached out for Cormac's arm. "Let it go!"

But he tore out of her grasp, as if he feared she would steal the chest from him.

He sank with an ominous gurgle. She dove down, tugging at his arm, trying to pry the chest from his hands, struggling to haul him back up again. But his grip was determined, and the weight of the chest proved too great. Temair had no choice but to let go, and he was dragged to the bottom of the river.

Hours later, they retrieved the chieftain's body. He was still clinging to the chest with a death grip. The *clann* agreed it was proof that Cormac treasured riches more than anything—even more than his own life.

CHAPTER 30

SEVEN WEEKS LATER

Temair advanced, studying her adversary carefully, scrutinizing him from head to toe. She could spot no shortcomings, no vulnerabilities. He seemed unflappable, unshakeable, unconquerable.

Her opponent approached her with the same assessing gaze. By the time he was through perusing her, she felt like he knew her every strength. And every weakness.

She gulped. Under his smoothly confident regard, she sensed her chances against his assault dwindling. This wasn't a battle she would easily win. And if she didn't, she feared a man of such power and skill would seize the advantage before she even had a fighting chance.

She took a deep breath, steeling herself against the temptation to simply yield to him before the engagement could begin.

"I've been waiting a long time for this," he purred.

She shut the chamber door behind her and arched a skeptical brow. "Ye've been waitin' since last night under the oak tree," she corrected. "And the night before that in the stable. And the night before that by the *lough*."

"True," Ryland said with a wicked grin, "but if *feels* like forever. Besides, this is the first time we'll be trysting as husband and wife."

Temair smiled. She thought it felt like forever too. Gazing at her incredibly handsome bridegroom in his wedding finery, she could already feel her heart quickening and her body tingling with anticipation.

She still couldn't believe how much had happened in the last several weeks. She'd gone from being a woodland outlaw, at the mercy of a merciless father, to the head of her *clann*, with the power to restore justice. She'd put her sister's soul to rest, righted her father's wrongs, and willingly wed an English knight.

An English knight who was laying siege to her even now, launching his first attack.

"Come to me, outlaw wife," he growled, carefully lifted the wedding wreath of myrtle and lavender from her hair and tossing it onto the bed.

She countered his assault by running the back of her hand over his jaw, marveling at its freshly shaved smoothness.

He caught her wrist, turning his head to place a kiss in her hand. When he made a small circle in her palm with his tongue, her fingers curled reflexively.

Not to be outdone, she lifted her free hand to his ear, tucking his hair behind it to trace the delicate folds with the tip of her finger.

He shivered. Then he lapped at the webbing between the fingers of her captive hand.

She gasped as an erotic spark fired to life within her. Hooking the back of his neck, she pulled him close and murmured against his mouth, "I'm goin' to rob ye, English."

"Is that so?"

"Aye," she said, licking at the corner of his lip. When he turned his head to kiss her, she pulled away. Picking up the *bata* she kept at the foot of her bed, she spun it once and placed the narrow end at his throat. "First I'm goin' to need your *brat*."

He stiffened, wary of her weapon. "My *brat*?"

"Aye. Give it to me now."

"You mean my mantle?" he teased.

"Aye, rogue, your mantle." She was still learning his foreign terms.

With his hands harmlessly aloft, he stepped back from the *bata* and then dutifully worked loose the silver brooch holding the mantle together at his throat.

She held out her hand for the brooch, and he placed it in her palm. She wiggled her fingers for the mantle, and he offered it to her as well. She cast both onto the pallet.

She peered down at his feet. "I'll have your *brogs* as well."

"My boots? But they're far too large for you."

"Hand them o'er."

"Fine," he conceded with a sigh, removing them and casting them at her feet.

"Your *inar*."

"I'm sorry," he said, his eyes twinkling. "My what?"

For a moment, she couldn't remember. "Your haub-

...surc-..." She poked at the garment with the *bata* and then finished triumphantly. "Your surcoat. Give me your surcoat."

He gathered up his long green wool surcoat and tugged it off over his head.

She took it from him, threw it aside, and tapped the *bata* against her lip, considering what she wanted next. "I'll take that...that..." She waved the *bata* at his undershirt.

"Not my tunic? Are you sure, lass?" He lowered his voice to a whisper. "I'm not wearing anything beneath it."

"Oh, I know," she assured him.

He fought back a grin and peeled the white linen tunic off, exposing his broad shoulders, his powerful chest, and the ridged muscles of his stomach below.

She felt the familiar ache of lust pulsing between her thighs. But she refused to surrender to her desires yet.

"Your *chausses*," she demanded, fixing her gaze on the tie that held them up at his hips.

"Interesting." Staring at her with hunger in his eyes, he pulled the tie slowly loose. "You've no trouble remembering the name of those."

Her cheeks flushed as she watched him slide the brown woolen *chausses* off—taking out one towering leg, then the other—and dropping them on the floor.

Her voice came out on a breathless whisper, "Now your *braies*."

He crossed his arms boldly over his chest. "Nay." His lips curved up in a wicked, willful smile.

She blinked in surprise. "What do ye mean, 'nay'?" Was he ceding the battle?

"I mean nay," he said. "I won't do it."

"Why?"

"Because, outlaw, if you intend to rob me of my last stitch of clothing, you'll have to come take it yourself."

Temair bit the inside of her cheek. He was a clever knave. He knew that once she came close, she wouldn't be able to resist him.

Still, she couldn't back down from his challenge.

Clinging to the *bata* as if it would somehow protect her, she crept forward to do the deed.

He made no move to help or hinder her. Instead, he watched her with a smoldering gaze and a smug half-grin.

With one trembling hand, she awkwardly untied the knot securing his *braies.* When they dropped to the floor, she saw that he was already primed and ready, like a beast about to charge. She inhaled sharply.

"Now you," he murmured.

She frowned and shook her head.

In the blink of an eye, he snatched the *bata* from her hand, spun it, and set it at her throat. "Now you," he repeated.

Her eyes wide, she could only sputter. "How did ye...that's not f-...bloody..."

"Your *brat*, wench," he demanded.

"Shite." Her breast heaved as she averted her gaze and unfastened her brooch. The scarlet *brat* dropped to the floor, but with the *bata* at her throat, she couldn't bend forward to pick it up.

"Now, outlaw," he said, licking his lips, "I want to take a peek at those lovely toes."

A frisson of desire coursed through her as she remembered two nights ago when he'd sent her to new heights of passion, nibbling on them. "Nay," she gasped.

"Oh, aye. Give me your *brogs*."

Swallowing hard, she slipped out of them, nudging them toward him with her toe.

"That's a beautiful *léine*," he said, lightly tracing the intricate silver embroidery over the bodice with the tip of the *bata*.

She held her breath as the *bata* grazed her breasts, awakening every nerve.

"Beautiful," he repeated.

She released a sigh. The *léine was* beautiful. Made for her sister, it had never been worn. The soft blue cloth was embroidered with silver thread, in knots that intertwined in a border with no beginning and no end, representing the eternity of marriage.

"Take it off."

"What?"

"Take it off."

"But I'm not wearin' anythin' underneath."

"Oh, I know," he said, echoing her.

She hesitated.

He dragged the tip of the *bata* down the front of the *léine*, ending just before he reached the spot that was throbbing for his touch "Do it."

She knew once she took off the *léine*, once there was no barrier between them, the real battle would begin. And she was feeling defenseless.

But she couldn't back down now. So with as little ado as possible, she slipped her arms out of the sleeves and pulled it off, shaking her head so her long, loose tresses would at least partially cover her.

At first she wouldn't look at him. She stared at the floor, at the bed, at the fire, anywhere but at the man with the magnificent muscles, the soul-searing gaze, and the bold manifestation of lust.

"Look at me," he bade her.

She shook her head. If she looked at him, she'd be lost.

"Look at me." He nudged her chin with the *bata*.

She shook her head.

Finally, he let go of the *bata*. It clattered to the floor.

When she instinctively looked up, he was gazing at her with such hunger, such adoration, such passion that she couldn't resist him.

They came together in a breathless embrace. Kisses and caresses led them to stagger to the bed. He pressed her onto her back atop their discarded clothing, and she hugged him close with her heels.

Their skirmish was brief this time. Their passion, like a tightly drawn bow, was already on the verge of release. A few dozen eager thrusts, and they soared together like a flaming arrow, lighting up the night sky with a glorious brilliance, then cooling and falling back to earth.

Much later, after they'd made love for the third time and she lay spent beside Ryland, Temair marveled over how much her life had changed—as a woodkern, as a wife, as a woman.

Yet it wasn't only her life that had been changed. Changes were coming to all of Eire as well.

The new English king was making his influence known. Already in some places, birthright had taken the place of honor price. In the north, the *clann* structure was disappearing, replaced by a feudal system of lords and vassals. The language was changing, as were the customs.

In some ways, it seemed wrong to her to let these changes happen. The Irish way of life was worth fighting for. And to Temair, who'd been born and raised in conflict, making her way with her wits and her weapons, resistance came in the form of pitched battle between the two factions.

And yet, making love with Ryland didn't feel like a battle at all.

"'Tis a curious thing," she breathed, "trystin' with ye."

He was too weary to raise his head. "Aye?" he mumbled into the mattress. "How so?"

"It feels like a surrender," she said, "but also like a victory."

"I suppose so."

"So who wins?"

His soft chuckle warmed her. "Both. Neither." He turned his head to look at her. "I don't think 'tis meant to be a war. 'Tis more of an alliance."

She lifted her brows. "Like the alliance between our two countries."

He closed his eyes and gave her a sleepy smile. "Aye. We bring together the best of each and make something stronger." He yawned.

She smiled a secret smile. He didn't know how right he was. "The way that two metals are forged together to make an unbreakable steel blade?"

"Aye."

"Or leather and wax melt together to make impenetrable armor?"

"Mm-hm."

"Warp and weft threads weave together to make a sturdy *léine*?"

"Mm."

"Or a husband and wife tryst together to make the babe I'm havin' in the spring?"

He sighed. Then his eyes flew open. "Wait. What?"

She grinned. She couldn't wait to see what their loving alliance had forged.

Well-respected by their father's warriors and well-loved by their mother's *clann*, their babe would doubtless possess the best qualities of its mother and father—the chivalrous heart of an English knight and the wild spirit of an Irish outlaw.

One day their children would be the caretakers of a glorious legacy—that of the chieftains of the O'Keeffe and the lords of de Ware.

CHANK YOU FOR READING MY BOOK!

Did you enjoy it? If so, I hope you'll post a review to let others know! There's no greater gift you can give an author than spreading your love of her books.

It's truly a pleasure and a privilege to be able to share my stories with you. Knowing that my words have made you laugh, sigh, or touched a secret place in your heart is what keeps the wind beneath my wings. I hope you enjoyed our brief journey together, and may ALL of your adventures have happy endings!

If you'd like to keep in touch, feel free to sign up for my monthly e-newsletter at www.glynnis.net, and you'll be the first to find out about my new releases, special discounts, prizes, promotions, and more!

If you want to keep up with my daily escapades:
Friend me at facebook.com/GlynnisCampbell
Like my Page at bit.ly/GlynnisCampbellFBPage
Follow me at twitter.com/GlynnisCampbell
And if you're a super fan, join
facebook.com/GCReadersClan

MACFARLAND'S LASS

The Scottish Lasses Book 1

SELKIRK, SCOTLAND
SPRING 1545

The pain was shocking, intense. Florie's first thought was that a wolf had sprung at her from the brush, sinking its fangs into her thigh. She screamed, but the sound was cut off as she twisted and fell, colliding hard with the earth.

Knocked breathless, for an instant she lay stunned. Then, fearing to be devoured, she kicked desperate heels into the decaying leaf-fall, scrambling, clambering, scraping dirt beneath her nails as she struggled to escape the unrelenting burn of the teeth embedded in her flesh.

No beast snarled or sprang to finish her, but neither did the stabbing pain in her leg subside. She wrenched about to see what demon had her in its jaws.

The sight left her faint with horror.

An arrow pinned her through a trailing link of her gold girdle and her skirts, its steel head buried in her flesh, its thick shaft bobbing as she writhed in pain.

The edges of perception blurred then. She felt herself

tilting, fading, falling into a cavern of seductive oblivion.

Rane's bowstring was still vibrating when the blood drained from his face and his arms dropped limp at his sides.

"Bloody hell," he breathed.

Casting off the bow, he charged forward into the open meadow, his heart hammering. He bolted for the trail, toward his fallen prey, hurtling along the pond's edge, around its perimeter, whipping past reeds and fern, snapping off bracken as he ran. When he reached his victim, he dropped his quiver to the ground and fell to his knees with a bitter cry.

Guilt threatened to unman him, and he ground his teeth against a wave of self-loathing.

Curse his hands, he'd shot a child.

Then he peered closer by the fading twilight. Nae, not a child. A slight, slender lass.

Though she lay as still as death, she wasn't dead. Thank Odin, he'd been able to redirect the arrow at the last moment, thus sparing her life.

He turned her carefully toward him, and she revived with a wheezing gasp, reflexively scrabbling at the outside of her thigh, where his arrow obscenely protruded.

"Nae!" he cautioned. "Leave it be!"

Her eyes widened, and he instantly withdrew his hands, trying not to panic her, raising his palms in what he hoped was a placating gesture.

The last thing he expected was the sting of a sharp needle through his open hand.

He grunted in pain, drawing back his wounded palm. Blood welled from the puncture. He sucked a sharp hiss through his teeth.

The needle had pierced him deeply. But he supposed he should have known better. After all, only a fool approached a wounded animal.

Her left arm arced toward him again with whatever vicious weapon she wielded.

He lunged aside. "Nae, lass! I mean ye no—"

His words were cut short as her right fist clipped his jaw.

"Ach!"

The needle returned to graze his bare neck, leaving a stinging trail.

"Son of a... Lass, cease! 'Twas an acci—"

She ignored his command, attacking him again and again, as if she intended to fight him to the death. Damn! If she didn't stop thrashing about, she'd drive the arrow deeper into her thigh.

"Woman!" he finally bellowed, startling her into momentary submission. "Put away your weapon. I'm friend, not foe."

Florie didn't believe him for an instant. Whether he was Gilbert's man she couldn't tell. 'Twas too dark to make out his face or the color of his cloak. But the villain had shot her. *Shot* her!

She'd managed to wound him with her brooch pin. She'd heard his grunt, felt the point sink into his flesh. But she hadn't inflicted enough damage to stop him. And if she didn't... If he turned her over to the law...

Fighting for her life, she stabbed forward with the brooch again. This time he was prepared for her attack. He caught her wrist in a steely grip.

Thrashing against his punishing hold, she tried to pry his fingers away with her free hand. But he gave her wrist a sharp flick, and the brooch flew loose, skittering out of reach.

"Lie still," he commanded. "Ye'll only make it worse."

Worse? What could be worse? Florie wasn't about to surrender, regardless of the wave of dizziness that assailed her...regardless of the dire stain widening on her best brocade skirts...regardless of the drops of blood, her blood, dripping onto the leaves of the forest floor.

Summoning up one last, desperate burst of power, she reared back her closed fist and swung forward as hard as she could, aiming for his jaw. But he ducked easily out of the way, seizing that hand as well.

"For the love o' Frigga, lass, lie *still!*"

The edges of her vision dimmed, darkening as her bones dissolved into submission, and she vaguely wondered who the devil Frigga was.

God have mercy. Maybe the archer had dealt her a mortal wound and she was dying, for she felt as weak as a bairn, with neither the strength nor the will to move.

"Nae, nae, nae, nae, NAE!" he shouted, giving her wrists a reviving shake. "Not *that* still!" His voice, for all its vehemence, sounded distant, dreamlike. "Stay awake, do ye hear me?"

"Ye go to hell," she mumbled.

He cursed under his breath, returning her arms to her sides, where they lay as limp and useless as empty sleeves.

"Ach, lass," he murmured, as if to himself, "what were ye doin', stealin' through the thicket like that?"

"Leave me alone."

"If I leave ye alone, ye'll bleed to d—" He shook his head. "I'm not leavin'."

From beneath eyelids growing heavier by the

moment, Florie could faintly discern the man's silhouette as he crouched nearby. He was unbuckling his belt.

Ballocks! Did the monster mean to swive her while she lay helpless?

"Get the hell away from me," she managed to croak.

He ignored her.

She heard the sound of fabric being shredded. The brute must be tearing her clothes from her. Tears of rage and frustration and anguish welled in her eyes. "Bastard," she whispered.

"Aye, I know. But 'twill be over in a moment. Lie still."

"Nae!" she groaned. She wasn't about to let the lout have his way with her. She tried to curl her weak fingers into lethal fists. "Don't touch me."

A dark fog crept in at the sides of her vision like a closing curtain. She fought to keep her eyes open.

"I'll be swift as I can," he promised, "but ye have to hold still." He positioned himself beside her injured leg. "I'll carry ye to shelter afterward. There's a priest up the rise from here, not far—"

A priest! That brought her instantly alert. "The church!" she blurted.

Sanctuary! By strength of sheer will, she seized his wrist in one hand with such ferocity that she almost knocked him off his haunches.

"Aye!" she cried, though her command came out on a weak wheeze. "The church... Go... Now..." If she could make it to the church... Pain gripped her again, and she winced, digging her fingers into the leather bracer around his forearm.

"Soon." He clasped a restraining hand over hers, his fingers sticky with blood.

"Now," she groaned. Leveraging against his wrist, she began to creep forward, determined to drag herself bodily up the hill if need be.

"Lass, be still! Ye'll drive the arrow—"

"Sanctuary!" she beseeched him.

"What?"

"Take me...to sanctuary." Lord Gilbert couldn't be far away. "They're comin'," she mumbled.

"Who?"

She gasped as searing lightning shot up her leg.

He squeezed her hand. "All right. I'll hurry, lass," he promised, "but the shaft's got to come out first." The cloth he'd torn he now rapidly wadded into his hand. Then he offered her his leather belt. "Hold this in your teeth."

She turned her head aside. She didn't want his belt. All she wanted was sanctuary.

But he pulled her jaw down with his thumb anyway, wedging the thick belt between her teeth. "Bite down."

She scowled. No one told Florie what to do. Then a strong wave of pain washed over her as he pressed the wad of linen against her wound, and she reflexively clamped down.

Blowing out a forceful breath and kneeling above her, the man curved his right hand around the shaft so 'twas braced under his arm. "Ready?"

Nae, she wasn't ready. But Lord Gilbert was coming. And this knave wouldn't let her go until the arrow was out. Praying the brute wouldn't betray her, that he'd keep his word, she ground her teeth into his belt and nodded.

"One...two..."

She fainted before he reached three.

ABOUT THE AUTHOR

I'm a *USA Today* bestselling author of swashbuckling action-adventure historical romances, mostly set in Scotland, with over a dozen award-winning books published in six languages.

But before my role as a medieval matchmaker, I sang in *The Pinups,* an all-girl band on CBS Records, and provided voices for the MTV animated series *The Maxx,* Blizzard's *Diablo* and *Starcraft* video games, and *Star Wars* audiobooks.

I'm the wife of a rock star (if you want to know which one, contact me) and the mother of two young adults. I do my best writing on cruise ships, in Scottish castles, on my husband's tour bus, and at home in my sunny southern California garden.

I love transporting readers to a place where the bold heroes have endearing flaws, the women are stronger than they look, the land is lush and untamed, and chivalry is alive and well!

I'm always delighted to hear from my readers, so please feel free to email me at glynnis@glynnis.net. And if you're a super-fan who would like to join my inner circle, sign up at http://www.facebook.com/GCReadersClan, where you'll get glimpses behind the scenes, sneak peeks of works-in-progress, and extra special surprises.